CRITICAL ACCLAIM FOR THE SIMONA GRIFFO MYSTERIES

"I love Simona Griffo! At last, a heroine who's tough enough to solve a murder and savvy enough to realize low-fat mozzarella really is tasteless. Pick up *The Trouble with a Bad Fit*—you won't put it down until the last bite."

—Lisa Scottoline
Edgar Award–winning author

"Zesty characters in [a] vibrant city."

—*Publishers Weekly*

"Mouth-watering."

—*Denver Post*

"Crespi's writing makes Simona seem very human . . . the result is a heroine who rings true."

—*Drood Review of Mystery*

"Quick-moving prose, good garment-district atmosphere, and a heady mixture of skeletons in the closet."

—*Library Journal*

"Reading Camilla Crespi is so delicious it feels fattening. I hope it isn't since I intend to keep doing it."

—Mary Willis Walker

THE TROUBLE WITH A BAD FIT

A NOVEL OF FOOD, FASHION, AND MYSTERY

CAMILLA T. CRESPI

HarperPaperbacks
A Division of HarperCollinsPublishers

HarperPaperbacks
A Division of HarperCollins*Publishers*
10 East 53rd Street, New York, N.Y. 10022-5299

This is a work of fiction. The characters, incidents, and
dialogues are products of the author's imagination and are not to
be construed as real. Any resemblance to actual events or
persons, living or dead, is entirely coincidental.

A hardcover edition of this book was published in 1996
by Harper Collins*Publishers*.

ISBN 0-06-109408-0

HarperCollins®, 📖®, and HarperPaperbacks™
are trademarks of HarperCollins*Publishers*, Inc.

Cover illustration by Marc Burckhardt

First HarperPaperbacks printing: April 1997

Printed in the United States of America

Visit HarperPaperbacks on the World Wide Web at
http://www.harpercollins.com/paperbacks

❖ 10 9 8 7 6 5 4 3 2 1

In memory of Lee David Pesky,
who had found a good fit.
We'll remember you.

The garment center—a.k.a. the garment district, the market, the fashion center, or Seventh Avenue—lies on New York City's West Side, between Sixth and Ninth Avenues from Thirty-fifth to Forty-second Streets. In these clogged blocks of aging lofts beats the heart of American fashion.

Cast of Characters

IN ORDER OF APPEARANCE

Simona Griffo Transplanted Italian. Chases an ad and a killer in New York City's garment center.

Phyllis Striker Longtime fitting model. A deadly muse.

Roberta Riddle Owner and designer of Riddle Solutions. Struggles to hold on to her hat and her design business.

Charlie Angelo Roberta's new partner. Into old-fashioned loyalty and new-fashioned chic.

Flossie Sarnowski Roberta's sample maker. Fiercely loyal to her boss and her son.

Stan Greenhouse Simona's police-detective lover. Not giving his new roommate her space.

Raf Garcia Stan's detective partner. Plays the good cop.

Gregory Price Simona's good friend at work. Always lends an ear.

Mario Lionello   Farsighted tailor. His thimble and thread sew up more than fabric.

Lourdes Montalvo   Riddle Solutions's new seamstress. Thinks her job is a miracle.

Ed Mannucci   Roberta's floor neighbor. Sells sportswear and fears *agida*.

Irene Connelly   Stan's ex. Has an uncharitable agenda.

Mr. Nite   a.k.a. Ernest Gold. Merits all his names.

Dmitri K.   Cabdriver and bodyguard. Owns a fashion business of sorts.

Jerry Sarnowski   Flossie's son and Roberta's production man. Works the dress and racing forms.

Kathy Breen   Cleaning lady. Reluctant to spill the dirt she collects.

Sally Mannucci   Ed's wife. Has a mom who forgets and friends who remember.

Willy Greenhouse   Stan's fifteen-year-old son. Turns out to be a good juggler.

Plus

An assortment of bosses, garment workers, cops, nurses, speeding cyclists, delivery boys, social workers, mothers, felons, and food.

1

"Garmentos stab you in the chest!" Phyllis announced.

Roberta Riddle ripped a muslin sleeve from the jacket Phyllis was modeling.

From the open workroom door, the tailor scowled. The sample maker nodded. The production manager jiggled his sneakered foot.

Roberta ripped out the other sleeve.

"What! Are you crazy?" Charlie screamed. He was Roberta's assistant designer, now a new part-owner. He had dared to alter one of her designs.

"This isn't a democracy!" Roberta threw the sleeves at Charlie's reflection in the mirror.

"It was perfect!"

"You don't get to vote!"

Phyllis popped a Tootsie Roll in her mouth. "In broad daylight we'll stab you!"

It was exclamation-point time at Riddle Solutions, Inc. In exactly one week the New York ready-to-wear spring/summer collection—Seventh on Sixth—would begin its ten-day parade in the tents of Bryant Park.

1

Roberta had designed a hundred outfits. Forty-three were ready.

Roberta ripped off the front of the jacket.

Flossie, the sample maker, smiled. She was short, stocky, concrete. "Even the buttonholes he changed!"

"I hate this!" Charlie wailed.

"I don't need a sound track!" Roberta had an attractive pointed face, cheeks colored by two rouge brush strokes in the Diana Vreeland mode, and a rosebud mouth glossed with scarlet lipstick. Her unadorned hazel eyes were pinched with fatigue and anger.

Charlie charged out, slamming the door shut.

This minor fashion drama was taking place in the showroom of a small ready-to-wear designer firm on the thirtieth floor of 530 Seventh Avenue, a prestigious address in the heart of New York City's garment center. Normally, a garment is draped in the design room, but it was Sunday. There were no buyers around, and Roberta wanted spectacle.

The L-shaped room was lacquered in dark red with paneled mirrors covering three sides. Rows of ceiling spots cast blades of light on empty clothes racks. Black taffeta drapes covered the windows and the sun-filled October day. A long, lacquered black table held lines of sharpened pencils and blank order forms.

A foot-tall jade Buddha exuded calm.

"The garmentos"— Phyllis stretched her arms out as Roberta draped new muslin over her naked shoulder—"we're so awful you have to love us!"

I do. I'm Simona Griffo. Being originally from Rome, I enjoy excess and for the past four and a half years I've earned my living doing print ads for a lot of "garmentos." That's why I was sitting on the floor of Roberta's showroom. I had an ad to pitch.

"There's all kinds in the industry," Phyllis said. "Fat business types who like to rub their gold and diamond rings against my softer parts. The designers, most of them faggots—"

Roberta pinched Phyllis's waist.

Phyllis chewed louder. "They swoon at fabric and hiss at women. If you breathe, one of 'em—I won't mention names 'cause I have to work for the fat jerk—sticks pins in you! For fun!"

Roberta, her trademark hat firmly in place, pinned darts and straightened her back as if trying to find another inch in her four-foot-eleven frame.

She was scared.

The first half of the nineties had been bad for the industry. Riddle Solutions was no exception. According to *Women's Wear Daily*—the fashion business trade paper, the retailers' bible—Roberta's designs were "tired." *Vogue*—the fashion bible to the world—had ignored her for the past five years. The rumor on the street was that Roberta's company was waist-high in unsold rags, that the Bryant Park showing—an expensive proposition—was a last-ditch effort to get back on the map, that she'd never make it. In the fashion business, substantiated or not, rumors kill.

The bad news didn't end there.

Mrs. Morewitz, who gave Roberta her start, had died six months before, willing her 40 percent partnership to Charlie Angelo, a twenty-six-year-old assistant designer eager to push Roberta into a closet and turn "tired" into "hot" single-handedly.

Roberta was showing for the first time since her husband's death five years before.

A week after the shows she would turn sixty.

Plenty to be petrified about.

Roberta leaned back, eyes squinting for a better look at the new shape.

"With boss lady here, everything's hunky-dory." Phyllis looked down at Roberta, who was nine inches shorter. "She doesn't stab me, I don't stab her. Right, sweetie?" A half-bitten Tootsie Roll protruded from her mouth.

The two women locked eyes. For a moment I thought they might strike each other. It was part of the general tension, I decided. Roberta looked away first. "Get rid of the candy. I can't use fat. Spit it out." She didn't drop a pin from her mouth, but her neck had turned as red as her Frisbee hat.

Phyllis sucked in her stomach. "She can't do a line without me." A self-satisfied smile crawled over her face. "I'm her muse."

The workroom door smacked against the wall and Charlie stormed in, his entrance repeated in the mirrors: five foot six at the most, curly bleached-blond hair, with coal-black roots and eyebrows for contrast, long-lashed eyes, and a square, sculpted face. Showing off well-worked biceps underneath a white T-shirt and an acid-yellow shearling vest over black leather pants. He breathed heavily.

Roberta ignored him. With a sweep of his arm Charlie toppled the jade Buddha and stormed back out, taking his reflection with him.

Phyllis laughed, giving me a see-what-I-mean? look. Roberta repinned a tuck. "Turn around."

Phyllis obliged, preening in the mirror she now faced. Somewhere in her fifties, with a frosted beehive lengthening an already long face that flattened out wide at the jaw, she wore a scar underneath her chin like a strap. She had never been attractive according to fashion-world standards, but she had the perfect measurements for a size-six runway sample: height 5'8", bust 35", waist 26", hips 37". Your average American woman.

"Roberta hasn't done a collection without me for thirty-five years," she said.

"If you don't lose weight, I will." When Roberta stood still, she was thin enough to pass as a fashion cutout. She was wearing a suit from her fall collection: a pearl-gray, A-line wool skirt cut to the knee, with matching textured hose that were no longer in fashion but covered her varicose veins, and a form-fitting, single-breasted jacket in charcoal gray highlighted by white brocade cuffs and collar.

Phyllis, dressed in bra, panty hose, and spikes, spit out in her hand what was left of the Tootsie Roll.

I cranked myself up from the corner and picked up the Buddha from the floor. Impatience was creeping in, and my knees were killing me from sitting cross-legged. I was scared, too. For the first time in a long relationship with HH&H Advertising, Roberta was being difficult. She had already rejected ten comps, facsimiles of the final ad; she had kicked the agency account executive out of the showroom and had told our number-one art director that he had pickles for brains. Last year Riddle Solutions spent what my CEO considered a "measly" $200,000 in advertising. The garment industry wasn't the only one that had suffered in the nineties. HH&H could not afford to lose another client.

I asked Roberta for one more chance, then cajoled a miffed art director, my immediate boss and friend, into coming up with three new ideas. My own job was at stake. The CEO, entrenched in the rarefied air of the seventeenth floor, had decreed restructuring, which meant early retirements, firing 30 percent of the agency, and reshuffling the survivors. I was one of the lucky leftovers, but the CEO, not understanding my usefulness in the creative department, was threatening to "promote" me upstairs with the Living Dead, account execs who get to work at eight A.M. in ironed suits and crisp hair, trailing antiseptic deodorant smells. I thrive in the late-starting, garlic-breath, T-shirts-and-jeans department of the creatives. I'm too hippy for jeans, but our mental attitudes match.

I sat down again. This time on a chair. "Riddle Nothings" was the theme line we'd come up with for Roberta's new easygoing knits, which she was counting on to bring her back to fame. Riddle Nothings popping out of drawstring pouches like bright-colored jewels. She had to like it. I stroked Buddha's soap-smooth pate for luck.

Roberta tugged, crimped, folded, and cut out arcs of cloth with foot-long shears that looked heavier than she was. Her every movement was careful and neat.

Phyllis was immobile. Even her mouth.

"Don't you cramp up?" I asked.

"Something awful, but then I model that finished sample, with the whole workroom looking up, everyone waiting for Berta's okay, so quiet you can hear a pin drop on this carpet. I stop, turn. She walks away, around, back, near. She taps her hat, we all stop breathing. Then it comes. The hiss. Like a snake. Except backward. She's sucking it in." Phyllis's fuchsia mouth dropped open. Gold flashed at the back of her teeth. "That's it! Wow!" She clasped her hands together. "I'm like a queen. Everyone's clapping. Laughing. Breathing again." She lifted an elbow to let Roberta pin an armpit. "It's worth the cramps, the sore feet, the varicose veins, the nips at the butt, the pinpricks." Her scar stretched with her smile. "I tell 'em where the sleeve's too tight, where the fabric pulls at the hips. I'm part of this, I created something."

"I feel that way with an ad campaign," I said.

Phyllis dumped her smile. "Yeah?" She wasn't interested.

Roberta slapped a fold back into place, turned slowly around, examining her handiwork. A rib cage–hugging shape, emphasis on the shoulders. Lagerfeld and Saint Laurent, at the Paris couture collections for fall, had decreed that tight was right. Everyone had to follow. The new look didn't hide an ounce. Which was fine with me. My budget only allows for knockoffs from five seasons ago.

"Flossie! Mario!" Roberta yelled. She was through.

I stood up. It was my turn. The acids in my stomach skipped rope. "Where do you want to see the comps?"

"In my office."

I rushed ahead to prop the weakest ad against the wall, saving the best for last. Once she'd picked one, I wanted to convince her to aim for *Vogue*. Roberta had to get on the fashion map again.

Think in a straight line, Simona. Pitch the comps first. I walked into Roberta's large office and tripped. The carpeted floor was covered with mounds of costume jewelry, handbags, scarves, hats, shoes—accessories for the upcoming show. I lifted a green stiletto-heeled pump and set it on a chair next to its mate.

I straightened up, relaxed my face, dropped my shoulder blades. This was my moment. I was going for that famous Roberta intake of breath. I reached for the first comp.

I cried out. Behind me, Roberta sucked in her breath. Not in approval.

In the center of her desk, on my stack of comps, was a rat. On its back. A brass letter opener stuck out of its chest. Blood covered the comp. Above its head, the ad's headline: WHAT EVERY WOMAN NEEDS!

My pizza lunch reared.

Roberta picked up an old *W* from a stack on a chair, opened it, and covered the rat. Now Claudia Schiffer's million-dollar face smiled at us.

"Who would do this?" I whispered.

Roberta shrugged. "I hate dead fur."

2

"Then she kicked me out." I was on my knees, six hours later, unpacking. Forty-eight hours earlier I had left my tiny studio apartment in Greenwich Village to move into Homicide Detective Stanley Greenhouse's two-bedroom brownstone apartment on West Seventy-seventh Street. In the office I had been congratulated as a Manhattan success story. They were referring to the two bedrooms, not the man.

"She kicked me out," I repeated for drama. Greenhouse was sitting in the only armchair in the living room, head buried in the paper. He'd moved my stack of underwear to the coffee table.

I raised my voice. "She high-heeled me, threw the dead rat at me, came after me with the bloodied letter opener."

A brown eye appeared above Friday's *Wall Street Journal*. A skeptical eye. "She politely asked you to leave."

"Yes." He was on to my Roman exaggerations. "Not that I blame her. She couldn't exactly pick a comp, not with rodent blood all over it. Something ugly is going on in that place."

The eye disappeared. "Leave it alone, Sim."

"I need her account. Forget being promoted, I risk getting fired. I'll be accused of not protecting agency artwork, of having wasted two hours."

"It's Sunday."

"I'll be accused of having compromised the integrity of the rodent population of New York City, and I don't know what else. The CEO is itching to save my salary. I can't leave it alone, Greenhouse!"

The wonderful, warm, solid, stubborn, sexy man I was now living with gave up his paper with a lot of unnecessary noise. "Stan, my name is Stan. I get Greenhouse all day. At home I want Stan. And you know—"

"Stan! I love you, Stan."

He looked distracted, worried. He had worked all day, too, plus his fifteen-year-old son, Willy, wasn't coming to dinner as expected. "And you know that if you get fired, I can carry you."

"To bed you can carry me anytime, but that's all. How much does a detective make, anyway? Only the rich read the *Wall Street Journal*, and *no one* reads it two days late." I had no idea how much money he had. We had decided to keep our accounts separate. Actually, I insisted on it. It gives me the illusion I can walk out without repercussions.

Moving in with a man at age thirty-eight was both exciting and anxiety producing. I had been living by myself for eight years. The first three in Rome, waiting for Italian law to turn my separation into divorce, and the next five in New York, trying to start a new life. A life that began to be fun when Greenhouse—Stan—walked in to take over a homicide investigation at the agency. But I have a long memory, and although I wanted to gobble Stan up, a kernel of wariness stuck in my throat.

"*Allora*, are you rich?" The brownstone apartment, in a nice but not excessively chic block, had belonged to his parents. Willy went to private school, but I'd always thought it was the ex-wife's money.

"I have a few investments, money my father left me. Do you care?"

My relationship to Greenhouse had always been skewed. Between the sheets we had from the start been a Fourth of July blaze. Before and after, Greenhouse was tenaciously private about the facts of his life. I had, for instance, discovered by chance that he was Jewish. He didn't practice his religion, and he'd never brought it up. I, normally curious about everything, had been tenaciously shy with questions on the subject of my new lover. I knew his divorce had been bad, too, and from the beginning I respected his need for reserve and caution. I was afraid of losing him, I told myself. A recent emotion-baring trip home had shown me another truth. I'd been as scared of commitment as he was.

I looked at Stan now, his hair tousled, his eyes kind and calm. A solid man with an old-fashioned belief in respect and honor. Behind him a brick wall, red and worn, one of the details I loved about his town-house apartment. He was wearing a ratty orange sweater that had been his father's, tan corduroys, bare feet. He looked tired, down. I loved him. I'd given up my rent-stabilized apartment—a tremendous act of faith—and moved in. I knew we would be fine. But I was still going to keep a separate checking account.

"I don't care how much or how little money you have," I said, "but is there enough to paint the walls?" I leaned down and kissed his big toe. "Pink gives me nightmares, and I only make enough money to repaint the bathroom." I had also insisted on paying half the maintenance, half the house bills.

He looked at me in surprise. "The walls aren't pink."

"What color are they?" A fire truck blared down the street.

"I don't know. Ask my mother."

Dawn pink, soft-blush pink, tomato-and-white-sauce pink, peach-juice-in-champagne-Bellini-cocktail pink. Pink. By the look of the apartment—a heavy mixture of Victorian and depression furniture—I suspected nothing had been touched since his mother, a woman I had met only over the telephone, had moved to Florida ten years before. I was already itching to make changes, to lighten up the place, but men require patience.

"Then how about clearing a drawer for my underwear?"

His eyes twitched to a stock-market coup jumping out at him from the page on his lap. "I've already given you half the dresser, half the closet."

"I need more." Five piles of panties and bras were teetering on the coffee table. Stan was used to American women, who wear their femininity on the length of their nails. Italians wear it on the lace of our underwear. Brought up to assume that the body needs cherishing, I have amassed frilly silk things as if they were food coupons. I'm no beauty by any definition. An overly long, straight nose, brown eyes, shoulder-length brown hair with a mind of its own. Five foot four when I remember to stand up straight. Hippy, heavy-breasted. An hourglass figure is the illusory way to describe my body. The fertility-goddess type, all breadth and width, which doesn't stop me from buying another frilly underthing that has to be hand washed and ironed.

Stan stroked my head. "Can we discuss your underwear some other time?"

"I know, you prefer me naked." I got no reaction. "Is Willy okay?"

"Too much homework. We'll get him next weekend. I'm scheduled to be off."

"Good. I'll cook whatever he wants."

"We'll go out." His tone clicked a warning in my ear.

"What's wrong?"

"Nothing."

"Stan?"

He frowned. "I want to read the paper."

I got up, picked up the first stack of underwear, and dropped it inside an old mahogany breakfront on his mother's good dinner plates. I dropped the second stack in a wicker basket in the fake fireplace. Greenhouse didn't even notice. I left the other piles where they were.

In the kitchen, a room with a table *and* a window—a luxury in New York—I thawed artichoke hearts in the microwave and thought of Roberta. Flippant remark about hating dead fur notwithstanding, someone had played a very nasty trick on her. I reached for the wall phone and called her office. Above the refrigerator, the Mickey Mouse clock read seven-thirty. With fashion week only seven days away, she'd still be working.

My art director boss, paranoid about his ideas, wanted his comps back, blood and all. Roberta hadn't let me take anything out except my purse. I cut up a large ball of mozzarella, the receiver cradled on my shoulder, and let the phone ring for almost a minute. By the time I gave up, I'd eaten half the cheese. Low-fat. Tasteless.

I went back to the cramped living room, lowered the newspaper long enough to drop a piece of mozzarella—peppered and now dripping olive oil—in Stan's mouth, and picked up the phone book from under one of my cartons.

I sighed. Roberta's home number was unlisted.

Stan's hand grabbed my wrist and kissed it. "Hon, I'm sorry. I'm in a foul mood."

"Feeling crowded already?"

"No. It's work."

I dropped down on his lap, tearing the stock-exchange page in the process. "A new case?"

"The trial."

The Anna Delgado case. He'd testified last week. I'd picked him up downtown afterward and he'd been so glum, I'd treated him to fried calamari and spaghetti with meatballs down in Little Italy.

"I helped convict a woman of attempted premeditated murder. But I don't think she's guilty."

"How did you help convict her?"

"I presented the evidence. The evidence pointed to her. I had no facts corroborating my doubts, and the police commissioner was sure we had the killer. Case closed."

"Didn't the police commissioner's wife leave him a year ago?"

"That's right. He isn't into women. How did you know?" He had a sweet frown I wanted to smooth with my cheek.

"Raf, your partner and my confidant. When I complain that you're in a bad mood, he sometimes tells me why." I wrapped my arm around his neck and pulled him to me. I knew little of what Stan went through on the job except that satisfaction came only at the very end, when a criminal was convicted. "What are your doubts?"

He sat silent for a while, his head against my shoulder, torn between the desire to unload his frustration and the need to shed the grittiness of his job on the front steps of his personal life, like boots you take off in the mudroom. I'd gotten angry with him for it at the beginning, but as we grew closer, I became grateful that he kept me apart. Our two jobs didn't mix. He tries to contain the extent of evil; I sell the fantasy that buying brings happiness.

I still have a childish desire not to face the unpleasant truths of the world, although that hasn't stopped me from getting involved with ugliness and seeking justice. I place no great store in vested authority—few Italians do—but I do trust Greenhouse and his work. I have to, to love him. And by loving him and respecting him, my sleuthing feels at times like a game, a Dungeons and Dragons played out in virtual reality. A feminist friend says I am acting out centuries of male brainwashing.

I kissed his hair. What I knew of Stan's case I had gleaned from the papers. Anna Delgado had enlisted a drinking buddy of hers to shoot her husband. The man took her two thousand dollars, and at two in the morning drove with the husband to the top floor of an open twenty-four-hour parking garage, locked the husband in the trunk of his own car, shot once, and left without checking on his work. The husband survived, the metal rim of the spare tire diverting the bullet, and the hit man turned state's evidence. His story was corroborated by a barmaid who had overheard Anna say that she wanted her husband dead. It read like an easy case. "What are your doubts, *amor mio?*"

The microwave pinged. "That I'll never eat again." Stan stood up, slipping me off his lap. He was unhappy. I would ask again, after dessert. Or in bed, when constraints get shed along with the clothes. There is no question of sharing cooking chores with Stan. He takes half an hour to slice one piece of bread. A perfect slice, crumbs nowhere to be seen. I cook, he cleans.

I took the phone book back to a chest in the hallway, where it belonged. Stan, as I said, is neat. "I need an unlisted telephone number."

"Sim." A warning tone. He'd agreed to keep our accounts separate, I'd agreed not to ask him to use the investigative powers of his job and office for my own purposes.

"Roberta Riddle. I need her home number. She's in trouble. She's alone. Her husband died five years ago or something. She's got my comps. I don't want to get fired. Come on, Stan. A phone number." I couldn't get that dead rat out of my mind.

The phone rang. Not Roberta. Raf Garcia, Stan's partner.

"Sorry, Simonita. I have to steal your hombre." He had a throaty, warm voice that always sounded at the edge of laughter.

I handed over the phone. I liked Raf, but I knew this wasn't the time for chitchat.

Stan listened, nodded a couple of times, hung up. I followed him into the bedroom, where he kept his gun.

"Where?"

"Your part of town." Stan got out of his sweater. I tossed him a clean shirt.

"The Village?"

"The garment district." He flinched as if he'd stubbed his toe.

"Where?"

Stan strapped his gun around his waist, reached for a jacket in the closet.

"Where, Stan?" I had a sudden vision of the brass letter opener dripping human blood.

He slipped his jacket on, made a great fuss with the buttons. "Three-fifty Seventh," he finally said.

I wobbled with relief. Awful of me. Someone was dead and I was happy because it wasn't Roberta. I followed Stan to the door. "That's at the beginning of the fur district, I think."

He leaned over to kiss me. "I'll bring home a mink."

I hugged hard. "Bring home you. What about that unlisted number?"

"We made a deal."

"I hate rules."

"Unless you make them."

I ran to the small balcony off our bedroom, actually the roof of the bay window of the apartment below. In the spring I planned to fill it with herbs and geraniums. I leaned over the railing to blow Stan a kiss. A row of scraggly sycamores lined the street, still holding on to their leaves. It was raining lightly. Raf drove up in a blue unmarked car, saw me, and waved. I waved back at both of them, feeling very much like a wife. I wasn't sure I liked that.

Stan looked up from under the white light of the street lamp. "Get Billie at the squad." Rain flashed silver over his sweet, contrite face. "She'll give you the telephone number you want."

Blowing him a kiss of thanks, I should have remembered that Stan doesn't readily break his own rules.

3

Roberta didn't answer at home either. I popped defrosted artichoke hearts in my mouth. I finished the mozzarella. That was dinner. I knew better than to wait for Greenhouse to come home. Stan, not Greenhouse. I love you, Stan. Come home soon.

Mickey Mouse said eight-ten. Roberta was probably out to dinner. No one was going to steal those comps. And if I lost the account, the world wouldn't come to an end. I wasn't Roberta's keeper and I wasn't going to get fired.

But why that rat?

Eight-fifteen. She had to be working. I tried again. This time a young man's voice answered after the first ring.

"May I speak to Roberta Riddle, please? I'm Simona Griffo."

"She's not here." The man hung up.

I remembered an old garment-center adage: "Always be sure your lights are the last ones out." I grabbed my raincoat and plunged downstairs.

17

* * *

Three police cars had stopped in front of 530 Seventh Avenue, radios crackling, top lights spinning red and white against the brick wall, the slick of the street. An ambulance was double-parked, its back doors gaping. Beyond one door I caught sight of Raf's blue fender and license plate. I handed the cabbie a twenty-dollar bill and ran, not waiting for the change. He yelled after me, but I didn't stop until a muscled arm hooked my armpit by the elevators. I explained about knowing Roberta Riddle and two of the detectives on the case.

"Sure," the uniformed cop said.

"Call up Detectives Greenhouse and Garcia." The phone was right behind him on the desk. "Tell them Simona's here." He let go of my armpit. That was all he was going to do for me.

"Come on, thirtieth floor, extension 3002." I grabbed the receiver. He yanked it from me, his face a big rubber ball ready to bounce whatever I might scream right back at me. I'd leave no dents.

I backed away slowly, past the bank of elevators, my eye on two men in civilian clothes plowing through the double doors. Crime scene unit guys, I guessed.

"Twenty-ninth floor," the guardian dog told them with a self-important nod, pointing to the fifteenth-through-thirtieth–floor elevators. The discrepancy didn't register. I edged forward two steps, waiting to see which elevator would open. I got lucky. The one nearest me. Some women and men came out, saw the police, and started asking questions all at once. The cop tried to answer them, one red-veined eye on me. The crime unit guys stepped in the elevator. I pretended one of them bumped into me. My bag dropped three feet ahead of me, at the foot of the elevator.

"It's all right. I'll get it. Thank you," I said, although

no one had offered. The elevator started closing. I picked up my bag.

"Hey, where do you think you're going?"

With two feet of space left, I slipped half in. The door retracted. The rest of me made it. The door bounced shut on the rubber ball of an angry face.

The crime unit men laughed, but they wouldn't let me off on the twenty-ninth floor.

"Twenty-nine? That's okay." I laughed, too. Their homicide had nothing to do with Roberta. "I want thirty. Riddle Solutions. The ready-to-wear collections are showing in a week. Lots of work to do."

"Hey, this building's closed!" someone yelled from the twenty-ninth floor.

The door to the showroom was locked. I pressed my face against the glass. Light washed out from under Roberta's office door. I rang the bell, I pounded. Roberta didn't answer. The black lacquer table now held a Chinese enamel planter with gracefully curving, creamy butterfly orchids. The jade Buddha was missing.

"Hey, miss, what do you think you're doing?"

I didn't bother answering.

The policeman ushered me into a corridor on the twenty-ninth floor, an exact replica of upstairs. Except for the empty gurney. "Where's Garcia?" he asked in a loud voice. "This lady was trying to break in upstairs."

"I was not!"

He pulled me by the elbow. I dug my rubber-soled rain boots in the vinyl. The ladies'-room door was open. There were too many men inside. The bathroom mirror flashed, then reflected Roberta's jade Buddha between the scuffed shoes of a cop. A corner had broken off. Its soap-smooth head was covered in blood.

One uniform handed me over to another. "Take care of her. I've got work to do." I was too stunned to protest. Whoever was dead was still in there, in the ladies' room.

The policeman now holding me seemed grateful for the distraction of my presence. He was young, his complexion the color of the pea soup of *Exorcist* fame. A rookie, I guessed, on his first homicide. He kept asking me who I was, what I was doing there, his clasp weak on my raincoat.

"Great set of latents," someone behind the door said. "Bloody latents."

"Maybe this time we have an open-and-shut case, the way I like 'em." Stan's partner's voice.

"Raf!" I craned my neck toward the bathroom. "Raf, Simo—" I saw her, still in her two-toned gray suit with the white cuffs and collar. I'd titled that collection "The White Touch." She'd really liked that. Roberta with her red hat.

Alive! Talking to Stan at the end of the corridor. *Grazie a Dio.* I waved my arm and yelled.

Stan turned around.

"Who's dead?"

He gave me a tolerant the-woman's-burned-the-roast-again look. "She's okay," he told the rookie.

"Don't worry," I told Stan. The rookie still held on to me. "You had me fooled completely. Inverting the number was clever. I never can remember the boundaries of your new precinct." He'd moved from the Thirteenth to Mid-Town South over a year ago. "I came here for my own reasons. Who's dead?"

Roberta walked slowly toward me, her ankles wobbling on her high heels. Over her shoulder, ten feet back, a glass door read: NITE LIFE, INC. The showroom was dark. As Roberta came nearer, I saw that her face was frozen. I rushed to hug her.

"Go home, Sim," Stan said. His tone was defeated, the color of his skin gray.

"Will you at least tell me who's dead?"

"Phyllis," Roberta said with the perfect composure that comes from a cold heart or shock.

"Your fitting model?" Why would anyone want to kill Phyllis? "How?" I had visions of her being speared like the rat, her "garmentos stab you in the chest" turning into prophetic words. Bad news pushes the blend button in my brain. I'd forgotten the bloody Buddha.

"She was hit on the head," Roberta said.

"Sim, honey—" Stan's shoulder was brushing my nose. The young policeman was on the other side of me, holding on to me still.

"Get that man some coffee!" I whispered to Stan.

"My Buddha killed her. An anniversary present from my husband." Roberta nodded slowly, the mechanical gesture of a wind-up doll. "Someone bashed her head in with five thousand dollars' worth of jade. She died with her underpants down. A mother's nightmare."

Stan let me take her home.

"Can you imagine dying like that? It's so humiliating." Roberta poured herself a whiskey.

I chewed on a dried apple slice. "Wearing a Bill Blass ball gown isn't going to dignify death." We were sitting in Roberta's vast, red-lacquered living room on Fifth Avenue, overlooking a dark Central Park. From my armchair I could see the fuzzy swoop of lights on the George Washington Bridge in the far distance. The window was wet with rain.

"Why would anyone want to kill Phyllis?" I asked.

Roberta threw off her heels and tucked her legs under one of the huge silk pillows of her wine-red sofa. The hat, too garish a red for the rest of the decor, stayed on her head. "She got fat!"

"I think you should lie down."

Roberta shook the ice in her glass. "Tinkle, tinkle,

little death, how I wonder . . . No, I'm fine." She stretched out an arm. "Really."

I sat back down.

Alarm hunched on her face. "They won't think I—"

"The best detective on the force is working on the case. Stan Greenhouse. If you didn't do it, he won't think."

"Of course I didn't do it! But God, everyone's going to be happy she's dead."

"Why?"

"She had bad manners." She was being sarcastic. "Greenhouse? He's the man you now live with?"

"Yes. Did you find her?"

"The cleaning woman did. Apparently, the bathroom doors on my floor were jammed. That's what your boyfriend, the detective, said. Both men's and ladies'. She had to go down one flight. The bathroom key works on all floors. The killer was waiting for her. No one works late on the twenty-ninth floor."

"She could have gone up one flight, too."

"No, on the thirty-first floor Nina Ricci has the penthouse, and the bathroom's inside, not in the hall like the rest of the floors. I wanted to—" Roberta put down her glass to stare at me, anger in her eyes. "Why did you come back to the studio?"

"I knew you'd be working late."

"That's right. The collection must go on. The operative word for over thirty years. For what? Mythmaking. Except I don't create anything that lasts more than a couple of seasons, if I'm lucky. All that paranoia, lock up the sketches, don't let anyone see the samples. What for? Chanel was the mythmaker. Me, I'm just a little woman with little ideas."

Roberta hadn't let anyone at the agency see the sketches or the finished products of her Riddle Nothing knits. She had told us the mood she wanted for the ad—

light and fun—she had told us the colors of the line, but had insisted we imagine the clothes. Fortunately, our other fashion clients weren't so paranoid.

As I sat down, I had noticed two clothes racks covered by white bulging sheets, incongruous in an elegant living room filled with Chinese art. I was willing to bet the racks held the closely guarded Riddle Nothings. "Is someone knocking you off? Was Phyllis selling your designs?"

"In her perverted way, Phyllis was loyal." Roberta stared at a point behind my head. "She wasn't stealing. It's hard to know anything for sure."

"How can I help you, Roberta?"

"I think I'm beyond help." Her eyes left the clothes racks and focused on me, sitting across from her, between us a glass coffee table crowded with framed photos of models wearing her designs. Her family pictures. I couldn't find a photo of her husband.

"I looked at the layouts," Roberta said, her voice level, sounding at ease. "I like the one the rat died on. What I could see of it."

"That rat was a threat of some kind?"

"Riddle Nothings is a perfect name. We'll have to find a good model. Someone like Cindy, but less expensive. Someone with a having-fun face." She leaned back against the sofa and was quiet for a moment. Two large drops fell from the corners of her eyes, leaving pathmarks on the rouge of her cheeks. No sound. I sat still.

"Phyllis was tired," Roberta said, opening her eyes. She used her cocktail napkin to wipe a wet spot her glass had left on the coffee table. She didn't bother with the tears on her face. "We were working late. She had started eating too much again and I got angry. Phyllis was a bitch, but I'm so damn superstitious. Everyone wanted me to get rid of her. She was thin then, when—

all those Tootsie Rolls means she was up to something again. No, she wasn't stealing designs. Not from me. Maybe from Arnold Scaasi." She made a gurgling sound with her throat, an attempt at laughter.

"Why not from you?"

"We had a special relationship. The police will think I killed her."

"Why? What reason could you possibly have?"

"I never thought of killing her. Phyllis was part of my life, whether she was in the studio or not. An extra bone in my body. All I had to do was call her and there she'd be. How often can you count on that?"

I offered to stay the night. Roberta refused. I insisted. "I don't think I can afford your ads," she told me as if that would get rid of me.

"We don't have to talk about that tonight." Following her to a white-lacquered bedroom, I offered to call a friend. She lay down on a black, raw silk duvet, her red hat still in place.

"I won't leave you alone."

Roberta finally asked for Flossie, her sample maker. As I dialed I looked at several paintings of the same scene. A breaker of rocks, a narrow beach, sailboats on the water. She saw me stare.

"My partner Elsa painted those. Manhasset Bay as seen from her house. They're reminders."

Of what she didn't say.

At three o'clock in the morning, I heard Greenhouse come home. He locked himself up in the bathroom for a long time. Locked. He'd never done that before. When he came to bed, he reeked of mouthwash, something he never used. I found his hand, ice cold from washing it too long.

"You're not feeling well."

"That rookie you were worried about," Stan said, "I gave him coffee and he was fine. I've been a cop for twenty-one years and I still throw up."

"It makes you human and wonderful, and I love you all the more for it."

He tucked both our hands under his arm. "It took me three years to learn how to hold back until I got home."

"Now you've got a sentimental, soppy woman on your hands and no privacy. I hope you never regret it."

"No, but don't tell Willy. The only other person who knows is Raf."

"And your ex-wife."

"Irene pretended not to notice. It didn't fit into her idea of a man. And she hated my being a cop anyway."

"I'm sorry." I kissed the wrinkles on the inside of his elbow. "All I can tell anyone, if they ask, is that I love you to pieces."

While we held each other close in a double bed that was too soft, Greenhouse filled me in on the murder.

Phyllis Striker had died of multiple blows to the head between seven-fifteen P.M., when she excused herself from Roberta's studio to go to the bathroom, and seven-forty-three, when the cleaning lady found her. The most likely murder weapon was the Buddha left beside her in the bathroom stall. According to Roberta, her studio was the only one working on the two floors in question. The other four tenants on the floors imported clothes from Italy and Hong Kong. They did not show at the collections, and therefore had no reason to be working late on a Sunday. When the police arrived, they found no one on the two floors except the cleaning woman, Roberta, and, of course, Phyllis. Flossie and the rest of the gang had been sent home at seven. A lot of people were working late on other floors but gave no information that seemed pertinent.

"What about the bloody prints on the door?" I asked. "Raf thinks it might be an open-and-shut case."

"How do you know?"

"I listen."

I got a nose nudge behind my ear. "Only when you feel like it."

"What about those latents?"

"That will take a while." They had to check Phyllis's fingerprints, her blood. If they didn't match, they had to take fingerprints of everyone who worked on that floor, on Roberta's floor. If nothing came of that, they'd proceed with the entire building.

"Nothing's open and shut," Stan said, "unless you catch the perp in the act, and nowadays even that is no guarantee the perp's going to do time."

Roberta had told Stan that she didn't know if Phyllis had enemies. She had draped her designs on Phyllis's body for over thirty years, but she claimed not to know her last name. Which didn't concur with what she'd told me about Phyllis being an extra bone in her body. I decided that shock had confused her.

"You don't think Roberta did it, do you?" Rain was pattering on the air conditioner outside the bedroom window. An unfamiliar sound. In the Village I'd covered my air conditioner with herb pots.

"I think I need to sleep."

"Thanks for telling me as much as you did about the case." The noise outside the window sounded as if some naughty child was up on the roof dropping pebbles.

"Consider it an exception."

"I plan to." I nudged my foot under his thigh for warmth. "I didn't come to live with you to share homicides of people I know."

Stan tightened his thighs to squeeze my foot. "Is Mrs. Riddle all right?" A kind cop, my Stan.

"For now. I got hold of her sample maker to keep her company. Couldn't we put a rubber mat on that air conditioner?"

"Sim?"

"Stan?" I spooned myself against his rear end.

"You're not going to get involved, right?"

"Too late for that. But if I find out anything of interest, I'll let you know. . . ." He tensed under me. "*Amore mio*, I was trying to be funny."

Stan shifted onto his back. "My stomach's all balled up." I wrapped my neck over his shoulder.

"It's only dead women that make me sick." Stan turned on his hip, his face inches away from mine. The room was dark, but I could see his eyes in my head, welcoming despite their seriousness. "Raf thinks I'm compensating for Dad."

His father was shot in the head for a gold watch in the elevator of his office building. Stan, a junior in college then, had hung out with the detectives on the case and a few months later had quit New York University and joined the force. The killer was still at large.

"Doesn't make sense to me," he said.

"It does, though. In the usual nonlinear way most of us deal with our lives." His thumb skated across my forehead. I pushed back my head to kiss it. "I'm sorry I was making light of this case. I'm nervous. I don't know how to handle myself. If I stick my nose in this particular murder, you'll be furious. If I don't, I'll feel I'm giving up something that is important to me and I'll resent it. Living together makes some things harder. Like doing whatever I please."

"Why is it important to you?"

"Because I like to make things right again. I see a bad situation and I fly in, Batwoman without wings. I guess it's my way of having a say."

"How about a compromise?"

I kissed his neck. The rain patter had turned into a machine-gun volley, but I was too comfortable to do anything about it. "What's the compromise?"

"Keep working with Roberta, ask questions on the spot if you want, since you're going to anyway, but no snooping where you're not welcome. Leave the investigating to Raf and me." He took my arm and wrapped it over his chest, turning his back to me again. I settled my body against his.

"That sounds sensible," I said. Skin to skin with the man I loved, what else could I say? "What are you going to do about that woman you think is innocent?"

"Find the killer."

"How?"

He mumbled, half-asleep. I kissed the nearest shoulder blade. I felt, despite the ugly events of that day, as if all would be right with the world. It is a feeling left over from childhood that comes just before sleep, when a mother or a father is holding you and you are living only in that soft, fuzzy moment, perfectly safe.

"You sweetheart," I muttered, closing my eyes. "About our compromise."

"Hmmm."

"I have a better one."

"Hmmm."

"Give me your body, I'll give you my heart."

We both fell asleep.

4

"Who do you think killed Phyllis?" Charlie Angelo pushed two fingers against his square chin. I had found Roberta's new partner waiting for me in my office the next morning. Along with a marketing planning manual the size of the Manhattan phone book and a note from the CEO, Harold Harland, the first H of HH&H. He wanted to discuss my future.

Charlie was interested in his own. "So who killed her? The police are going to think it's somebody from the company. The murder weapon came from our showroom."

"I have no idea. I met Phyllis yesterday." I dropped the marketing manual on the floor, next to Charlie's black-lizard cowboy boots.

"You were there last night. The detective on the case is your boyfriend."

"You must have talked to Roberta." I'd called both the house and the office before leaving the West Side, too late for one place, too early for the other. "How is she?"

"I couldn't get hold of her. Mario told me about the detective boyfriend."

"I'm sorry this happened."

Charlie had dark circles under his eyes and he hadn't shaved. I didn't know whether he was anxious or had been partying all night. He was wearing black velvet pants, tight enough to choke his manhood, a white button-down shirt with the sleeves rolled up, and a raw silk milk-chocolate brown vest that I would have loved to steal. His hair was appropriately mussed, his jaw clenched.

I, on the other hand, had humidity-frazzled hair, beige gabardine floppy slacks that needed an iron fix, and a navy-and-white-striped shirt my mother had just sent me from Italy. I think it was a present for my move into Greenhouse's apartment, not that she would admit it. She believes that at the age of thirty-eight and a half, I should acquire a new husband, not a roommate. I had, to her old-fashioned chagrin, dumped my former husband for burning his penis at both ends. I had not been the woman holding the match.

"I didn't know Phyllis much." Charlie hunched forward, elbows on knees, and sipped the coffee I'd brought him. Getting coffee for clients is a habit the CEO frowns upon as not being managerial. He thinks power is measured by how loud a snap he can make with his fingers. I know power is measured by the square footage of your office, by the presence of a window, by the existence of a door. I was in a closet, which is how I'd started out at HH&H. In four years I'd progressed from $22,000 a year to $38,000 and from an open closet and canned air to a closet with a door and canned air, the perk partially due to my having solved an office murder. I could now pull up my panty hose without an audience and afford to send my clothes to the cleaners. My next goal was a glass rectangle with a view of the wall of the building next door.

"So what do you think?" Charlie asked. His finger-tips were white against the gray of the mug. He wore a heavy turquoise and silver ring I hadn't seen before.

"That gossip in your business is worse than in mine and that I'll find out about the killer in the newspaper same as you." Is that why he was sitting in front of me, one bouncing knee generating enough energy to light a runway show? To pump me for information I didn't have? Up to now I hadn't given Charlie Angelo much thought. We'd only met a couple of times, exchanged a few words. He could be dismissive and charming.

"How can I help you, Charlie?"

"You don't think Roberta . . ." His hand gave a bleached curl an unnecessary squeeze.

"I don't." I didn't know. The most innocuous, respectable-looking people can turn out to be killers, but I wasn't going to express any spreadable opinions. "Why would Roberta want Phyllis dead?"

"I don't know. Look, you probably think I can't wait for the police to lock the old lady up so that I can take over. All right, you saw what happened yesterday. I got mad. I want to be a designer and Roberta's holding me back. We're not exactly getting along, but I owe her."

"You've worked for her how many years?"

"Three. I'd still be draping polyester knockoffs for a volume house with a top price of eighteen dollars and seventy-five cents if she hadn't dropped in one day and hired me." Charlie tipped the chair back and stamped a boot on my wall. "She's scared stiff of putting any piz-zazz in her designs!"

"What if Roberta is accused? What would happen to the business?"

His leg dropped. "Instant fame. I called *Vogue* this morning and got an appointment with an editor in five minutes. She's coming next Wednesday. With the foldouts we're doing in the fashion magazines, we'll really start rolling."

"Foldouts? Roberta talked about a four-color, one-page ad in two magazines." The space in *Vogue* alone was going to cost them over $55,000. The back of the front cover or the back cover would add another ten thousand.

"I convinced Roberta that she's got to work on her image, to think of fashion as performance. We're ready to commit three hundred thousand dollars!"

"Roberta sent you to tell me this?"

"No, I thought you knew."

I instantly panicked. She was ready to fire the agency. There was no other reason I could think of for not telling me. The ad business is wall-to-wall viral paranoia. "Do you have retailers behind you?" Magazines usually give stores a twenty percent discount on ads.

"Saks and Neiman Marcus, maybe more." Charlie started swinging in his chair, rubbing his ring. "With enough ads, we could generate a request." That meant one of Roberta's pieces would be included in a fashion editorial. He grinned. "I hear the buzz already swarming up the avenue."

His optimism was infectious. Paranoia was replaced by possibility. For a moment I relished the look of oozing gratitude on the CEO's face when I told him the ad budget had shot up 50 percent. "We can use the same layout, just quadruple it." Was $300,000 enough?

"Yeah, four or five models. Red nails, red lips, stiletto heels, kohl on their eyes. Power women! It's sexy, it's *now*. See if Steven Meisel can shoot it for us. That would be fifteen thousand dollars well spent. Women as sex subjects." Charlie aimed his square jaw at me. "I like it!"

Roberta appeared in my mind, sitting on her sofa with her hat on, tears as big as last night's raindrops gliding down her cheeks. She'd said she had no money. "Excuse me a minute. I'll be right back."

"Sure." Charlie looked glued to the chair.

I walked into Gregory's office around the corner. He merits door and window. He's been the in-house illustrator for over twenty years and is the only truth in advertising I know. An honorable and gentle man, and my best friend. Accustomed to my sudden noisy intrusions, Gregory didn't look up from the Magic Marker squiggles he was making.

"Wicked. Pure Picasso." I kissed his forehead and dialed Bobbi Scotch's number. She worked in a Seventh Avenue buying office and was living with the head of our studio department. Her hobbies were sample sales, lipsticks, and gossip. They got her out of chronic bad moods.

"Isn't that something?" was Bobbi's comment on Phyllis's murder.

"What do you know about a bank loan to Riddle Solutions?"

"Got turned down by Chemical and Citibank both. About two months ago. You know she's factored?"

"Yes." A lot of smaller apparel manufacturers turn over their receivables to factors in exchange for 75 to 80 percent cash up-front to meet their overhead and pay the vendors. There's the added advantage of no bookkeeping or bill-collecting headaches.

"I hear her factor wants to pull out for next season." Bobbi's lips smacked. I imagined them a glossy, pearlized pink, her favorite color. "I also hear she's trying to get private backers."

"Trying?"

"If she's scored, it hasn't hit the streets yet. Carlisle is having a great sample sale. Seventy percent off. Wanna go at lunchtime?"

"No thanks. I've just moved into a closetless apartment."

"Meaning the boyfriend gives you no space. When I moved in with Henry, I took over the kitchen. I got me a walk-in closet and I don't have to cook."

We laughed. I hung up and kissed Gregory again.

"What's up besides murder?" He snuffled. Falling leaves kill his sinuses.

"Maybe three hundred thousand for the Riddle campaign. Foldout, all the fashion books. Fifty-four thousand in agency commissions, which are desperately needed."

Gregory sniffed and squiggled with his marker. He reacts to facts. I gyrate at the mere hint of possibility. It's my aerobic exercise.

"A little encouragement, please," I begged. "You'll miss me if I get booted upstairs."

"I'll buy a radio."

5

———— ❦ ————

Back in my own office, Charlie was reading the marketing manual, specifically the strengths and weaknesses analysis page. His eyes looked glazed. From boredom for sure.

I swung into my seat, drying my hands as if I'd just been to the bathroom, and wished for the ability to analyze the new situation. "Who do *you* think killed Phyllis?"

"Her girdle; how should I know?" Charlie dropped the manual on the desk. "Sorry. That's not funny." He looked sincere, which made me warm up to him.

"Did the police fingerprint everyone in the showroom yet?"

"I wasn't there." He pulled at his hair in the back, near his bald spot. "Why would they do that?"

"They found bloody prints on the door to the bathroom."

His eyes canvassed the walls of my room, papered with photo-shoot schedules, budgets, models' head sheets. "Phyllis must have left those."

"The medical examiner says she died on the spot, in the bathroom stall. She wouldn't have had the chance to reach the door. Those have to be the killer's prints."

"Who would be that dumb?" He did a good imitation of a smirk, which did nothing to cover up what was now clearly a bad case of anxiety.

"Maybe the killer had to leave in a hurry. Do you have any idea who put that rat on Roberta's desk?"

"I did, that's what everyone in the showroom thinks. But I didn't. Rats give me the creeps."

"Who, then?"

"My guess is the landlord. The guy next door to us, Ed Mannucci, he's a fancy sportswear maufacturer. Raking it in. He wants to take over the whole floor, and he's willing to pay a lot more. The landlord's offered Roberta some nice space on twenty-three for ninety thousand a year instead of a hundred, but she won't move from the thirtieth floor."

"So the landlord, to encourage her to leave, left her a nice present." How? When I'd dropped the layouts on Roberta's desk, there was no dead rat in sight. One door of her office led to the showroom, the other to a small corridor that led to the design room, a cutting room, and the small production office. "Maybe someone came in from the shipping entrance."

"Hey, you don't think that whoever played those tricks on her also killed Phyllis?"

"Tricks? The dead rat is not the only present?"

"Roaches, dog shit, stuff like that."

"Did she go to the police?"

"That would be too sissy for Roberta." Charlie smiled and I thought of a child, hair plastered down with water, sitting in the principal's office, with that same ingratiating smile on his face, trying to live up to his name. Angelo. Maybe everyone in the showroom was right. He was the trickster. To wear "the old lady" down and get her to quit. Then he would be the designer.

I wondered how much Roberta trusted Charlie. "What do you think of the knits?"

Charlie sat up, squared his shoulders. "Sure. Great stuff. I mean it could use a lift here and there, but considering—"

"It's been hard for us to come up with any ideas." I propped the new layout for Riddle Nothings against my bulletin board. It looked great. At the top a green satin pouch, lined with blazing pink, reversed, spilling out a model in a plain white teddy followed by Roberta's floating knits in the same lime green.

"Roberta gave us the concept," I said. "Ease and comfort. We know she's always been big on the practicality of her clothes. So we worked on that, added a little fun, but we haven't seen anything. If you can give me an idea, it would help me find the right models."

"Okay, I'll admit it." He crossed a leather boot over his knee. "I haven't seen them either."

"You didn't cut the samples?"

"No, she hired a freelancer. The guy downstairs, Mr. Nite, recommended someone." Charlie's motor knee kicked in. "Roberta gave the excuse that we had too much work preparing the dress line, which was bullshit."

"Someone's knocking off her designs."

Charlie shook his head. "Yeah, so what? Happens all the time. And why pin it on me? I want to design my own. I hate her not trusting me! I really hate it."

"How did you become a partner?" Six months ago, the news that he had inherited the 40 percent partnership sent off ripples of surprise. Aileen Mehle's "Suzy" column in W had asked, "Now what did he do to merit that?"

"Mrs. Morewitz had no kids. Dead husband. No

cousins or nephews, at least not that she talked about. Funny, huh? I always think Jews have big families like us Italians. We're a lot alike. Tight families, Mama in control. Food a big thing."

"Mediterranean origins."

"I'm a queen from Bensonhurst. Not many of us around. Who'll admit it, I mean." He was punching his words again, his confidence eroding with each stressed syllable. "I got the best parents. Didn't get upset much, except Ma, she wants grandchildren. The funny thing about Mrs. Morewitz? I met her three times, maybe."

"Then why did she leave you her share of Riddle Solutions?"

His face turned somber. "Beats me."

Was he lying?

Flossie, the sample maker, sat in front of her sewing machine feeding fabric to a needle. It was afternoon. I'd finally reached Roberta on the phone. She had sounded her old self, abrupt and yet friendly. I asked about the increased ad budget. She told me to come over. I flew. In the showroom two salespeople were taking orders for the resort/cruise line from a gaggle of impatient buyers. I noticed that the butterfly orchid plant was gone. In the shipping department, three men were boxing reorders on the fall line. Rumors be damned. Business looked brisk.

Roberta wasn't in the studio.

"Where did she go?" I was impatient to find out if we really had three hundred thousand to spend, eager to flaunt the coup to my CEO and dump the marketing manual in the garbage.

"She's got a lot on her mind maybe," Flossie said, sounding appropriately disapproving. Not much taller

than Roberta, she was a stocky woman in her late sixties with thick, curly gray hair and a round, lined face
always accessorized by drugstore Benjamin Franklin
glasses. "She's got to find a replacement fitting model.
Finish the line, that's a hundred outfits. Edit them
down to sixty. Finish picking the runway models. Fit
them. Make up her mind about the accessories that
keep coming in. Rehearsals start in two days.
Tomorrow she's picking the music for the show. So
maybe she forgot."

No mention of Phyllis's death. I wanted to pull up a
chair and ask everyone questions, but Stan's presence in
the case had the weight of a gravestone on my curiosity.
"How is Roberta taking it?" Flossie had spent the night
with her.

"For breakfast she ate half an onion bagel, a little
cream cheese." Flossie's hand grazed over beige linen.
"We're doing fine."

Next to Flossie, three other women bent over pale
fabrics at their sewing machines. Two were Chinese
seamstresses hired part-time for the spring collection.
Lourdes Montalvo had recently been hired full-time.
The workroom had four windows facing Thirty-ninth
Street. Across the street was the premier building of the
garment district—550 Seventh Avenue, home to Bill
Blass, Hanae Mori, Michael Kors. Donna Karan occupied six floors.

"The police came this morning, took all our fingerprints like we were thieves," Mario the tailor said, his
Italian accent weak and his tone dire. He stood behind
one long table, sewing the armpit of a jacket, the silver
thimble on his finger catching sunlight with each arch-
ing stitch. A stooped, thin man with dyed black hair
tight against his scalp and loose skin drooling from
under rimless eyeglasses, he wore a faded blue cotton
duster. At the far end of the table, a portable radio

played Dvorak's *New World Symphony*, apt music for a room of immigrants.

"The detective locked himself and Mrs. Riddle in her office," Mario said, "and when she came out, an hour later, she looked like something I sweep up from the floor. It's a shame what they do."

I was quick to come to Stan's defense. "The police are only doing their job."

Mario lifted his head, eyes rheumy. "I think of the death. Every minute every one of us thinks of it." The sewing machines started a fly-against-window thump. "I also think there is no morality left in the world."

"Where's Charlie?"

On the other side of the room was the assistant designer's table. Dotted-white pattern paper was strewn everywhere. Behind the cutting table, sheafs of patterns hung stiffly on numbered hooks on the wall, each number representing a style. Fabric swatches framed the window. In the corner under a sweep of dusty daylight a headless mannequin wore the right half of a yellow linen jacket. No Charlie.

"He might know where Roberta is," I said.

"Hah!" Flossie announced, looking at me as if my brains had gone for a walk. "That young schnook doesn't even know how to thread the right needle . . . "

The youngest seamstress giggled.

Flossie opened her mouth wider. "*And* maybe we think about Phyllis being killed, and maybe not, but one thing is for sure. This business is no different from Broadway. We got a show to put on."

"He was just here," Mario said. "He'll be back."

"I think of me." Lourdes Montalvo gave Flossie a quick, scared glance as she swung a pink skirt under the needle. "Phyllis got me my job, I am grateful, but I don't like her and I am scared!" Lourdes was in her late twenties, with a quiet moon-shaped face curtained by thick black hair that shone under the fluorescent lights. Mario snipped with monster scissors, his sagging eyes on Lourdes. Flossie and the other two seamstresses stopped sewing.

Lourdes took the attention as a sign of encouragement. "I bet the police arrest Mrs. Riddle and we all lose our jobs."

Mario's scissors dropped to the floor. Dvorak's largo changed into the fast-paced third movement. Flossie's chin snapped up. "What do you know? Nothing you know!"

"I know plenty!" Lourdes said. "Phyllis was mean to Mrs. Riddle and Mrs. Riddle fire her and then Phyllis is dead. I know plenty! I know she has a nervous breakdown once and closed the place up. She could do that again. What about our jobs then?"

"Phyllis was getting too big." Mario lifted the jacket he was sewing as evidence. He was looking at me as if I were the accuser. The scissors were still on the floor. "I have to tighten everything for the runway model. That's why Mrs. Riddle fire her. She never had a breakdown. Mrs. Riddle is strong. A strong, good woman."

Flossie jerked the handwheel of her sewing machine and stood up. "One day, if you don't watch it, Mario, you're going to cut that long tongue of yours—and enough with that noise, it's driving me crazy!" She snapped the radio off. "I do most of the tightening around here, and as for you, Lourdes Montalvo, you know nothing, and even if you should know, you don't go spreading your mouth in front of strangers."

"Flossie, I'm a friend," I said.

"Maybe you are." She sat back down, her eyes peering at me over the top of her glasses, uncommitted. "I hear the detective on the case is your boyfriend, so maybe not."

Mario picked up his scissors and turned the radio back on, louder this time. "We like to be a family in this showroom. That's how Mrs. Riddle runs it for thirty-five years. Like a family."

Flossie hummphed. "With such a family I'll go into a nursing home."

"Who played the tricks on Roberta?" I asked. "Charlie claims he's innocent."

Flossie bent over her linen dress.

Lourdes changed a pink bobbin to a beige one. Mario snipped nonexistent threads. In their minds, I had already left.

I decided to call my art director, tell him to stop holding his breath, I still had no news.

I went into Roberta's office, narrowed my eyes to get past the blinding shine of rhinestone jewelry—glitter was in—amassed on chairs and floor, and finally found the phone buried under a dome of green and purple bras, all push-ups, another *dernier cri* in fashion.

I peeked. I'm a broad-backed 36C with a color range of white and black. Green might have added a jazzy note to my nights. The sizes varied from 32As to 32Bs.

Disappointed, I picked up the receiver. The display showed the previously dialed number. An easy number to remember since it was Roberta's office number, except for one digit. I left a message for my boss.

On the way out, the receptionist slipped me a note.

"The dead rat and the other stuff—Ed Mannucci." It was signed *Lingua lunga*. Long-tongued Mario.

The garment center is too busy a place to be elegant or pretty. There are some handsome Art Deco buildings, 530 and 550 being two of them, but what hits the eye are the fast-food shops, the tacky clothing stores, the growing litter on the street, the long line of trucks trundling over potholes, the rush of men pushing hand trucks loaded with cartons of trimmings and fabrics, more men propelling metal racks packed tight with one style of plastic-covered plaid skirts or pink rayon blouses or whatever. Gum-popping women walk the sidewalks crunching flyers of the latest sample sale into your hand, others push past you, high heels clicking, late for their next buying appointment. Men with gelled hair stand on street corners in their Gucci loafers and double-breasted suits, flashing gold Rolexes, showing off the breadth of their shoulders and their latest deal.

Someone has gone to the trouble of putting up fake green street signs. Compassion Avenue. An ironic concept on an avenue where jobs are made and unmade on the turn of a fad.

So much energy, I thought as I sprinted past the florist's kiosk and the larger-than-life bronze statue commemorating the linchpin of the garment center—the worker, yarmulke on his head, stooped over his sewing machine. Where was woman and her sewing machine? I crossed Fortieth Street with the green light, on my way to the subway station on Broadway to catch the N or the R back to Union Square and my office. The careening messenger didn't even sound his warning whistle, he just rammed his bike right into me, sending me sprawling on my ass.

"*Stronzo!*" I yelled after him, calling him a turd, a strong insult in Italy. His legs, thin and white, pedaled furiously. Seen from the back, hunched over, he looked headless. Therefore unrecognizable.

"There ought to be a law," a woman said, helping me up. She was overdressed, which gave her away as a tourist.

"There is, but what's that mean nowadays?" I

thanked her, grateful to her and the fact that I'd left the new layout in Roberta's office. Dirty slacks and a hole in my panty hose I could deal with.

"He, like, wanted to get you," a young black man said, walking beside me, his feet hidden by the folds of his drooping grunge pants. "You okay?"

"Sure. Thanks."

He twirled a cellophane-wrapped tray of cold cuts, concentric yellow, pink, and white circles dotted with toothpick-skewered, pimiento-stuffed olives. My eye always zeroes in on food.

"The jerk was in a hurry." I resolved to treat myself to a slice of pizza. "We all are."

"Naw, I saw him aim that front wheel. Someone don't like you."

I had no reason to believe him.

Three hours later, pizza slice settled in my stomach, models' portfolios stacked outside my office door for a pickup, their head sheets pushed to an empty section of my desk and the dreaded marketing manual perused, then hidden under the mess on top of my file cabinet, I fished into my purse for the elusive subway token that would get me to my new home. The phone rang. I let it ring, fearful that my CEO was popping an eight o'clock breakfast meeting on me to drill me on operations systems. On the fifth ring, my *brava ragazza* upbringing took over.

"HH&H, Simona Griffo speaking." The perfect good girl.

"Five thousand dollars is all I can give you!" Roberta.

"Five thousand dollars barely pays for a photographer."

"Not the ad. For you."

"You're going to pay me five thousand dollars?"

"That's right."

"What for?"

"The police believe Charlie murdered Phyllis. You'll discover the real killer."

6

Roberta had an errand to run in the Village and asked to meet me at the Union Square Cafe on Sixteenth Street. A perfect place in which to handle important news—friendly, warm, with some of the best food in town. It was also two blocks from my office on Fifth Avenue and Eighteenth Street. A striped-shirted bartender smiled a handsome welcome. I ordered Risotto d'Oro, rice simmered in carrot and celery juice, with flecks of minced vegetables—a Cafe specialty. Solid food eats the mold off my gray cells. Roberta ordered a scotch, straight up.

"First of all," I said, "why are you so sure Charlie didn't kill Phyllis? Second, what's the incriminating evidence against Charlie? Third, why me?"

She studied the amber color of her drink as if it might inspire her next collection. A wide, black-felt hat, lampshade style, shaded the top half of her face. Blond-rinsed curls coiled out from under the back of her hat. She had foregone the trademark rouge slashes on her cheeks, perhaps in a sign of mourning. Her size-four body was fitted into a tight, black wool suit. She had tucked Manolo Blahnik black suede high heels behind the rung of the bar stool. She wore nude-colored hose, varicose veins exposed. At her feet the signature black nylon Prada bag with hand-finished leather piping that could carry a week's wardrobe. Behind her a massive dusty-rose halo of dried hydrangeas amplified her presence. Roberta looked so fifties I half expected to see long black gloves and a matching cigarette holder. A diminutive, aged Holly Golightly, I thought, with almost the same Audrey Hepburn elegance.

"Charlie is a sweet, eager young man who wants to be the next Halston. He's no killer. Those fingerprints on the door are a mistake!"

That was great evidence for the witness box. I sucked on my rice. "The bloody fingerprints on the bathroom door are his, then?"

"That's what the police claim."

"Is it Phyllis's blood?"

"I don't know. Charlie says he wasn't there at all."

"If those are his fingerprints, he's lying. How well do you know him?"

"Will you take the assignment?"

"Roberta, if you care that much for Charlie, the best thing you could do is to get the best team of lawyers you can afford—"

"What do you mean, care that much for him?" Her hazel eyes had all the warmth of marbles rolling through a March blizzard.

I was momentarily confused. "I mean that you obviously care since you're willing to spend five thousand dollars to prove he's not guilty. A good team of lawyers will cost you much more than that, but—"

"This is strictly business. I'm showing in eight days. The collection isn't finished. With this murder hanging over Charlie's head, he's going to be thinking straight lines as in jail bars. My lines are curved. Caring doesn't enter into it."

Why didn't I believe her? "I'm not a bona fide detective. If you want, I'll try to find someone good."

"Simona, do you want me to beg?" Roberta put a laugh in her voice, but it was clear that she was upset. "My fitting model has been killed. My name is spilling all over the crime section of newspapers. The police are interrogating my workers, and I'm incapable of doing anything to clear up this horrible mess. I must concentrate all my energy on the collection. I have a company to save. Can't you see I need a nosy friend in my camp? Just ask questions. You can say I sent you. I'll confirm it. A detective would scare people off. You're a friend."

"This has nothing to do with my having a boyfriend who just happens to be one of the detectives on the case?"

"No. I think I can count on you not to have divided loyalties."

"He tells me nothing of his cases." Would I tell him of mine?

"Will you do this for me?" Roberta's eyes pleaded. Her teeth gnawed at her lips. She was scared for Charlie, for herself, I didn't know for what or whom else. I savored the last morsel of golden rice against my palate. Something in my chest knocked hard—my heart or my crusading spirit, wanting out as badly as Robin Williams in Aladdin's lamp.

I swallowed. "All right, I'll see what I can find out. What's Charlie's alibi?"

"He was in the workroom all day, cutting samples."

"Is that where you were?"

"No, I worked on Phyllis in the design room. Lourdes, Mario, and Flossie were in the workroom with him. I sent them all home around seven."

"Fifteen minutes before Phyllis went to the bathroom."

"That's right."

"Did they leave together?"

"You'll have to ask them." She reached into her bag for her checkbook. "God, I forgot to pay the rent. Today's the last day." She ripped out a blank check and folded it under her Swiss Army watch, then poised her pen. "Two *f*s in Griffo?"

"Put the five thousand into our ad budget. Speaking of ads, what about this new budget Charlie mentioned?"

"You're an *oytser*!" She dropped her checkbook back into the bag.

"Raw or cooked?"

She smiled. "*Oytser*, not oyster. In Yiddish that means you're a treasure."

"So are you. Charlie dropped the word 'foldout' and the nice sum of three hundred thousand dollars." My direct boss, Bertrand, had wanted the core locusts of the agency to descend on Roberta immediately. Somehow I'd gotten caution to prevail. Bertrand accused me of wanting to hog the show, which was perfectly true. I was enjoying the power. "We can finally do an ad campaign with legs."

"Three hundred thousand dollars?" Roberta's eyes glazed over.

"What's wrong?"

She squared her shoulders. "I love the idea of 'What Every Woman Needs Is a Riddle Nothing.' And the concept of 'every' is good. I'm aiming for a bigger market. I want to steal some clients from DKNY, from Liz Claiborne, Ellen Tracy, Vittadini. I'm still going to be upscale, but I need to increase volume to survive. The comp the rat was on is the ad I want. My clothes dropping out of drawstring pouches. I've even had some pouches ordered in primary colors for the show."

"Great!"

"But Charlie's a *luftmensch*. A dreamer."

"He said it was a joint decision, not a dream."

Roberta pursed her mauve-colored lips. "For a moment I dreamed, too. We simply don't have that kind of money."

"A backer didn't come through?"

"That's right." She circled a finger around her glass, unwilling to say more. "We will go ahead with the ad. In *Vogue, Harper's Bazaar,* and *Town & Country.* I'm sorry to disappoint you."

"I'm sorry your backer reneged. For both of us. Look, I'm fine. You gave me an okay for a one-shot. Three magazines. The account is safe for another season." And maybe she'd saved me from moving upstairs with the Living Dead. "Your Buddha was used as the murder weapon. Could anyone outside the studio have gotten hold of it?"

"It was stupid to use the Buddha. It immediately implicates Riddle Solutions and its employees."

"Maybe that's what the murderer wanted. The statue was worth a lot of money. It was an anniversary present from your husband. Maybe the killer wanted to involve you directly."

"You think? I say it was impulse, whatever was handy, without thought to consequences. I keep the studio door locked, and my receptionist swears she saw the Buddha in its usual place on the table when she left at six."

"Did you let anyone come in after that?"

"No, I didn't. The others say they didn't either."

"Who brought the plant of butterfly orchids I saw last night? It wasn't there when I left."

"The florist's boy came before six o'clock."

"On a Sunday?"

"It's a week before the collections. Besides, for most of us the Sabbath is on Saturday."

"Sorry." I could taste the egg running into my mouth. "How well do you know Charlie?"

"He's worked for me for three years now as an assistant designer. That's a misnomer, by the way. Assistant designers do not design, they're technical, they implement. The same relationship a contractor has to the architect. Usually the assistant does the draping of the fabric on the model, cuts the fabric, and makes the pattern for the original sample. At Riddle Solutions, I do my own sketching and my own draping. Charlie calls me a control freak."

"He wants to be a designer."

"He's good at structure. That's what he should stick to for now."

"Do you know anything about his personal life? His relationship to Phyllis? If he's innocent, why would he lie to the police about being in that bathroom?"

Roberta twirled her glass, careful not to spill the scotch she hadn't touched.

"Charlie is greedy, ambitious. And insecure. In other words, young."

"He didn't hesitate to tell me he was gay."

"That might be the only thing he's sure of. He's extremely talented, but he needs discipline to mature. That's why I'm holding him back. I might even be a little jealous. He's got his whole life before him. We argue a lot. He didn't understand my need for Phyllis. I told him I had no choice if I wanted to stay in business."

"That sounds ominous."

"It isn't. Phyllis was my muse."

"You called her a bitch."

"Yesterday she complained to you about a designer who likes to stick pins into his models. Phyllis's specialty was sticking metaphorical pins into people."

"Give me an example."

"She picked on weaknesses, sore spots," Roberta

said. "Mario, whose wife went back to Sicily twenty-five years ago with their son and never wrote or spoke to him again. She'd say, 'How old's the boy now, Mario? He must be the spitting image of you.' Flossie, who worries about her son playing the horses. 'I gave him a hot tip, Floss, and he put three hundred on Going Nowhere.'"

"Did she pick on Charlie?"

"She didn't like his being gay. She considered it a waste of a handsome man."

"What pins did she stick in you?"

Roberta's hat tipped down, a full black moon, as she picked up her bag to root around inside. "She picked on my hats, on my devotion to work. She could be quite vulgar. I paid no attention." Her hat shot back, and Roberta, flushed from having bent down or from avoiding unpleasant truths, dangled two keys from a gold ring. "Charlie wants me to pick up his mail."

"Where's Charlie?"

"He's still with the police. Tonight I'm taking him out to Café des Artistes for a survivor's dinner. Charlie lives on Twelfth Street. He's just broken up with someone, which has made him testy. He's healthy, thank God. I lost my last assistant designer to AIDS." Roberta called for the check, paid, and told me to start my investigation with Flossie. "I've already told her not to keep anything back."

"I need a bio on your employees, plus addresses and telephone numbers. Only the ones who were in the studio last night. And something more extensive on Phyllis."

Roberta stood up. "I don't know much, but I'll write something up tonight and fax it to your office in the morning." I followed her out onto Sixteenth Street. Roberta slipped on black suede gloves.

"Didn't any of your employees protest Phyllis?" I

asked as we ambled to the corner of Fifth Avenue. Across the street Emporio Armani had its white shades down. They were changing the window display. The air was cold. It was six-thirty, the night held at bay thanks to daylight savings time. Only a few more weeks and I'd be going home from work in the dark. Suddenly I missed Greenhouse. How was I going to tell him I'd been hired to prove him wrong?

"My staff knows work comes first. We're all unpleasant to each other under stress, but we have the same goal in mind. To create the best collection possible. A fitting model's personality doesn't matter to a designer and therefore can't matter to anyone else in the studio. Phyllis was an excellent fitting model. She always knew when something wasn't right. Except this time. This time she had no idea." I sensed Roberta shivering. I clasped her elbow.

"Charlie told me you don't trust him to see your knits line."

A sigh lifted Roberta's chest. "I don't want Charlie to interfere. My old partner, Elsa, was silent. I like it that way. I miss her, too."

A doubt wafted by me, like a bad smell too weak to define.

"Roberta, if I'm going to help, you have to tell me the truth. Why don't you admit that someone's stealing your designs?" A clomping sound preceded a clutch of students with regulation Doc Martens and black clothes. Their artists' portfolios flapped against their thighs as they puffed on cigarettes. One blue-haired girl stared at Roberta's hat and raised her thumb in approval. The Parsons School of Design was three blocks south.

"Not on the scale you're thinking of." She raised her hand for a cab, a gentle balletlike gesture. "Every successful designer is knocked off. It's a sign of our fame.

Even the bad ones get copied. That's what this business is, variations on a theme someone else composed."

A cab with his off-duty sign lit cut across traffic and slammed on his brakes in front of us. Cruising with the off-duty sign on is a New York cabbie's trick to avoid picking up "undesirables," that term including drunks, rowdy teenagers, and minorities who might have "dangerous" addresses. It is against the law to refuse a passenger.

"Roberta, the knockoffs have appeared even before your shows. That means someone in the studio is behind it. Who? Could Phyllis have been involved?"

"I don't know." Roberta gave the cabdriver Charlie's address, only four blocks away. The cab spurted away, off-duty sign back on.

"I thought the police would arrest me," Roberta said, flagging down another cab, as instinctive a gesture on New York City streets as brushing your teeth in the bathroom.

"Why would they do that?" I had the answer from Lourdes, but I wanted Roberta to tell me. A sincerity test.

"I fired Phyllis last night." She folded herself in the cab with a rapid, graceful motion. "Talk to Flossie's son, Jerry. He's my production manager. He brought Charlie to the company."

I jumped in after her. Under her lampshade hat, Roberta looked startled. "You fired Phyllis?" Her response was a brief flutter of eyelashes. "You just finished saying that she was your muse, that you couldn't stay in business without her."

"I work in an art that glorifies mood moments, that subsists on quicksilver changes."

"She was with you for thirty years."

"I lost it. Besides, I'm a Gemini. My emotions are not expected to be consistent. You are just as irrational,

I think, which is why I like you. As for Phyllis, we had a horrible fight about her weight, which I think Kathy, the cleaning lady, overheard. And I'm sure she was more than eager to tell the police. Dear Kathy doesn't think I tip her enough at Christmas."

"What about the dead rat? Is there a connection with a dead Phyllis?"

"Forget the rat!"

"Why won't you leave the thirtieth floor?"

"Because I like it there, I will not be maneuvered out! I started Riddle Solutions on the thirtieth floor and I'll stay there no matter how hard that idiot Ed Mannucci and the landlord push. I positively thrive on adversity!"

"They're behind the tricks, then."

"Nonsense!"

The cab jerked to a stop. Someone yelled, "It's her. The boss." A camera flashed as Roberta got out. "Mrs. Riddle, where's Charlie Angelo? Is he involved? How did it feel to see your favorite model with her head bashed in?" A young woman reporter pushed a notepad in Roberta's face while I paid the driver. "Was she wearing one of your designs?"

Roberta adjusted her hat and started to answer in the same sweet, soft voice I had heard her use on potential buyers. As she spoke, she clasped my hand. For a second I simply thought she needed support, then I felt keys press against my palm. She let go. I closed my fist and stepped away. Roberta kept the reporter busy with composed expressions of grief punctuated by well-placed plugs for Riddle Solutions. I nonchalantly walked inside an award-winning sixties building that blended into a row of historic town houses.

"Picking up Mr. Angelo's mail." I waved the keys at the doorman. He nodded, his attention riveted on Roberta and the reporter. Behind him, a fountain trickled. I didn't know why picking up Charlie's mail had become an urgent, secretive project, but I did as Roberta bid.

And I studied the mail. An American Express bill, an appeal from Gay Men's Health Crisis, what looked like an invitation from the Costume Institute at the Metropolitan Museum of Art, an envelope with no return address, hand-addressed in a curlicued script, and a letter from a company called Happy Futures, which probably offered gold mines in Antarctica.

7

"What happened to your rear end?" Greenhouse stood at the door of the bathroom, still wearing his raincoat. The sky had been cloudless when he'd left in the morning and had stayed that way all day. Stan likes to be prudent.

I was in one of my skimpy silk things, leaning over the sink to rinse out my mouth.

"My end had a quickie with New York asphalt." It was past eleven. I'd gotten tired of waiting for him and had just finished brushing my teeth. I wanted to say "You could have called" but didn't, knowing full well that when I'm hot in pursuit of something I forget, too. Still, it was hard. I'd put off tackling the cleaning lady over at Roberta's showroom, wanting to be home or thinking I should be home when Stan came in. I was a little confused. I'd never roomed with a lover before and wasn't quite sure what the parameters of our relationship were. I was also nervous about having accepted Roberta's offer. I was official now. A real detective. And the first thing I'd done on the job was to go home and continue unpacking. A leaning tower of sweaters now graced Stan's dresser.

"Does it hurt?" He looked so worried that I had to give him a kiss.

"The spot where I fell needs a hand about your size . . . Oh, Maria Cordova called, Anna Delgado's mother." Stan had testified for the prosecution and an unusually harsh jury had given Anna ten to twenty-five years for hiring the man who bungled killing her husband. "She wanted to know what you were doing about getting her daughter out of jail."

Stan let go of a dust-clearing sigh. "How did that woman get my phone number?" He—we—had an unlisted number.

"She works for the phone company. She sounded desperate."

"She has reason to be."

I went back to the sink to clean my face. "Why do you think Anna Delgado is innocent?"

"A gut feeling."

"Ha! You always tell me intuition is out. Facts, evidence, that's what you want me to go by."

"I'm trying to keep you grounded to this planet *and* out of danger. I'll give you a fact—the husband and the hired killer just made a deal for a four-hundred-thousand-dollar advance to write a book."

"There's no body!" I wiped tissue across my face.

"There's sleaze, that's enough."

"What other reasons do you have?"

"I'm beat, Sim."

"Can you help her?"

"I've got three cases on my desk right now, but some friends are looking into it. God, it's bright in here."

I bared glisteningly clean teeth. "New lightbulbs so that I can bite you better. It's a miracle you didn't slit your throat while shaving."

He smiled, his face fuzzy with fatigue. "You remind me of a cat peeing in all the corners to mark her territory."

"*His* territory. Males do that."

"I bet you put a rubber mat on the air conditioner, too."

"But I haven't painted the walls yet." I decided not to mention the too-soft mattress.

"I like the walls."

I slipped inside his raincoat. Pink, purple, red, the color of his walls didn't matter. And any bed would do with this man in it. "Willy called." Stan's son had sounded surprised when I picked up.

"You'll get used to me," I'd said in a light voice. "I promise." I'd told him his dad wasn't home yet. "I missed you Sunday night."

"Yeah, sorry about that."

It had taken the better part of a year to get Willy to accept me as an important presence, if not in his life, at least in his dad's. He had greeted the news of my moving into Stan's apartment with what I sensed was relief. There was someone else around to take care of Dad. When Stan told him about me, Willy had reciprocated the confidence by telling Stan of his own unrequited crush on a girl in his class.

"You unpacked and everything?" Willy asked over the phone.

"All over the furniture."

"Use some of my drawers if you want."

What a sweetheart! "I'm not taking even an inch away from you, but thanks, you don't know how wonderful that offer makes me feel. Are you coming over soon?" Willy hadn't answered, saying he was in a rush.

"He sounded glum," I said to Stan.

"I know. I called him from the squad room. The kid's got too much homework." Stan did not respond to my touch.

I pulled back. "Are you hungry?"

His shoulder left the doorjamb to reveal a hand clasping a spoon and a pint of pistachio chocolate-chip ice cream.

"That's why you didn't hug me back!" Looking at that sweet, tired face, at the impish glee in his deep brown eyes, I decided food was not what I wanted to offer. The first night I moved in we made crazy, long love in every room and every surface big enough to hold us. Willy's room we left as inviolate as a chapel. That was six days ago. Greenhouse had led me to believe that one of the advantages of living together was easy accessibility to stress-reducing exercise. I had lots of stress.

Wiggling a shoulder, I let a lace strap fall. Green ice cream held more appeal for my American hunk. *Know your client,* the marketing manual instructed.

He's cute, sexy, lovable, stubborn, obsessively neat, circumcised. I love him. I hitched up the strap and gave Stan the news.

"She offered you five thousand dollars?" He made the mistake of laughing.

"I'm not taking the money, and it's not a joke. Roberta doesn't think Charlie's guilty."

"I'm sorry. I don't mean to put you down, but Roberta can think what she likes and pay all the money she wants. Charlie Angelo's fingerprints are on that door, covered in blood, and he's denying it. If he's not guilty, it sure looks suspicious."

"Phyllis's blood?"

"Haven't gotten the report yet."

"What about motive?"

"We're working on it." He walked out of the bedroom, down the hall, shedding his coat, his jacket, his tie while all the time holding on to his ice cream and his spoon. I padded after him in bare feet and absurd underwear. "I'm going to ask some questions, Stan. Nothing more than that."

He hung up his coat on the wooden tree in the entrance. He folded his tie, draped his jacket over his arm. Maybe he was counting to a hundred. Stan turned slowly around, his face shut down for the night. "Sim, what makes you think you'll change?" He sounded exhausted.

Listen to disagreements was another bit of marketing wisdom. *They may indicate management problems.* "I won't let this come between us."

"How do you propose doing that?" The ice cream was beginning to drip down his hand.

"By letting you eat that whole pint of revolting green ice cream while I make mad love to you."

He didn't laugh at this offer. "And tomorrow?" He licked his fingers.

"Same as tonight. You can change ice cream flavors if you want." Stan sucked his palm. "Then when we get tired of that, you do your detecting, I do mine. And we will not compare notes. *Affare fatto?* It's a done deal?"

"Do I have a choice?" His lips were green. I leaned over and kissed them.

We didn't make it back to the bedroom, but Stan and the carton got licked clean.

At five-ten the next morning, awakened by an ambulance siren, with my head cuddled under his armpit and his thigh warming my knees, Stan told me about his son and the latest wrinkle.

"His mother claims our living together is morally corrupting for Willy."

I jumped up. "How dare she! Does Willy think that?"

"No, of course not." Stan pulled me back down, nestled my head back under his armpit. A cold breeze lifted the curtains. Stan covered me with the blanket.

"Poor Willy." That explained why he hadn't come over Sunday night. Why he'd sounded so odd on the phone the night before.

"Doesn't her boyfriend ever spend the night?"

"She says never. I didn't want to ask Willy, but I had a chat with the doorman. The man does stay over. Did. He hasn't shown up for three months."

Irene and Stan had been divorced for nine years. She'd left him to find herself. She had found a new job in a pharmaceutical firm, and a few years back, when new love had not come her way, she had tried to use Willy's unhappiness to convince Stan to give their relationship another chance. I broke off with him at that point. After we got back together, Willy started to be the problem. Last Christmas, after Willy and I had spent a week together, unexpectedly alone, we had become friends. Now Irene was back, making noise. I had never met her and didn't want to. Sometimes I had wished Stan had come childless. Sometimes I had wished Willy lived with his dad and Irene did not exist. Moving in, I'd envisioned evenings with Willy and Stan centered around food and movies, Sundays off in the car to go apple picking in upstate New York or to visit the Bronx Zoo. I was not being excessively romantic. I knew I would be grateful for the times Stan and I could be alone, the responsibility of a fifteen-year-old safe in the hands of Willy's mother.

"Now what?"

"I met with her tonight. I couldn't budge her. And Willy gets caught in between. A no-win situation."

"What does Willy say?" Divorced lover, ex-wife, and one child: it was like trying to cook three soufflés at once. You knew that at least one was going to collapse.

"She's made him promise he won't come here. Willy couldn't see a way out, so he agreed."

Parental blackmail. "I'll go out with a girlfriend on the nights you two get together."

"Not good enough for my ex-wife." He turned over and cupped my chin with his hand. A Band-Aid rubbed against my jaw. "She wants public places only."

"You hurt yourself?"

"Last night at the scene of the crime. Against that damn bathroom door."

I kissed his thumb. "Am I allowed to come along to these public meetings?"

"The subject has not come up. I talked to my lawyer. She doesn't have a legal leg to stand on, but I don't want to fight her. The one who ends up suffering the most is Willy."

"Hey, from my end, it's not such a bad proposition. No cooking." I consider cooking an integral part of loving, but I was trying to flash light into a dark hole.

Stan dug in his chin on the top of my head, a way not to let me see his face. I waited, knowing whatever he was going to say did not come easily. I waited so long I thought he was going to call off our living together. "What is it, hon?"

"Should we get married?"

I hugged him and had no doubts. "I love you and you love me and we'll probably have a wonderful marriage one day, but I think we both need to make sure the fit's right. One divorce is enough in a lifetime. Getting married to please Irene's moral sense isn't a compelling enough reason."

Stan kissed my forehead. I sensed relief. "I love having Willy here. Watching him sleep at night. Seeing him brush his teeth and checking the doorjamb to see if he's grown any taller. This past six months Willy's sprouted almost two inches." His voice held surprise and pride.

I crawled over Stan to cover him with my body, wanting to make the ache go away. "I'll talk to her."

"You'll make it worse."

"Let me try. How much worse can it be?" We held each other for a while, arms and legs wrapped tight. Then worry eased into sleep.

8

"How can I help you?" Ed Mannucci asked with a smoke-gnawed voice. MANNUCCI SPORTSWEAR ran across his glass showroom door, the large block letters alternating red, white, and blue. I'd caught Roberta's floor neighbor just as he was leaving. It was six-fifteen. My day at the office had been a breathless, lonely marathon of trying to keep every art director in the place satisfied.

Linda, my assistant, had called in to announce that she was in her fourth month of pregnancy and was taking the day off with her husband to celebrate passing the miscarriage zone. I congratulated her and cursed the phone. Five new print ads needed budgets ASAP. A model for tomorrow's costume jewelry shoot had come down with the flu. Our client, Baubles Delight, Inc., refused any other face and insisted on rescheduling, which meant rebooking photographer, model, makeup person, and hairstylist. Three trainers and their cats showed off their antics on my desk for our pet-food account. Jericho, an eight-pound ginger tabby, spilled vinaigrette dressing—part of my lunch—over the CEO's marketing manual. Jericho jumped to the top of the yes list. Roberta faxed me the bios of those employees who had been in the showroom at the time of the murder— Flossie, Charlie, Mario, and Lourdes. She'd added Jerry's. I barely glanced at them, Roberta's problems taking a backseat.

I called Stan's ex-wife and introduced myself. "Irene, I'd like to talk to you, if I may." I had to lick my lips to stop them from crackling. "About Willy."

"I have nothing to say." It was the first time I'd ever heard her voice. It was soft and elegant-sounding, even if her words weren't.

"What you're doing is not fair to Stan or Willy."

"Stan is your business now, but Willy is mine. I don't appreciate your interference and neither does Willy. Good-bye." She hung up and I looked down to spot the knife she had just lodged in my stomach. "Neither does Willy." Was that true? Maybe she'd made that up, just to be mean. Willy and I had become pals. I remembered that wonderful company name, Happy Futures, and wondered if I should apply for a job there.

I reiterated that thought after I rode up to the seventeenth floor to meet with boss Bertrand and the CEO over Roberta's account. Instead of thanking me for successfully persisting and getting an ad out of her, the CEO queried me about his manual. I sputtered something about target groups, brand awareness, product definition. Buoyed by his satisfied smirk, I declared my love for the creative department, and before he could lecture me on the needs of the agency, I raced down and out to grab a cab to the garment center, a cab HH&H was going to pay for. I considered my detective work a way of keeping up client relations.

My goal at 530 Seventh Avenue had been to talk to Kathy Breen, the cleaning woman, but she hadn't come to work yet. Jerry was down at the factory in Chinatown.

Flossie, Mario, and Lourdes were neck-high in fabric and thread. Roberta had popped her head out of the design room to say that it was exclamation point time again and no one was allowed to breathe. The hat of the day was a Jackie Kennedy pillbox. Yellow. The mourning period was over.

"Charlie?" I'd asked.

"Getting grilled by your boyfriend. Find out what's going on." The design room door swung shut.

So here I was accosting Ed Mannucci of Mannucci Sportswear. Along with the company name, he'd had his phone number printed on the door. The same number I had seen on Roberta's phone display the day after the murder.

"I wanted to talk to you about taking over Roberta Riddle's lease," I said after introducing myself.

"Good. Good." Mannucci was a florid man in his mid-fifties with an orangy tan that looked bottle-made, a gray toupee to match his real sideburns, brown pants that showed two inches of black silk socks, and a double-breasted jacket he'd bloated out of a thousand pastas ago. "Roberta's finally changed her mind?"

I hesitated. "I don't know about that."

"Then what do you know?" His voice got scratchier, his tan deeper.

"That someone's been playing nasty tricks on her."

"Yeah?"

"A rumor says you enjoy handling dead rats." I had only Mario's word for it, but it was worth pursuing.

He pointed a finger at me. "You were here the day of the murder."

"How did you know?"

"What's a glass door for, if not to look through?"

"You were here then?"

Ed Mannucci raised his hand to indicate that I should wait. He headed for the men's room at his end of the corridor, his steps short, his body heaving from side to side—a graceless penguin. When he came out I noticed that he had straightened his toupee and a burgundy silk handkerchief was now in his breast pocket.

"You were working here on Sunday?"

"Checking over the orders. Half an hour. No more. I saw you come in."

That meant four o'clock. "You must know a lot about Roberta's company if you look through glass doors."

"The john door works again, that's what I know. Damnedest thing. You got to figure it was the murderer who jammed that door, no one else would waste time doing that kind of trick."

"Sending cockroaches via Federal Express is a waste of time, too."

"Depends what you're aiming at." He pushed the elevator button. "The murderer used Crazy Glue, the kind that peels five layers of skin off you if you should aim wrong. Squirted right into the keyhole. Management had to put in new locks. You could kill someone with that stuff. Tape their mouth and squirt it up their nose." He stepped into the elevator and I followed, not really sure I wanted to be alone with this man's imagination.

"When did you notice that the door was jammed?" His cologne didn't help—flowers decaying in a funeral parlor.

"Four-thirty, thereabouts. I always go in before hitting the streets." He straightened up, adjusted his chin over his shirt collar, retucked his pocket handkerchief. Had Mannucci had real hair he would have patted it. "In my business, it's important to look right."

"You didn't check the ladies' room by any chance?"

"Jammed, too."

"You went down one flight?"

"I went home. You Italian?" He'd spotted my accent,

faint but consistent. Before I could answer, the elevator stopped on the sixth floor and a well-dressed man and his gray fedora hat walked in, both nodding in greeting. He brought with him a waning scent of sugared oranges. Small-boned, short, his face was pale and greatly wrinkled, with startling dark blue eyes.

"Mr. Nite!" Ed said, and grinned, dropping a heavy, gold-ringed hand on the frailer man's shoulders.

Mr. Nite shook his head. "Terrible. It is terrible what happened." His accent was German or Austrian.

An image flashed across my mind. Phyllis dead in the bathroom and Roberta walking toward me, the letters MR. NITE spreading out above her head. "Phyllis was killed on your floor!"

"Terrible," Mr. Nite repeated, bowing his head as if in prayer.

Ed Mannucci's hand dropped down for another back pat; this time Mr. Nite wavered under the weight of it. "Maybe you're spreading bad rumors about me?" The tone was fake-jocular.

"That you're making too much money?"

Ed displayed a set of capped teeth big enough for a horse. "I am, I am. That cotton fleece warm-up suit with the crazy colors and the patchwork pockets you liked so much, remember?"

Disapproval set on Mr. Nite's face, deepening his wrinkles. "The one for which you did not pay your supplier? The nightmare?"

Ed laughed. "That's the one. It's jumpin' off the racks. I'm in my fifth reorder. You should quit evening wear. No one buys that stuff anymore. People are too scared to go out at night."

"So then they stay home and wear my lingerie," Mr. Nite said, pride in his voice. "Congratulations, Mr. Mannucci. You don't deserve it, but you got yourself a runner."

The elevator door opened on the ground floor with its glistening beige marble and its polished brass doors and Art Deco details. In the morning the mail was strewn across the long wall for each showroom to pick up. Now the floor was empty except for a jumbled trail of scuff marks. The barbershop was closed.

Ed jabbed Mr. Nite's arm as we stepped out. "I better not find out you're spreading bad rumors about me and dead rats."

Mr. Nite shook his head and walked away.

Ed pointed to his back.

"I never met him before in my life," I answered to the silent question. "And why would he spread those rumors? Your businesses don't compete."

"He hates my guts. Doesn't like my business practices."

"They're that bad?"

He grunted. "I make more money than he does. What part of Italy you from?"

"Rome. Look, let's talk over a drink. My treat."

"Me, I'm a quarter Sardinian, a quarter Irish, the other two quarters from the mountains of Abruzzo. Tough combo." He took my arm.

On the way out, I reminded the doorman to let me back in later. Roberta had told him I was her new employee.

Ed suggested we go to Arno's, a block away, where I could have my drink and he could have his dinner. "And no girl's going to pay when I'm around."

I smiled my assent. Being called "girl" does not threaten my womanhood and I love it when someone else pays. Besides, I was trying to keep him happy.

Arno's maître d' called Ed by name and ushered us to the last empty table, marked RESERVED. The waiters smiled greetings.

The restaurant was a large, square room with white

table-clothed tables spread well apart. Etched gods and goddesses cavorted in the mirrors along the walls. In a corner was an immense vase of white spray mums and gladioli. The place was old-fashioned, out of place in nineties New York with its array of sleek, trendy restaurants. It was only eight years old, the Venetian waiter told me as he tugged on his short-waisted tuxedo and waited for our order. It had replaced a kosher restaurant.

"That was good, too," Ed said, ordering a martini, baked clams, fusilli in a cream and mushroom sauce, and a veal chop. "But the garment center isn't only Jewish anymore. Italians, we've always been here, but now we got Puerto Ricans, South Americans, Chinese, Blacks. *Justice*, the union paper? It stopped the Yiddish edition back in fifty-nine. Now we can read it in Mandarin." He waved at the busy bar area, crowded three deep with people of many nationalities. "It's a minestrone. You know why? The needle trades is a business where a man doesn't need a lot of education to make money. I bet you went to college."

"Barnard."

"How much do you make?" He rolled his shoulders back, the jacket too tight.

"Enough."

"Thirty, forty max. If it was more, you'd tell me. Me, I gross twenty-five million a year. That buys a lot of veal chops."

I ordered a glass of Pinot Grigio and chomped on a breadstick. "What's a runner?"

"A winning style I'm going to keep cutting season after season until it stops selling. Mr. Nite should be so lucky. He's a butter-and-egg man."

"His cholesterol count is high?"

Mannucci laughed. "Naw, it means he dresses real nice. Hair always combed. Suits a good cut. Shiny, manicured hands. To keep up appearances, look like you can afford butter and eggs. I'm the one making the money in that building. Not him. And sure enough not Roberta Riddle. Now who's spreading this sh"—Ed's gold bracelet jangling on his wrist—"I don't use bad language in front of ladies, but if I did, every face in this room would turn marinara red with the filth comin' out of my mouth." He took a long drink of his martini, then looked around the room. "Who is it? Maybe Mr. Nite, maybe not." He seemed to be talking to himself. "It's not Charlie. Flossie and Jerry got no interest. It's gotta be Roberta."

I reached for my wineglass.

Ed looked back at me, surprised. "So she thinks I would cut up her shipping orders, dump a dead rat on her desk to get her to move out?"

"No, Roberta thinks that idea is nonsense."

"I'm a gentleman. I don't do that kinda stuff. Not Ed Mannucci or anyone who works for him." He gulped his olive, his eyes popping with anger.

"You seem to know a lot about the incidents." A tall showroom model with flame-red hair, false eyelashes, and no fat let out a deep laugh at the bar. A hairy hand stroked her butt.

"The whole building knows about 'em. No one keeps a secret in the district. I know who's got hemorrhoids, who's sleeping with who. Patsy over there with the tomato hair? She eats like a pig, then throws up in the john. The man who's got his hand on her is over seventy, a fabric salesman, dyes his body hair, can't get it up. You can make a deal with him on a handshake. So what do you want? A pretty girl like you doesn't ask a man out for a drink with no return in mind. And don't give me *agida* with this murder mess."

I explained about trying to help Charlie. He chuckled. I told him I wanted to know who had played those tricks on Roberta, that maybe they were linked to the murder. Did he have any ideas? "Charlie Angelo says everyone thinks he did it."

Ed munched on a chunk of bread. "Naw, Charlie's an okay guy. He's got a lot of talent that woman won't recognize. You know what I think? Roberta's doing it to herself."

"Why would she do that?" The baked clams arrived, smelling deliciously of garlicky oil. I regretted not having ordered anything.

"She's looking for sympathy, setting the employees against Charlie. He scares her. Charlie's got more talent in his little finger—"

"How do you know?" I leaned over to sniff better.

"I seen some of his designs. I know. I got a good nose for design and I got a good nose for what people want to put on their backs. The fancy people and my people both. Listen, get one thing straight here. And I already told the police. I don't have to threaten Roberta Riddle. She's in trouble, everyone in the market knows that. Someone's selling her designs over to the moderate dress houses and her clothes are running off the racks for a hundred and twenty dollars before her models even hit the runway."

"Who is selling her designs?" I chewed on my third breadstick.

"I don't care. It's fine with me. Her money's low, her factoring company wants out. Not even a retard would back her up. So all I got to do is wait it out. This murder's the last crack of the whip. It's gonna lie her down flat. She's gonna have to sell, and Ed Mannucci of Staten Island, New York"—a thumb hit his chest—"is going to be right there, in the front spot, the money already counted. Which doesn't mean I killed Tootsie to push Roberta over the edge. I made sure the cops understood that."

"You're in sportswear. Why buy Roberta out?"

"I'm in whatever I wanna be. I like the idea of owning a fancy designer shop, and my wife's crazy about it." Ed bit into a clam.

"Charlie thinks the murder and all the media attention is going to help Roberta, not make it worse."

"Charlie doesn't know what he's talking about."

"How well did you know 'Tootsie'?"

"Phyllis? Turns out she went to school with my wife. I met her when she had a little place over in Westhampton two blocks down from us." Westhampton, on Long Island, was the summer retreat of most of the garment-center manufacturers. The top designers, to set themselves apart from the plebeian crowd, preferred to get their tans farther out on the island, in wealthy Southampton or the more artistic and equally wealthy East Hampton. "That's when Saul was being good to her."

I took a sip of my Pinot Grigio. Sesame seeds were stuck between my teeth. "Saul who?"

"Saul Herman, Roberta's husband. Phyllis was his mistress for almost thirty years."

9

"Simonita!" Raf Garcia, Stan's partner, was combing his hair in front of the ladies'-room mirror on the twenty-ninth floor of Roberta's building. Sunday night's scene of the crime. The yellow plastic police tapes were gone. The brass faucets shone, the mosaic white tiles sparkled. The place looked almost new.

"*Ciao, bello.*" I breathed through my mouth to avoid the smell of ammonia.

"I hear you're gonna give us a hand on this one."

"I don't want my roommate and his handsome partner arresting Charlie Angelo and ending up with shrimp, chicken, and rice all over their faces."

Raf laughed. "You left out a few ingredients like chorizo, scallops, lobster, onions, capers—"

"*Basta!* I haven't had dinner yet." Raf considered himself the best paella maker in the five boroughs. I could only vouch for Manhattan. Around five ten, with a thick frame armored by obsessively trained muscles, Raf had a fighter's squashed nose and a sloppy grin that kept spilling over everything he said. He always played the good cop when trying to break down suspects. I refused to imagine Stan as the bad cop.

I had left Ed Mannucci with a napkin tied around his neck, bulldozing into cream-soaked fusilli. At that point Ed didn't want to talk anymore, mentioning *agida* again. I'd told him I'd buy him Tums for his trouble and asked him if Roberta knew about Phyllis and Saul. When the police found out, she might move into the number-one suspect slot. *Addio* collection and client.

Ed had slurped up a fusillo, the cream splattering my way. "Maybe not. She wouldn't be caught dead in Westhampton with the rest of us. Too much of a snob. She's got her fancy Fifth Avenue pad, she doesn't move from there." The only sound he made after that made me bless my mother for having insisted on table manners. I left with new information and a new color pattern on my beige jacket.

Hoping to know more about the fight between Phyllis and Roberta, I'd tackled Kathy, the cleaning lady. She'd told me she'd seen enough of cops and went back to mopping the stairs. The questions I asked were met by the sound of dripping water. Which had left me checking the doorknob of the bathroom, wondering how Stan had cut himself.

"What are you doing here, Raf?"

"Talking to the cleaning lady one more time, trying to get friendly. She hates cops. I got grunts for answers."

"She wouldn't talk to me either. What's she got against the police?"

"I looked her up. Her brother's been arrested for holding up a grocery store. Anyway, she says she found the body. Gave us the time and that's it."

"You think there's more to it?"

"Just checking and rechecking. That's my job. I also like to get a better feel for the scene of the crime. Look at things from the killer's point of view."

"And comb your hair for a date with Tina."

"That, too."

"Have you come up with anything?"

"Three gray hairs."

I laughed. Even if Raf had found something, he wouldn't tell me. Until the prosecutor had a grand jury indictment, not even a suspect's lawyer was privy to any police information on the investigation. I gave my own hair a quick check for gray. So far, so good. "Where's the love of my life?"

"Willy called the squad room and wanted to talk." Raf offered a Mars bar from the breast pocket of his red and blue Hawaiian shirt topped by a wide yellow tie. Raf and I had always shared the same tastes in food, if not in clothes. "It's a bummer, huh, about his ex-wife?"

"*Un macello*, my mother would say. A slaughter. If only Irene had protested before I gave up my lease!" Raf tried to drop the Mars bar in my hand. "No thanks. I'm on a low-fat kick."

"Simonita, this is treason!"

"Sorry." I jiggled the doorknob, pressed my palms along the door. "Have you gotten the blood analysis on those fingerprints yet?"

"What I can tell you is that a screw from the doorknob stuck out. With a sharp edge. That's what Stan's finger got caught on. The janitor fixed it ten minutes ago. The screw had been loose at least a week."

"And maybe Charlie's finger got caught in the same way, hours before the killing. And the blood analysis will tell you if those incriminating fingerprints are covered in her blood or his."

"He could have cut himself on the Buddha he used to kill her with."

"Ah ha! His then."

A smile washed over his face. Raf, the good cop, was giving me the answer.

The results showed that the fingerprints on the door 'were made with Charlie's blood, not Phyllis's. I peeked into the first bathroom stall where Phyllis had been killed. A two-inch length of lip from the porcelain lid of the water tank was missing. A corner of the Buddha's base had also broken off, I remembered. The broken-off cross section of the water-tank lid was still clean, which meant the piece had broken off recently. The killer's blow had probably struck it, breaking both lid and jade base. But the toilet tank was low.

"She must have been struck more than once."

"Come on, Simonita, let me take you home."

Struck again when she was already down. A vengeful killer. "Well, you've analyzed whatever was on that Buddha, and if you don't find any trace of Charlie's blood, you don't have a case."

Raf cracked a knuckle, rolled a shoulder. "Maybe." He's not good at standing still. "I'll drive you home. Tina's waitin'."

I peered down the corridor to figure out what Charlie had been doing in the ladies' room of the twenty-ninth floor, and why he denied being there. The corridor ended at Mr. Nite's showroom door. I loped down to stare behind the plate glass. The hallway lights fell inside for a couple of feet, revealing ink-blue carpeting tall enough to need a lawn mower, the claw and ball of an antique table leg, and the bottom half of a small turquoise-enamel Chinese planter.

I heard Raf's sneakered footsteps. "Tina's waitin', Simonita."

"Got a flashlight?"

"What'ya looking at?" Raf slipped a pencil flash in my hand. I turned it on and aimed at the planter. Butterfly orchids, creamy white with deep-pink hearts, suspended gracefully on reedlike stalks. The same planter, the same orchids I had seen in Roberta's showroom the night of Phyllis's murder. I turned off the flashlight.

"The flowers mean something to you?" Raf asked.

I shook my head. I wasn't sure what they meant. Maybe everyone had received similar vases, a gift from a grateful retail merchandiser or the contracted weekly arrangement from a florist who had run out of ideas. But it did give me a reason to talk to Mr. Nite.

At my insistence, Raf dropped me off at Seventy-second Street where Amsterdam and Broadway cross.

"Come on, Simonita, it's only five more blocks, let me drive you."

"No, you're late, and I need to shop. Bye. Give Tina a hug."

"Keep your eyes peeled."

I didn't. It was only seven-thirty. The streets were crowded, people still gurgling out from the old subway kiosk on the center island. Yellow cabs flowed downtown to drop their charges off at Lincoln Center, or the theater district, or the latest downtown dining spot. Men and women hurried home loaded down with briefcases, with bags containing food or proper office shoes. The main arteries of the Upper West Side—Riverside Drive, Columbus Avenue, Amsterdam, Broadway, and Central Park West—do not have the small-town quaintness of the Village. The old buildings on the West Side are large, imposing, the new ones towering apartment complexes. The streets are vibrant with people. The area was still unfamiliar as a home base, but I didn't feel threatened. I was tired. I'd accomplished a great deal at work and very little for Charlie's defense. At this point I didn't even know if he really needed one. The fact that his fingerprints were made with his own blood and not Phyllis's was in his favor. Maybe Greenhouse would come home and tell me that Charlie had an airtight alibi, that Willy's mother had decided my permanent presence in Stan's apartment would show Willy the healthy, positive power of love.

I passed my new bank, a landmark building that was now the Apple Bank. I had chosen it because of its wide marble floors, tall arched windows, vaulted ceilings, and wrought-iron chandeliers. It stood for tradition, the Old World, an old European vault in which to retreat from hectic New York. Across the street was more Europe—the Ansonia Hotel, an apartment complex built in 1904 in the Parisan style, that had housed the likes of Enrico Caruso, Arturo Toscanini, and Theodore Dreiser. It is one of New York's architectural gems marred by the modern touches of street-level shops.

I spotted the blue awning of the Fairway market, *the* produce supplier for the West Side, open from seven A.M. to midnight. The thought of eating buoyed me. I walked on the sawdust-covered floors, perusing the aisles, avoiding the nudge of elbows and food baskets. I still wasn't sure where to find what. I smelled deliciously runny cheeses and aimed for the healthier foods. I ended up with arugula, tomatoes, and a crusty loaf of Italian bread. A block farther up I bought shrimp at Citarella. Stan was probably eating with Willy, but when he came home I would tempt him with thick slabs of lightly toasted bread covered by a diced mixture of tomatoes, shrimp, and arugula, lightly sautéed in a little garlic and olive oil. If he didn't eat, I planned to clean up both plates. Moderate amounts of all foods, my mother had taught me.

At the supermarket I bought more pistachio chocolate-chip ice cream for Stan's down moods. I looked forward to relaxing while I chopped and stirred, to watching his tired face, feeling his rough cheek against mine as we hugged hello. We were going to be okay together. Irene would relent, the killer would be found, and the CEO would understand that the creative department of HH&H would wither without me.

At the corner of Seventy-seventh, I said hello to the man who was rummaging through the street garbage can. The five-cent can and bottle recycling law has spawned a brisk business for the homeless.

"What's the richest city in the world?" he asked. Each night he came up with a new one. "Generosity."

I gave him a dollar.

"It doesn't take a Rockefeller to help a little feller." He went back to rummaging. Behind him, the Fishs Eddy shop displayed thousands of shiny plates, cups, and saucers, each with an emblem of a long-gone hotel or club. Once they had sold the genuine, hard-to-find article. Now the plates were reproductions.

I passed Stan's garage. It charged $290 a month to park a small car on the main floor, a price that I was told could get you a one-bedroom apartment in another part of the country. That price didn't include the $18^{1}/_{4}$ percent tax the city charged. I checked out the firehouse, Engine 74. Both trucks were in. I prayed that neither of them careened out into the middle of the night. Eventually I would sleep through their sirens. I crossed Amsterdam Avenue for my last lap home, hurrying past the chain-link fence of the small playground now closed for the night. Two blocks farther down, at the end of the double row of street lamps, Central Park looked like a black hole.

A cold cross breeze hit me full in the face. I shivered. New home sweet home and the warmth of a deliciously smelling kitchen was what I wanted.

Something thrust hard against my back, sending me reeling toward the ground. Before I hit the sidewalk I saw sheathed legs, felt my shoulder wrench. I was being mugged!

Stan's words burst in my ear as my hands and knees hit the sidewalk. "Don't resist, don't ever resist!" I let go of my purse, the packages. I played dead, eyes shut tight. Go away, please go away.

The mugger dragged me by the collar of my coat. I opened my eyes. I was lying on my purse. He was trying to get to my purse. All I could see from the sidewalk were black Rollerblades. I don't know if I was screaming. I was too busy pushing the purse out from under me, trying not to leave strips of my face on the asphalt.

The mugger jerked hard. I did cry out then. I can still hear it in my sleep. I cried out from the pain, the fear, from the sudden revelation that my life could end so quickly and stupidly.

A cab braked to a stop. "What this?" an accented baritone asked.

"Shit!" The mugger twisted around. "You take that home with you!" He gave me one last tug and was off in the opposite direction from the cab, back around the corner, his body bent down for speed, his legs slicing the sidewalk.

What was I to take home with me except bruises? Shrimp were scattered around me as if they'd been caught in an unexpected low tide. The bread had fallen into the gutter, where I was going to leave it. The Rollerblades had pulped most of the tomatoes. I could take home the arugula, Stan's pistachio chocolate-chip ice cream, my purse, and a dented me. Thank God there was still a me!

"You need help, lady?" the cabdriver asked. His mouth was covered by hair and he sounded Russian.

"You saved me!"

The cabdriver blessed me with a rueful look, a Slavic specialty, and drove on. He'd eyed a fare on the Columbus Avenue corner.

* * *

I stayed put. *Non c'è due senza tre.* There's no two without three.

When Greenhouse came home half an hour later, I had washed off dirt and a little bit of blood, taken two painkillers for my shoulder, and put on slacks to cover knees that looked like grated Parmesan crusts. Stan hadn't eaten. I offered him take-out roast chicken from Chirping Chicken and coleslaw encircled by a dark-green homemade crown of arugula. We ate in the kitchen, Stan not questioning my sudden cooking by telephone.

He had seen Willy. He had spoken to his ex-wife one more time. Irene wouldn't budge. Willy had begged him not to bring in the lawyer. "It makes us look like jerks" was his comment. I wanted to substitute "her" for "us," but kept my mouth shut. The mugging had subdued me. I mentioned my own unsuccessful call to Irene and then we let our conversation wander into the blander topics of new movies we wanted to see and shirt buttons the Chinese laundry had gobbled up.

By the time Stan dug into his ice cream, I had geared myself up to tell him about the mugging incident, knowing he would immediately think someone was after me, an idea I was trying hard to reject. When I opened my mouth to speak, he abruptly looked up from his dish, a chocolate chip nestling in the corner of his mouth. He smiled for the first time that evening.

"I'm sorry, Sim. How was your day?"

I smiled back, tucked my hands under my thighs, and said, "Would you believe that my assistant is finally going to have a baby?"

10

By seven-fifteen the next morning Stan was gone, leaving the smell of cinnamon trailing from kitchen to bedroom. He pours it in his morning coffee, which would be enough to give me babyless morning sickness. I am convinced that this intense dislike is linked to some traumatic incident in my childhood that I can't recall. My mother insists it's genetic. Her mother's brother's oldest son hates the stuff, too.

After a broiling shower I opened windows wide, did a few shoulder rolls to ease the stiffness in my shoulders, patted body lotion on my scraped knees and bruised thigh, and got dressed for the day. First item on the agenda: an eight-thirty breakfast with Flossie at a deli across the street from 530. I had even prepared a list of questions. The CEO's manual advised planning all action in advance, and basing all action on fact, a philosophy that went against the grain of my being. Roberta's suspicions are correct. I am solely motivated by emotion, intuition, and the mood of the day. BUT. I am always willing to try. That is America's valuable lesson. One can change, grow, completely reinvent oneself. In contrast, a Roman's cherished expression is *nun se po' fa'*. It can't be done.

The phone rang. Flossie.

"I woke up with a flood in the living room. I'm waiting for the plumber, so come to my place. I'll make French toast with challah. You've never tasted so good."

That was change number one.

The phone rang again. Roberta.

"What did you find out, Simona?"

I told her that Charlie's fingerprints were *not* covered with Phyllis's blood and that the cleaning lady refused to speak to me.

"Give Kathy a twenty. She needs it. I'll reimburse you."

I promised I'd try again. I added that I was meeting Flossie.

"Good! I'm still at home. *WWD* is sending over an editor. After three years! I'm going to show her the Riddle Nothings. She'll be thrilled, I know it."

"Good luck." I glanced at my Amex bill on the dresser. "Roberta, what about Charlie's mail, did you read it?"

She'd hung up. I scribbled "remember mail" on my bill and noticed that one day I'd spent eighty-seven dollars on food at Balducci's. A farewell-to-Greenwich-Village party I'd given myself and my upstairs neighbor. My stomach felt a pang of nostalgia.

On the subway, I read Roberta's fax on Flossie.

"Flossie Sarnowski—been with me at least twenty-five years. She must be seventy by now. Still sews divinely. Widowed shortly after I employed her. She took two days off. The first and last time she didn't come to work. She's loyal, hardworking, and much too devoted to her son, but then I'm childless. Sometimes I wish she didn't believe she was in charge, but that's my fault. I have let her know she is indispensable."

Flossie lived at Penn Station South, an urban renewal development that had been sponsored by the International Ladies' Garment Workers Union. It spreads from Eighth to Ninth Avenues and from Twenty-fourth to Twenty-ninth Streets.

"I'm one of the original tenants," Flossie told me in her small living room while I helped her roll up her sopping shag rug. From the ceiling slow drops of water plinked into a garbage pail. In one corner sat an old Singer sewing machine. Black with silver flowers etched on its body, it gleamed like a worshiped relic of the past.

"I took my mother, may she rest in peace, to the inauguration of the complex. That was in May 1962. President Kennedy was there, and my heart, it was going to burst, he was so handsome. My mother, she liked Eleanor Roosevelt, and there she was in flesh and blood with that grin of hers, like a horse. It was something not to forget."

We hung the rug over the balcony railing where the sun could get to it. It was one of those Indian summer days, brilliant blue sky marked only by a finger smudge of moon. The fourth-floor apartment faced south. On the corner a whirlpool of kids waited for the school bus. Wary mothers watched, standing still like rocks on a shore. All around us were trees and identical red-brick buildings that shot up twenty-one floors. Below, a well-kept lawn spurted pools of yellow and rust chrysanthemums. Newspaper-toting men who had retired from work a long time ago already occupied the many benches.

"An oasis in the middle of the city," I said.

"We've got playgrounds, our own senior center." She was dressed in a flowered housecoat thrown over a navy-blue wool skirt and a gray sweater, leather slippers on her feet. She had insisted that I put on a similar housecoat to protect my clothes before we moved the rug. "We even used to have our own paper, the *Penn South News*. You have to pay the cooperative an entrance fee to be able to rent here. Back then the fee was seven hundred dollars a room. We got three rooms, so that makes twenty-one hundred. But both my husband and me was working steady, I always worked steady, so it was all right and the rent was low." Flossie stopped to wave at a woman bent over her cane, her baseball cap worn too low over her forehead for her to spot Flossie. "A hundred and twelve dollars. Utilities included. Air-cooled. Now I'm almost seventy and the rent's over four hundred. Thank God we don't increase at the same rate. I'm talking too much." She ran her fingers into the wet pile of the rug. "I'm upset. I had a beautiful rug, now I have a *schmatta*. A rag, to you. All right, so it's not the rug I worry about."

I followed her back to the kitchen. "What can you tell me about Phyllis?" The bio Roberta had sent was flimsy.

"I didn't kill her." She looked at me above her half-glasses, a grudge in her sharp brown eyes.

"Roberta told me that Phyllis was in her early fifties, single as far as she knows, lived on Ninety-third and Broadway, worked with Roberta since her first collection thirty-five years ago. That's not much information after that length of time. Do you know any more about her?"

"I'm the sample maker, not an employment agency." Flossie banged a cast-iron frying pan on the stove, flicking on the gas flame. The challah bread had already been cut into inch-thick slices, the eggs beaten in a glass plate. The coffee was ready. I spotted a small canister of the dreaded cinnamon.

"You don't have to feed me, Flossie. It all looks wonderful, but coffee is enough for me."

"I'm feeding me. You just happen to be here, and what I give you is good, nothing like what you get out there, where you never know what's walked across your plate. Take some coffee and fill up a chair! You make me nervous standing here."

I poured coffee into a BEST MOM mug and sat by the speckled Formica table, a relic of the fifties, already set for two. The frying pan was heating. Waves of warmth hit my face. In front of me, uncooked strips of pale bacon were draped over a chipped blue plate. "What happened the night Phyllis died?"

"She dropped her pants for the last time." Flossie dipped the bread into the beaten egg and reached out to me with her free hand. I handed over the plate of bacon.

"What I know about Phyllis? She came in, stayed a couple of hours, then left. This for a couple of weeks four times a year. Spring, summer, fall, holiday/resort. When she was nervous she chewed Tootsie Rolls. For a couple of years her hair was red. What should I know? I was in the back, going blind with stitching, going deaf with Mario's radio."

"Sunday night in the studio. Where was everyone located?"

"Roberta and Phyllis were in the design room, Charlie, Mario, and me in the workroom. Lourdes, too. That one's getting to be a real good seamstress. Phyllis brought her in about six months ago. She didn't have a lot of experience, and I didn't want to hire her. But what Phyllis wanted, Phyllis got. So we got Lourdes. She's doing fine."

"Thanks to you."

"Who else? And flattery doesn't work with me." She dropped bacon in the frying pan and knocked a spoonful of butter into another skillet.

"Why did Phyllis get what she wanted? Did she have a hold on Roberta?"

"So what is it? To help Charlie you want to get Roberta in trouble?"

"I'm trying to understand."

"Nothing to understand. Phyllis had no manners, and Roberta is too soft-hearted."

"Sunday night Roberta sent you home at seven o'clock."

"No, I walked into the design room and told her we were tired, it was time to go home. The other two girls I sent home earlier."

"By the time the cleaning lady found the body at seven forty-five, you were all gone?"

"I was. Can't speak for the others."

"What about your son, Jerry?"

Two dripping challah slices slid into the buttered skillet. In the other pan the bacon sizzled. A delicious smell swelled under my nose. "What about Jerry?"

I held back a sigh. I was going to get a lot of fat for breakfast. And no trust. "Where was he Sunday night?"

Flossie spun around, fork poised in the air. "No one's going to pin anything on Jerry. Twenty years he's been with Roberta and she works him to the bone, but you don't hear a peep out of him. Charlie pranced in, started acting as if he owned the place even before Mrs. Morewitz left him the forty percent, trying to push Jerry aside, and Jerry still working himself so that he's got no meat left on his ribs. And the other night, we all could have bashed that woman's head. That's what I told your boyfriend, the detective. We didn't leave right away. Mario had his opera on, enough to drive you crazy, he was doing buttons. We do those by hand, and Mario has a way with buttons, the thread lined up like the marines. So I sent him, the radio, and his buttons to the cutting room. Lourdes kept going over to shipping for the phone. Her two-year-old had a hundred and two. And Jerry was in the subway somewhere between 530 and the factory in Chinatown. He was coming up, going down. We had a problem with zippers. One style from the fall collection, shipped to Neiman, Bergdorf's, Nordstrom, and I don't know where else. Four hundred and fifty dresses came back. *Meshuggeneh* zippers. They wouldn't zip."

"No one can alibi Charlie or anyone else in the studio."

"That's another thing I told that boyfriend of yours, don't try to pin it just on one of us. I know Charlie left his fingerprints in the bathroom, and Roberta, she worries, but there were others around that night that might have done it."

"Who?"

"Ed Mannucci, for one. He and Phyllis"—she flipped a bread slice—"she was after him. She was always prancing next door in her slip, trying to get Ed to sell her some sportswear, she said. She was only going to resell to some jobbers in New Jersey."

"That's hardly a reason to kill her."

"Then what about Roberta firing his wife? Sally Mannucci was the head salesman, doing good, too, then last year, faster than I can thread a needle, she was out on her tush."

"The reason?"

"What I think? Phyllis wanted her out."

"Phyllis got Lourdes hired, Phyllis got Sally Mannucci fired. That's a lot of power for a fitting model."

Flossie scowled. Her glasses had fogged up from the heat of the stove. "Now last year, next door at 550, they had a thief. Hid himself on top of the elevator. Anyone can come in during normal office hours. Later you have to sign in, but if you come in early, you just stay. Who's to know? Maybe that's where you'll get your murderer. On top of the elevator." Flossie took her glasses off to wipe them with a dish towel.

"Maybe Sally Mannucci was stealing designs?"

Flossie stopped her wiping. "Who told you that?"

"Just a possibility."

"No one steals."

"Did Ed Mannucci swear terrible revenge in his wife's name?"

"He stopped talking to Roberta. We walk right by him, I say my good morning, and his face shows nothing, I'm not there. Sometimes it scares me, makes me feel like I'm dead already. At my age, that's a thought that comes visiting a lot. His workers, too, he doesn't let them speak to us. Me, I wouldn't care about any of this, except for the not saying hello maybe, but Jerry really likes those crazy outfits Mannucci makes."

"If there was no communication between the two neighbors for almost a year, why did Ed Mannucci's phone number appear on Roberta's office phone display just yesterday?"

"Do I know? No."

"If after a year Mannucci was still in a murderous rage about his wife being fired," I said, "he'd have killed Roberta, not Phyllis. Do you have any ideas why Phyllis was killed?"

Flossie, glasses restored to the tip of her nose, flipped the challah slices. The cooked side was a lovely speckled brown. "Yogi Berra said it. 'I not only don't know anything, I don't even suspect anything.'"

I tried to picture Flossie as the murderer. She didn't like Charlie. In her eyes at least, he had displaced Jerry in Roberta's favor. How did she feel about Phyllis taunting her about Jerry's gambling? How loyal was Flossie to Roberta? I didn't quite see her brandishing a Buddha in the air to avenge a cuckolded boss or anyone else. Except Jerry. If Phyllis had done something terrible to her son, I imagined Flossie capable of killing with her fists. But she was a lot shorter than

Phyllis. She would have had to stand on the edge of the toilet bowl.

I finished my coffee. "Working at Riddle Solutions must be especially difficult now that money is tight."

"Roberta expects hard work," Flossie said, "and I like to give it. My mother sat me in front of a sewing machine when I must have been no older than five. 'Kiss it,' she said. 'It's going to keep a roof over your head.' My parents had a notions shop on the Lower East Side, First Avenue and First Street. Women would come in to buy buttons, thread, zippers. They'd go home, maybe make mistakes, bring their mistakes to my father. He'd say 'Leave with me. I fix.' He had the Polish smile that could melt the fat off the chicken, but he was terrible with the thread. My mother did the work in the backroom. I helped with the hemming. By the time I was seven, water poured through the tips of my fingers I had so many holes in them, but my stitches could hold the Red Sea together." Flossie leaned against the counter and rubbed her hand across her forehead. "Someone you know dies, and there you are thinking you're going to be next. You end up wanting to talk your life back, like it's some radio serial you can turn on every Sunday night."

"You're raising a glass to your own life."

"*Bubkes*, I'm giving myself heartache. You're here to find out about Phyllis, not me, and I'll tell you this. She was no lady and she got what was coming. You want maple syrup or sugar with your French toast?"

"Sugar, and no bacon."

"Good. More for me." She delivered two plates and sat down. "It's all those years of keeping kosher while my mother, may she rest in peace, was alive. Mind you, I still don't eat pork, but bacon, bacon's a gift from God."

I lifted a forkful of moist, golden French toast and took a bite. "*Meraviglioso!*" Flossie smiled.

I swallowed. "Do you think Roberta knew that Phyllis and her husband were lovers?"

"I didn't ask." The smile was gone. Her bacon nibbling grew audible. Probably Roberta did know. But Saul had died five years ago. Not a reason to kill Phyllis now.

"The night of the murder, Roberta told me Phyllis was an extra bone in her body," I said after another mouthful of challah. "Then she claimed she didn't know her last name."

"Phyllis Striker. It's in all the papers."

"I know. I just find it odd that Roberta wouldn't know."

"It used to be something else when Phyllis started working. That's the name Roberta doesn't remember."

"Phyllis did get married, then."

"No, she served time. She thought changing her name would make everyone forget. Herself mostly."

11

I pushed a newly formed pile of photographers' portfolios off my desk and started to dial Greenhouse at the squad room. I wanted the name Phyllis was born with, and I wanted to know more about the car accident that had sent Phyllis to Riker's Island on a two-year manslaughter charge. Roberta's bio of Phyllis made no mention of it, and Flossie had clammed up with the arrival of the plumber, claiming she didn't know anything more. The accident had happened before Flossie started working for Roberta. She only knew about the accident because once she'd asked Phyllis about the scar on her chin. Phyllis, drunk on too much champagne after a successful fall show, had told her. No one ever spoke of it in the studio.

I asked her one more question. What did she know about Roberta's fight with Phyllis the night of the murder?

"With that noise from Mario's opera, who could hear anything?" Then the plumber had started chopping down the ceiling, scaring Flossie into abandoning conversation and bacon. I'd gone back to work.

My assistant, Linda, appeared in the doorway of my office in her first maternity outfit. Two days before, her stomach had looked flatter than mine. I stopped dialing to give her a hug, congratulate her again, beg her not to quit her job once the baby was born. I fished into my purse and handed Linda a gift-wrapped package—an old English teddy bear pin—to celebrate her pregnancy.

She said she liked it, she thanked me. Linda is not one for effusions, at least not around me. She thinks I do enough emoting for the whole floor.

I went back to the phone. Linda dropped the *New York Times* on my desk, part of our daily routine. She's a crossword fanatic and gets the paper first. I get it for lunch. She'd left it open to the crossword page.

I glanced at the page, thinking she wanted to show me something.

"I need help," Linda said. She's tall and trim, with an elegant face that belongs in a nineteenth-century English portrait. If I got booted upstairs with the account execs, Linda would fill my spot with ease, efficiency, and no humor. She rarely needs help.

"Foreign word?"

"Indispensable in Rome. Eight letters. With a *z* on the seventh."

"That's easy. *Pazienza.* Patience."

"Thanks. How was I supposed to know that?"

"Works for New York, too."

"They should have said that." Linda started to take the paper back.

"No, wait." In an article above the puzzle, the name Pfizer, Inc., had caught my eye. I tore out the crossword, handed it to Linda, and kept the paper. I shut the door and dialed Greenhouse at the Mid-Town South Precinct.

"What's up?" Stan's voice was tense. "Are you all right?"

"Bad moment? I just had a question." Not the one I'd started out with. The personal took precedence.

"You never call the precinct."

"I don't like to be recorded. I'm fine."

"What's up then?"

"Does Irene still work for Pfizer?"

"Yes. Why?"

"Still in charge of corporate contributions?"

"Y-y-e-e-s." Extreme caution.

"It says in the paper of record that Pfizer is sponsoring a fund-raiser tonight for a youth employment agency called Young Start on the USS *Intrepid*, and since I know you're working on several cases at once and you're bound to be late—"

"Sim! Don't even think it."

I got angry. "Stan, I'm not going to be a sitting duck while your ex-wife takes potshots at my morality nor am I going to be proposed to only because you want your son to sleep over. I am just as affected as you are, even if Willy is not my son. I've got to talk to her. Women can get together and make sense of things, you know."

"Irene is not being rational right now."

"I'll appeal to her emotions, then. What I really called you about was—" No, I wasn't going to ask. That was our pact. I do my thing, he would do his. I wasn't going to risk our relationship. Besides, I didn't want his help. So what if he could get a complete bio of Phyllis just by pressing a few keys in his sophisticated police computer. I had my mouth and my feet. I would walk around in the garment district and ask about the accident. Call up Arnold Scaasi to see if he remembered what his fitting model's name was thirty years ago. Do some digging downtown at the criminal records department. A little hard to do without a date or a name. I could try the tax assessor's office. Maybe she paid taxes on property from way back then. I could then look up the property. I'd be really lucky if she hadn't changed the name on the deed. But then maybe she didn't own any property. What happened to birth certificates when you changed your name? My eyes were beginning to glaze over at the thought of all this research. I'd have to take a week of sick days. Then a name clicked into an empty slot in my brain. Mario Lionello! Roberta's tailor. He'd worked for Riddle Solutions from the beginning.

"I wanted to know about Charlie," I said finally. "How's it going?"

"He's in trouble. I'm sorry."

"Bad?"

"What happened to your hands last night?"

"What do you mean?"

"And your shoulder? You walked around like a winged bird."

"You noticed." *Amore mio.*

Big sigh on the other end. "Cops tend to keep their eyes peeled. Chirping Chicken was the clue."

"Ah, the stomach talks. I got mugged."

"Why didn't you tell me?"

"You were tired, upset. I've complained about your pink walls, your mattress, your air conditioner, the light in your bathroom. I didn't want to complain about being mugged on your street. I fell on my purse. He gave up when a cab pulled up, and my shoulder's fine now." Actually I'd just swallowed two more painkillers. "Why didn't you say something once you noticed?"

"I kept waiting for you to talk, I was worried about Willy, I don't know. Please don't do that. Not tell me things. I've done enough of that for both of us. That's the reason for living together, sharing things. At least, that's how I'd like it to be."

"Me, too. How bad is bad for Charlie?"

"We're about to charge him. He should go up

before a grand jury within forty-eight hours, which won't happen, but he will go up sooner or later."

"You have that much evidence against him?"

"The grand jury will decide that."

They didn't have enough evidence. I could tell by the lack of conviction in his voice. Someone higher up was pushing for an indictment.

"What's wrong with my mattress all of a sudden?" Stan wanted to change the subject. I played along, surprised that he wanted to stay on the phone this long. Usually Stan's phone conversations are limited to what, where, and when.

"I thought I'd told you. That mattress is best for short-time use. After six hours my back hurts."

"Stress. You're scared to live with me. And maybe you should be. Tell me more about the mugger." He *was* worried.

"Nothing more to tell you except that he was on Rollerblades." I knew he was now going to ask if any complaints had been filed on a Rollerblade mugger. It made me feel good and at the same time irked me. I didn't want to need his protection. "Phyllis killed someone with her car years ago. Are you looking into that?"

"Sim. Please. One detective in the family is enough."

"Have you thought of retiring?"

"Listen to me. One time you almost got pushed under a bus, another time you almost flew off a volcano, another time—"

"Almost is the key word. Got to run, the boss is calling." I blew him a kiss and hung up. I hate being lectured to.

I called Young Start. Tickets for the fund-raiser were still available. Two hundred and fifty dollars for a guaranteed awful meal and a not-so-guaranteed chance to face Irene. *Perchè no?* The cause was a good one. I wrote out a check and messengered it over. I called a florist a few doors down from 530. Then I called Roberta.

"I know," she said after my hello. "His lawyer just called."

"What's the new evidence?"

"It seems that last week he gave Phyllis a check for thirty thousand dollars, which she promptly deposited." Her voice was pitched high. "He claims he was paying back a loan, but the police claim there is no trace of that loan. They see it as blackmail."

"What has he got to hide?"

"Nothing."

"That you know of. What was in the mail I retrieved for you? It was obviously something Charlie didn't want the police to get hold of."

Not even a breath from the other end.

"There was a letter with no return address," I persisted. "It could have been from Phyllis. Something giving him a motive to kill her."

Finally I heard a long release of breath. "The letter was from his ex-lover, one he'd been expecting. It was sexually explicit. Charlie didn't think the police would be appreciative. In fact, he was afraid they would use that information to taunt him."

"Stan wouldn't do that."

"How was Charlie to know?"

"What's his ex-lover's name?"

"You'll have to ask Charlie."

"What can you tell me about Phyllis killing a woman with her car and going to jail for two years?"

"Flossie told you."

"You wanted me to find out things, right? I need Phyllis's real name, when it happened, how, who the victim was. Someone might have borne a nasty grudge all these years and finally killed her. A death for a death."

"It was so long ago."

"How long?"

"Twenty-seven, twenty-eight years ago. There was a little blurb in the paper. The *Post* or the *Daily News*. Someone pointed it out to me. Phyllis never even called. I wasn't fitting at the time. It must have been right after one of the collections. I don't remember the season."

"You don't know anything else about it? I find that hard to believe."

"Events affect me only if they affect my work. I'm sorry. What I remember is that when Phyllis came back, I threw her a party. I have no idea what her last name was then. To me she's always been Phyllis."

"Mario was with you then. He might know."

"His wife was leaving him around that time, taking their son with her. He could hardly sew a straight seam, much less pay attention to the fitting model."

I had one last question. Roberta's birthday.

"June fifteenth. Why do you ask?"

I didn't tell her.

12

I reread Mario's bio. Mario Lionello. Sixty-five years old. Refused to retire, saying he still had to support a family back in Sicily. He had come to this country when he was twelve years old. He was descended from a long line of tailors. "He's farsighted, but he can still sew up a dream," Roberta had written. "A bitter man, but my most devoted worker."

I called him. "Phyllis Striker. She used to have another name before she went to jail. Do you remember it?"

"What difference does it make what she called herself before or after? To me she was Phyllis. That's it." He sounded more belligerent than bitter. "I have work to do. We show in a week. It's like Mount Etna in here." Callas singing "Casta Diva" poured into my ear.

"Can you tell me anything about Phyllis's accident? When was it? When did she go to jail? It might be related to her death."

Mario breathed heavily, maybe in an effort to remember.

"Roberta said twenty-seven, twenty-eight years ago? Can you be more precise?"

"No!" he barked. "Leave it alone. Mrs. Riddle is a good woman. Charlie is okay, too. You leave us alone."

"Roberta asked me to help! It was around the time you and your wife split up."

He heaved a breath. Callas got lowered. "Roberta"—the sound of her first name was raw in Mario's mouth. He had always called her Mrs. Riddle—"Roberta is a good woman, a strong one, but not as strong as she thinks. There is no longer morality in this world. Roberta is loyal. She does not accept that people do bad things. Even good people, who should know better. It eats her heart out."

"Who did bad things? Phyllis? Charlie? What bad things? Help me, Mario."

"If you wish Mrs. Riddle good, leave it alone." No more brandy tones from Callas. No more Mario. He'd hung up on me.

I was left with a new question. Why did your wife leave you, Mario?

At lunchtime I was in the subway, on my way to the Mid-Manhattan Library on Fifth Avenue and Fortieth Street. I was uncomfortable in the crowd, my eyes wary of my surroundings, my nerves taut. I've been bumped around by various people and events in the course of thirty-eight years, and I've stuck to optimism as my defense. But that day in the subway I was anxious. I wasn't sure I could blame it all on the Rollerblading mugger. Roberta's need to involve me in Phyllis's case was picking up a distinctly bad smell. She was playing games with me, and, thanks to Mario and his brief speech on good people doing bad things, the possibility that she was the killer crossed my mind.

Only briefly. Why hire me to discover the fact? She could simply pick up the phone and confess. Unless she was stalling for time. In seven days her models would sashay down the runway in their Riddle Nothings. A rebirth of fame. Then what? If she was guilty, handcuffs? Charlie would take over the firm? He'd love that.

I'd tried to get hold of Charlie, but he was in a holding pen at the precinct, with his lawyer, out shopping, making up with his ex—I never found out which. No one at the studio knew where he was. His home phone didn't answer.

At the core of my bad mood was Irene. My life as a roommate was at stake. Stan and Willy couldn't be reduced to seeing each other in public places or on vacations without me. If Stan's ex-wife couldn't accept me as an integral part of her son's life, I would have to stop living with Stan. But if I did, I wasn't sure I was woman enough to stay in the relationship. The other choice was marriage. To a cop. Something I wasn't ready for.

Someone pushed me. I cringed.

"Lissen, lady!" A large African-American man was being squeezed between me and the post by a mob of schoolkids. "I'm not after your purse."

I felt instantly guilty. "I'm sorry. I have a bad shoulder. I really do." He did not look mollified. He'd had white ladies cringe once too often.

I got out at the next stop, pushed myself through the new turnstiles, starting gates to open air. On Forty-second Street the sun was still holding forth. When I reached Fifth Avenue, the lions of the main library looked sleepy in their wisdom. I turned downtown to the Mid-Manhattan Library and its trove of newspaper microfiches.

I was armed with Phyllis's original name. After speaking to Mario, I'd called Ed Mannucci. He'd only met Phyllis in Westhampton in the seventies and didn't know about the accident or her original last name. I had asked for his wife's work number, remembering she'd gone to school with Phyllis.

"What for? You want to give my whole family *agida*? Sally's got nothing to do with the murder."

I had tried to explain that I only wanted Phyllis's last name. He hadn't believed me.

"Then I'll call her tonight at home. You're in the phone book."

I had gotten her work number. Sally was the top salesperson at Très Français, an evening-dress house owned by Canadians. She was the high-energy type. Her voice crackled into my ear.

"Oh, sure, Phyllis changed it, thinking no one would know she'd done time for smashing into some poor girl. I think it was a girl. Yeah, a girl. I remember something about a baby."

"A baby got killed, too?"

"I think so. Don't quote me. I just remember a baby being in there somewhere. Maybe the girl was pregnant. That was way back. I was already working at Macy's, selling underwear. They used to have the best retail training program. From there I went to Saks, classier place. I was selling designer coats, which is where I met the Anne Klein salesman—" Sally would have liked to tell me her whole life, including shoe size and address of nail parlor. I kept bringing up the missing name.

"Something Italian. How'd you get my number?"

"Your husband. He didn't want to give it out."

"He's so protective. So you want this name? What for?"

I'd explained again about the possibility that Phyllis's death was linked to the accident.

"Well, I could look her up in the yearbook, but she was older than me. At least four years." I hadn't asked how they could have been in high school together.

She'd promised to ask her mother, who lived in Port Washington, ten minutes away from the site of the accident. An hour later, while a new, hungry-mouthed photographer showed me a meagre portfolio of under-water shots, Sally Mannucci had called back.

"I told you it was Italian. Cirni. My mother didn't remember, so I called my friend Janice in Palm Springs. She graduated from high school with Phyllis."

I'd asked her to spell Cirni, the American pronunciation throwing me. Then I'd asked the year of Phyllis's accident.

"Mom can't remember that either, except it was February. She always goes to Florida in February. She was real upset about missing the accident. It was either when I had Joey, that's my first kid, a real cute brat, or when I got pregnant with Meg."

"What year was that?"

"I had Joey in sixty-seven and Meg in sixty-eight. Both cesareans over at Doctors Hospital. God forbid my mother should miss her month in Florida. Painful! The gas alone—"

I had thanked her and hung up before I got to know the gory details. I had my name, and in a rush of optimism gave the photographer the name of a top photo agent. He'd left happy. I'd dialed Sally again.

"Sorry, I'm late for a meeting, but I had to ask. Why did Roberta Riddle fire you so suddenly?"

"Because she found out I'd lived two doors down from Phyllis in Westhampton and never told her anything all those years." I'd waited for more, but anger had made her terse.

"Then Roberta knew about Saul and Phyllis?"

"Of course she knew. What wife doesn't?" She'd sounded as if she was speaking from experience.

On the second floor of the library, the line for news-papers and microfiches was ten students long. The viewing machines were all busy. *Porco Giuda!* That's Judas pig, a politically incorrect imprecation that should have both the animal activists and the pro-traitor lobby up in arms. *Porco Giuda* anyway! I had hit a school-project day. I had two years of newspapers to go through trying to find a mention of Phyllis Cirni's accident, and in ninety minutes I had to be back at the office to review a budget with the Maxell tapes account exec. I got in line, eager to know who Phyllis had run over. The possibility of a baby being killed made the accident more relevant. I could picture grieving relatives ready to avenge their loss. For twenty-six, twenty-seven years they'd looked for Phyllis, not knowing her new name. Then one day, a coincidence, a chance encounter, whatever, someone found out she was the one. And Phyllis died.

The scenario looked good to me, especially while waiting in line. After ten minutes, the one employee behind the desk was still hunting for the same lost magazine.

I looked at my watch. It was time to call in a favor that wasn't due me. My friend Jonathan, ex-reporter, would-be author, who two years ago had convinced himself he had a crush on me. I'd told him about Stan and he'd told me I was crazy. Why date a man who had death as a partner? A question that recurred too often in my thoughts. We now had a phone friendship. Every couple of months he'd call to say hello. He'd sold his writer's soul to a fancy PR firm that had an expensive and convenient hookup with Nexis. Jonathan could access newspaper information.

I left the line and called. Jonathan was out of town, but Christie, his secretary, knew me. "How old is the information?"

"Sixty-seven, sixty-eight."

"Nexis only goes back seven years, but we send

people out researching articles all the time. I'll slip in your request." I gave her what I had. "Tomorrow okay?"

"Wonderful, thanks, and say hello to Jonathan."

"How's the cop?"

"Wonderful."

"So's Jonathan."

I got off the phone before she gave me a lecture on what I was missing. Christie thought cops weren't marriage material. Her tastes ran to surgeons or financiers. I called Roberta's studio again. I tried Charlie's apartment. He still wasn't to be found. I wanted to ask about the $30,000, about his mail, about why he had been in that ladies' room. The room with the perfect view of Mr. Nite's showroom.

I dialed information and got Mr. Nite's telephone number. I called, introduced myself as a friend of Roberta's, and asked if I could come over. I was only a few blocks away.

No, Mr. Nite said. It was a beautiful day, he liked to have his lunch in Bryant Park, would I please join him? He would enjoy the company. The park was only two blocks away, behind the main library.

"*Perfetto, si.*" His foreign accent made me want to speak Italian.

A private foundation has renovated the park, named after the poet William Cullen Bryant, and repossessed it from the drug pushers. It is now a welcoming two-block oasis between Fortieth and Forty-second Streets and Fifth and Sixth Avenues.

People of all walks of life rested, ate, read in this garden with a central lush lawn edged by bushes, flowers, and a carved stone balustrade. A U-shaped hem of sycamores, ivy, flagstones, and gravel completed the park. Green, slatted café chairs reminded me of the

Luxembourg Gardens in Paris. Looking east, toward the white marble temple of the main library, I could imagine being back in Europe, but then my eye scaled the sky. The trademark skyscrapers were strictly New World.

Behind me, on Sixth Avenue, the national debt clock flickered a too-long row of increasing numbers, warning that the family share on that day was $52,579. At street level, food stores huddled to stuff anyone with junk food in exchange for a few dollars. In the park itself, three kiosks offered more expensive fare: focaccia sandwiches, pasta, Häagen-Dazs, cappuccino. Lunchtime. I was hungry.

"*Ach*, the lady on the elevator," Mr. Nite said, surprising me in my tourist reverie. I introduced myself. He shook my hand. His was hot. Sheathed in a buttoned-up camel coat, gray fedora on his head, and with a cashmere scarf around his neck of the same intense blue of his eyes, he looked larger than I remembered him. Imposing in his elegance. He still smelled of sugared oranges. Not a butter-and-egg man. A gentleman from a past era.

"A friend of Roberta's and a friend of Mr. Mannucci's also?" Surprise was in his voice, as if he deemed it impossible. While I explained my mission on behalf of Roberta, he listened with a wistful expression on his narrow face.

"You have eaten?"

"No."

"I hoped maybe not. Potato knishes." He lifted a paper bag. "A gentleman around the corner sells good ones. Please. Allow me." He fished inside the bag with a napkin and offered me a yellow-gray lump of dough. "It is good to share food. It makes friendship."

I regretfully slid my glance away from the sign advertising a focaccia sandwich with chicken, tomatoes, and arugula and accepted with thanks. In my view, potato knishes are suicide aids. Walk into water with one in your stomach and you're sure to sink.

Mr. Nite also chose the two chairs we would sit on, dusting them off with a sweep of his handkerchief. I thanked him again. He was at least seventy years old and steeped in the Old World belief that women need coddling.

I sat down, the wrapped knish hot in my hand. "I'll be to the point, Mr. Nite—"

"Ernest Gold, that is my name, although my hair, it is of silver." He lifted his hat to show me his white hair, smiling at his own joke.

"Mr. Gold." I explained about Charlie's fingerprints in the ladies' room on his floor. "Could Charlie have been spying on you?"

"Why would he do that?" He was interested, not surprised, probably wondering how much I knew. The cocky let's-pitch-an-ad feeling got hold of me.

"There's some connection between you and Roberta, and Charlie wanted to find out what it was. He's a new partner, he's insecure, he doesn't think Roberta is giving him his due. He knows the company is in trouble and maybe that you're advising her, advising her against him."

"How do you connect Roberta and myself?"

"The night of the murder, Roberta got butterfly orchids. Tuesday evening those butterfly orchids were in your showroom. I called the corner florist, he stays open on Sundays the two weeks before the shows. I told him Roberta never got her flowers. He mentioned your name. You sent them, didn't you? Why? It wasn't Roberta's birthday, I checked that, too."

Ernest Gold stroked his nose with a small, well-manicured hand. "What are you trying to prove?" Now he looked perplexed.

I sat back. "I apologize. What I'm trying to prove is

that Charlie had a fairly innocuous reason for being in that ladies' room before the murder. And that reason was to spy on you and Roberta. Maybe you were reaching an agreement about the company. Or maybe you were fighting, because she returned the flowers. Charlie might have been pleased by that."

Ernest unwrapped his knish package. "Forgive me. I am hungry." He took a bite, hiding behind a raised hand so that I should not see the unbecoming spectacle of an open mouth.

I took small, discreet bites, out of politeness and distaste for what I was eating. "I'm sorry. I didn't mean to pounce on you like that."

"But you did mean it. You wanted what? A reaction, I think. I am, at my age, cautious. But it is good to be so electric. I admire this. It is the best of America, this energy. I left Budapest when I was fifteen, 1938, two weeks after *Kristall Nacht*, when Jewish Berlin was destroyed. My parents understood what was the future for Jewish youth. They sent me to live in London. Not a good place during the war, but better than Budapest. After the war, I came here. I was lucky. I knew about fabrics, designs, how to sell them. I was good. Almost as good as my parents. They owned a small department store in Budapest. My first years, a baby, I was in the arms of models, designers. And clothes! So many beautiful clothes. I was very pampered. Now I pamper others." He took another bite of his knish, this time letting me see his hungry mouth. I took a larger bite of mine. Trust for trust. The story would come.

A mime in black tights and whiteface followed a package-laden woman, mimicking her sore-feet waddle. Her male companion, equally laden, tried to stifle his laugh.

Ernest followed the mime's act with his eyes and smiled. "Last week he chose me. A little pinched, a little flat foot, the shoulders frowning. I laughed, it was so much me. He is good. America is good also. Where else can you come here a poor man with an accent and still build a business so you have a good coat on your back, a warm *schmatta* on your neck, and some money in the bank? Where else?"

"You had a talent."

"Talent is not enough. My parents, my relatives, they had talent also." He eased his hat up on his forehead and stood up.

I liked this man. He could tell me nothing about Roberta, he could smoke a cigar under my nose, stuff me with knishes and cinnamon. Still I would like him, his smell of sugared oranges and the kindness of his wrinkled face. I waved my half-eaten knish. "We haven't finished sharing food."

"*Ach, no.* Only I get a Coca-Cola, two Coca-Cola?" I nodded. "To break down the knish in the stomach, and we talk about Ernest Gold and Roberta Riddle, née Berta, now I will spell the surname, you pronounce. *P-B-R-Z-Y-B-Y-C-Z-S-K-I.*" He dotted each letter with a finger shake, as if he were keeping time to music. "Difficult, no?"

I laughed. "I'm Italian, I do vowels."

"A Polish name of great nobility. Pronounced *Shebasceski*. Not so hard once you know." He squirreled off to get our drinks. I watched the mime, looked at the chess players setting up, the potbellied businessmen sitting back with their impeccable jackets on their knees, the tourists removing shoes and consulting maps. In less than a week this park would be covered with white tents and fashion crowds eager to participate in the week-long frenzy of Seventh on Sixth. Now it looked benign.

A cold jab behind my neck. I started to turn around, thinking Coke can.

"Don't!" a voice warned. A hand slipped under my armpit and hoisted me up from the chair. "Walk!" he commanded. His knees knocked against my own as he headed me across the gravel, then flagstones, toward Sixth Avenue. A man of my own height, I thought, trying to keep from panicking. If I yelled, would he shoot?

"Take my purse and go."

He jabbed my back this time. "No running, no yelling." He had an accent. Hispanic. Hey, wasn't I clever? Around my height and anywhere from Latin America to Mexico to Puerto Rico. Maybe even Spain. I had him nailed.

Mr. Nite, please see me! Yell for me!

I could smell cigarettes, sweat. His. My own.

I passed a chess player and screamed at him silently. Look up! Look up! I'm in danger. The chess player raised the queen.

People laughed. The man pushed me to walk faster. People laughed harder. Buoyed by the optimism of that sound, I pretended to trip over a raised flagstone. My knees crumpled. More laughter.

My assailant spun around. "What the fu—?" I wrenched myself free.

The mime stumbled into the man, then sprang back, a released coil, his black-painted lips breaking into heaving, silent guffaws, part of his act. I wanted to run, but was too surprised, couldn't. My assailant's face blurred with panic. The laughter stopped. The man's gun jerked at too many targets. The mime threw himself on the flagstones. I shouted. Someone else screamed. The man ran to Sixth Avenue. I kept shouting, pointing at the fleeing figure as a security guard ran up. Another guard gave chase. Two policemen joined him. Another stayed with me. When I was through explaining what had happened, Mr. Nite was gone.

*   *   *

Non c'e due senza tre. No two without three. Was this another random attack? Possible in crazed New York, but not probable. I didn't look wealthy. I was wearing a man's tweed jacket I'd bought used in a Soho side street, and tan gabardine slacks old enough to hold my shape on a hanger. No jewelry except for my grandmother's antique enamel earrings whose greatest value was sentimental. My valuables—three tokens, driver's license, and twenty-five dollars plus loose change—had rested in a scruffy purse the size of a hand. Wealthier tourists had sat around the park with that overwhelmed look the first sighting of Manhattan can give you, a look thieves thrive on.

Someone was out to get me.

"You alone?" the desk sergeant asked, nudging a *Playboy* under a file.

"I was alone for a minute or two. The man I was with went to get Cokes at the kiosk." I flipped through my second stack of mug shots of thieves and rapists who had struck in the area, my spine icing over. I was sitting in Stan's precinct, Mid-Town South. Not on his floor, thank God. If he knew about this latest incident, he would lock me up somewhere, out of harm's way. Or have me protected by some bored young cop aching for headier stuff.

"That's what they go for," my sergeant said. "Women alone." His eyes flickered over my shoulder. Behind me a French man and wife were berating each other for inattention. Their Nikon had been snatched.

"As a rule." The sergeant's eye sacs were blisters sagging with fluid. "Naive will do it, too."

My neck shot back, a crane about to strike. "I am not naive."

"You got a nice face. The sister type. I was always picking on my sister."

"Silly me. I've always imagined myself the sultry-vamp type."

His blisters squeezed into folds. He was smiling. "You got lucky."

"Yeah, I didn't have to finish my knish." I'd dropped twenty-five dollars into the mime's bowler hat. He'd given them back in silence. I'd followed with a hug. "I should have grabbed him," he'd said, then he'd slipped out of my grasp to charge after the self-congratulatory strut of a three-piece business suit. I was left with immense gratitude and a white cheek.

I gave up on the photos. "I don't recognize anyone."

"Join the rest of 'em." His *Playboy* was waiting. "Sign here." He handed me his report.

I'd tried to get a good look at the gunman when I'd picked myself up from the stumble, but fear isn't a good witness. He was taller than I'd guessed, his torso taking up most of his body. His head had been covered by aviator sunglasses, a baseball cap, and a lot of wool around his chin and mouth.

"You gotta sign."

I was hesitating because I had given the desk sergeant my old Greenwich Village address and phone number. I didn't want anyone at the precinct to recognize Stan's address. I signed. I hate lying. To the police.

"Thanks." I stood up, wanting out, back to the advertising world, crazy only in its pursuit of the ultimate sell. *And* I did not want to run into Stan or Raf.

In a cab whose shock absorbers had been through the Revolutionary War, I wondered what my destiny would have been if the mime hadn't chosen us for his act. Each pothole jostle shook another question loose.

A good beating to teach me to mind my own business?

Where, in broad daylight?

Had there been a parked car, waiting for us around the corner?

The roof of a nearby building?

An empty elevator shut off at the basement level?

The pothole from hell sent my head dashing against the roof. The cabdriver hunched over his steering wheel, determined to hit them all. I gasped for breath.

Why had my assailant waited until Bryant Park to pull out his gun? It was well patrolled by its own security guards.

Unless someone had told the gunman he'd find me there. Mr. Nite. He was the only one who knew.

Why had he disappeared?

13

―――― ⊙―♦―⊙ ――――

"Talk to me, Roberta." We were sitting in the creative director's window-wrapped corner office, models' rejected portfolios strewn on the floor. I'd told Roberta about the Bryant Park incident and asked her to come to our office. Although she didn't think I was the victim of some sinister plot, Roberta understood my reluctance to venture out into the big wide world just yet.

For forty-five minutes my boss, Roberta, and I had done the final screening on a preselected series of portfolios, looking for possible defects—too-thin legs, knobby knees, flat buttocks, wide waists, stiff smiles, big breasts (they were back in, but Roberta said they ruined the line of her clothes). We finally picked the Riddle Nothings woman—a Nadja Auermann look-alike. Nadja was the supermodel of the moment. German, with snow-blue eyes and legs the length of Manhattan, she'd shot herself to fame by dyeing her hair moon white. Nadja commanded $15,000 for a day's ad shoot. Margo, from Switzerland, got $3,000. If we shot her right, no one would know the difference between them.

The blue of the sky was turning in for the night and my boss had left us for another client's cocktail party. "I'm hounding other people," I said, "but you're the one who knows more than anyone." Margo, artful freckles on her nose, stared up from my lap. "Talk to me, Roberta."

"You think I killed Phyllis?" The rouge streaks looked gaudy on Roberta's white face, her lipstick too bright. Her eyes had the transparent smoothness of the green glass found on beaches, a smoothness hard earned from the battering of time and waves. What and who had Roberta fought all her life?

"I think you are not leveling with me," I said. "I'm getting *odor di zolfo*, the smell of sulfur, on this case. A small example. You told me Jerry introduced Charlie to the company. Charlie said you came looking for him. Which is it?"

"I may have run into Charlie in some showroom." She'd changed her hat to a black velvet skull-hugging cap. On one side, strands of jet beads cascaded to her shoulder.

"All right, I'll give you a big example, then. Phyllis and Saul?"

"They're both dead. Saul accidentally, in case you're wondering. Five years ago, a massive heart attack that no doctor could doubt. I knew they were lovers, almost from the start, but I was too busy to pay much attention. Now you know why I thought the police would arrest me. Not only did I lose my temper and fire her minutes before she was killed, but she was my husband's lover for almost thirty years. Someone was sure to think I'd bashed her head in. "

"Why wait thirty years? Give the police more credit than that."

"Time doesn't change anything. I've wished her dead often enough, and I should be the number-one suspect. Instead, Charlie leaves those very confusing fingerprints. I should be happy, the focus isn't on me. But I'm not."

"Did you fire Sally Mannucci because she didn't tell you about Saul and Phyllis?"

"She quit."

"Sally claims you fired her. So does her husband."

"Maybe that's what she told him. Sally's mother set Ed up in business. He'll believe anything Sally says. She's giving him another reason to resent me."

"Did you call Ed from your office Monday?"

A flicker of anxiety in her eyes. "I haven't spoken to him since his wife quit without giving me notice. Why do you ask?"

"I used your phone on Monday and his number was on the digital display."

Roberta took the portfolio from my lap and snapped it shut. "Anyone can come into the office and use my phone. Anyone at all."

"But you're worried about someone in particular. Charlie?"

She stood up and smoothed the jacket of her tightly tailored tuxedo suit; she rearranged the portfolios on the coffee table until they fanned out like a deck of cards; she fingered the jet beads of her hat.

"I'll tell you," I said. "Ed Mannucci wants to take over your sixty percent of the business so that his wife can boast about having a fancy ready-to-wear line of her own. Charlie would keep his forty percent and finally get to do the designing."

Roberta sat down again. She looked unhappy and suddenly graceless. "Ed's after Charlie to put pressure on me. Charlie's been waffling, but if you saw Ed's telephone number on my phone display, it may mean—"

"It doesn't mean Charlie accepted, just that he had a conversation with Ed on your phone."

"How do you explain Charlie telling you that there was three hundred thousand dollars for the ad campaign? He knew our backer had reneged. Ed must have offered that money."

"No one can force you to sell."

The beads of her hat trembled. "You're damn right! Riddle Nothings will turn the company around. WWD is putting me on the front page. And the *Vogue* editor raved."

"You didn't show Riddle Nothings to Charlie because you were afraid he'd sabotage the line in some way."

"There's too much riding on those knits."

"Why did Mrs. Morewitz bequeath Charlie her percentage of the company?"

"Elsa liked him. She thought he had talent. She had no heirs."

"She could have left the forty percent to you."

"But she didn't."

"Were you surprised?"

"We discussed it beforehand. Elsa knew she was dying. She'd had angina for years. She was eighty-seven when she died. A wonderful battleship of a lady who believed women should have a bigger say in this industry. When she backed me, there were women designers, but not many women manufacturers. Adele Simpson had done it. A few others. Elsa was a firm believer in the strength of women."

"Then why not leave her share to another woman?"

"I don't know." She lied with elegance, her expression guarded, calm. Her fingers skated over the jet beads of her hat as if she were slightly bored with the proceedings. Charlie and Phyllis, two linchpins in Roberta's life. One was dead. Because of the other? In spite of? Had Roberta manipulated their lives? Or was she their victim?

I could have asked but didn't. Stan's partner, Raf, had taught me not to belabor a point.

"Throw out lots of questions," he'd said. "They get so busy trying to keep their answers straight, they trip themselves up." Raf believed cop tips covered all contingencies.

"How does Mr. Nite, Ernest Gold, fit into your life?"

"He's providing the lingerie for the show."

"Is that why he sends you orchids and you send them back? He's in love with you, isn't he?"

"Listen, Simona. Please. Don't depend on me to tell you the truth. I'm not being dishonest. I'm involved. I'm scared. I'm used to playing alone. For thirty-five years I've defended myself and my business with clenched teeth. Mrs. Morewitz gave me money, moral support, and asked nothing of me. Saul gave me nothing and asked everything. When I didn't give it to him, he went elsewhere. I was on my own again. Now I have Charlie, and he's in trouble. I don't trust myself to help him. I need you."

"How can I help if you don't level with me? I don't even know your agenda. I'm not sure it has anything to do with Charlie's innocence."

"It has everything to do with Charlie. Ernest told you I wasn't born Roberta Riddle. My real name was not made for fashion headlines, and it is by no means aristocratic. I chose Riddle because of my grandfather. At the turn of the century Zeydeh Shlomo peddled his talents on the Lower East Side carrying a sewing machine on his back. He made enough money with his fingers to bring a young wife over, have five children, and feed them all. Zeydeh Shlomo died when I was six and he was sixty, a few days before Pearl Harbor. He died of a cut in his heart—Hitler in Poland—a cut no Singer could sew up. My eyes remember a severe-looking, mustached man in a yellow photograph. My heart remembers his riddles.

"Why is the ocean so salty?"

I laughed. "To boil pasta, of course!"

"Because of all the herring in it! Why is the moon more important than the sun?"

"It inspires romance?"

"It lights up the dark!" Roberta let herself smile. "Riddles are part of our heritage. My grandfather was trying to teach me that there are no logical answers to life. Certainly not for a Jew." Roberta's eyes flitted to the window. In the distance the twin towers of the World Trade Center looked ready to lift off for an interplanetary mission. "This murder is a riddle I'm not able to answer."

"I think you can."

"I'm delegating responsibility. I have a legitimate excuse." Roberta stood up and slipped into a silver raincoat. "I have a show to put on." She kissed my cheek. "Ernest, Mr. Nite, apologizes for leaving you in Bryant Park."

"For a minute I thought he'd set me up."

Roberta looked horrified. "He was the one to call the police!"

"He did? Why did he leave?"

"Another one of our riddles. Because the sight of a uniform, any uniform, breaks his heart. Because his parents were taken away from him at gunpoint. Because he did not want to throw up in the middle of the street."

"*Oh, dio*, I am so sorry!" I followed Roberta to the elevator, filled with shame. "He told me a different story, about *Kristall Nacht*, his parents sending him to London."

"We all distort the truth to fit the dictates of our hearts." The elevator door opened. She stepped inside. "It's our only defense."

The door shut and I stood there staring at vast expanses of gray paint. What did I know of Roberta? She was dedicated to her work, ambitious, unsentimental, not overly sympathetic to the weaknesses of others. Loyal to her workers. The perfect career woman. Strong. And yet, just as she stepped into the elevator, I had seen a crack in the green glass of her eyes. I realized that I knew nothing of what her mind thought or her heart hoped for. I was at the edge of a story, trying to look in. Roberta thought I was a disinterested party in Phyllis's case. That's why she had picked me to help. She was wrong. She was a client of the agency. Keeping her happy was part of my job. If I did it well, I'd get my wish—to stay in the creative department.

I walked over to the prop closet to get the black sample dress long ago forgotten by a client; *the* dress for last-minute invitations and utilized by most of the females of the creative department. It was an out-of-style trapeze dress with the advantage of fitting sizes eight to twelve. Perfect for Irene's fund-raiser.

Apart from being confused, I was having what a psychotherapist might call an episode of paranoia. I had no intention of going back to the apartment and exposing myself to the outside world on the way. Besides, I didn't have the time, and my one evening dress was still in the depths of a packing carton. I had reserved a car from the agency's usual car service to take me to the USS *Intrepid* and then retrieve me. It was a safety measure and, I admit, a vain one, too. I wanted to impress Irene in case she was looking. Stupid, I know. A side effect of having Irene's ex in my bed. Adopting Roberta's defense, I was distorting the truth.

I dressed, I started to put on makeup in the office bathroom, then left when a dead Phyllis started appearing in the mirror where my face should have been. I shined my shoes with a paper towel. I brushed my hair. I tucked my bra straps out of sight. I pulled up my panty hose. I told myself I looked confident, sophisticated, beautiful.

The London Town car—a sleek, black, funeral special—was being driven by a chunk forcefully extracted from some Russian mountain. He looked enough like Stalin to send your blood to Siberia. He swung open the car door. His mustache sniffed. I had too much perfume on. "Free" by Janick, another agency client. I felt as free as the count of Monte Cristo.

"You lady with shrimps all over sidewalk."

I looked up. "You forgot the tomatoes and the bread." I hadn't recognized the hair over his mouth. "Thanks for appearing out of the blue!"

"Taximan's job."

I got into the backseat. "What happened to the yellow cab?"

"Belongs to my cousin. I fill in when he sleeps." The front seat sank back as he got in. A gnarl of eyebrows cut the rearview mirror. "You okay?"

I lifted a shoulder to prove it and winced.

The mustache narrowed into a smile. "Pepper vodka. One bottle, you very okay."

A soft man with mean looks. What I needed.

"How about driving me around for a few days?" I would ask Roberta to pay for it. She had offered five thousand dollars. This might cost her five hundred at the most. "Pick me up, take me to the office. I need someone to keep an eye on me."

"From man with wheels on shoes?"

"Maybe others, too."

"Boyfriend? Crime of passion?"

I explained about Phyllis's murder, the cyclist colliding into me, the Rollerblader, the gunman in Bryant

Park. He thought about it as we got stuck on the Westside Highway, heavy with suburbanites eager to get home to Westchester and Connecticut. From the rearview mirror, his mustache aimed at my face throughout our ride. A big cat putting out feelers.

"Hair," he said.

I clutched a strand. "I brushed it. It doesn't get any better than this." Brown, shoulder length, thick enough to break combs. Indomitable.

"When you cut, you sell me. Good business. Russian women, lots of hair." He went back to Moscow every Christmas to load up on inexpensive tresses that he sold to wig makers here.

"Capitalistic enterprise." He grinned. He wanted my hair and thirty dollars an hour. He'd use his cousin's wife's car.

"Fifteen dollars and no hair."

"Twenty and option to buy."

"If I cut it, you got it."

He stopped the car in front of the aircraft carrier USS *Intrepid*, now part of the world's largest naval museum. He swung open the car door. "It'za diieel, it'za a pliieeshr. I was born and reared in Moscow. Thirty-two years old. Six feet three-fourth inch. Two hundred sixty pounds. My name Dmitri. Violent, proud, sensual, cruel, but generous. Like Karamazov brodder."

I got out, glanced across the river at New Jersey dropping its night lights into the Hudson, let my eyes rest on the towering warship. Dmitri got my name and thanks. I was free to focus my fears on Irene.

I hadn't thought of Willy being there. Of course Irene had brought him. This evening was all about youth, its future, the problems facing the less privileged. An apt subject for a boy who went to private school. His future, if not guaranteed, was at least half-paved. And even if Irene had not thought to invite him, Willy would have wanted to come. Privilege had not insulated him.

We were both standing on the hangar deck of the aircraft carrier. Willy was peeking into the midnight-black pit of the carrier operations theater, looking edible in a blue blazer with a missing button on the sleeve and gray flannel slacks. I was hiding behind a Curtiss SB2C–3 Helldiver carrier-based scout bomber. I'd read the sign five times, hoping Willy would fly away. My first instinct had been to wrap my hands over his sweet blue eyes and whisper "Guess who?" My second instinct was to sew that button back on to prove how useful I could be. Maybe I should be the one to fly away. If he saw me, he would instantly understand what I was after. My presence would mortify him.

With Willy's back still to me, I made a dash for the middle of the carrier, where the bar was set up. I hoped to find Irene. I had seen pictures of her in Stan's albums. Blond, blue-eyed, freckled like her son. Far too pretty. I would recognize her.

All around me, a sparse, racially mixed crowd of well-dressed men and women sipped drinks and munched on triangles of spinach-filled phyllo dough while they examined the glassed-in exhibits of model tanks, missile cruisers, the Black presence in the U.S. Navy.

Partying on a warship for the future of American youth—the New York irony du jour. A ball at the Plaza had raised money for the homeless.

I wandered farther into the stomach of the ship, trying to fortify myself. For three dollars I could get four-and-a-half minutes in a thrill simulator. I passed. A glassed-in wax effigy of Franklin Delano Roosevelt followed me with a beady eye. I sought comfort in a displayed menu: oyster stew, olive pickles, roast young turkey, cranberry sauce, snowflaked potatoes, lettuce and tomatoes, applesauce and ice cream, fruitcake, mixed nuts and candy, orangeade and cider, hot rolls and butter, ending with cigarettes and cigars. A Christmas menu from Fort Barrette, I read. 1941. A meal that never was. A sign above my head admonished me to remember Pearl Harbor.

Around a tight corner a TV screen showed newsreels of World War I. "Our strength lies in being ready for war," the kaiser said. I agreed. That's what I was here for.

I spotted Irene at the stern of the carrier, in the dining area. Her blond hair glowed under the spotlight affixed to a hanging helicopter. Hair that fell below her shoulders with a slight wave at the tips. Dmitri would salivate at the sight. Irene wore a cream-colored, shortsleeved satin shift. She was slim, her arms muscled, her feet narrow, her nose pert, her wrinkles minimal, her lipstick discreet, her pearls glowing, her nails oval and buff-colored like her stockings. She was *Town & Country* perfection, and I could hardly breathe, she looked so much like Willy. The pain of that fact took me by surprise. Looking at him, I would always see her.

Then Irene turned around and recognized me. How, I do not know.

"What the hell are you doing here?" Perfection splintered into anger. I couldn't blame her, but her reaction armed me. I began to doubt that morality was the issue at stake.

"I don't want to embarrass Willy or you. Could we please go outside? I will only take a few minutes of your time."

"How did you get in?"

"I paid two hundred and fifty dollars like everyone else. For a good cause." I waved the program I'd rolled up.

Irene grasped for a smile as a couple greeted her. She made small talk, her eyes reaching beyond my shoulder. I hung by her side, introduced myself, praying with her that Willy was far away. She finally let go of the people and walked away, around a corner, down a narrow corridor. Outside, our heels were too loud on the metal gangway. We clattered around the stern. The Hudson had picked up more lights on its way to the Atlantic. She stopped in front of a stairway, as if to make sure of a quick getaway. She smelled of tuberose.

"I'm not here to argue with you or embarrass you, Irene. I'm divorced, too, and I'm still picking glass splinters from my feet—"

"This has nothing to do with my divorce!"

"It might. That's all I'm asking you to consider. I know you're a churchgoer, and by church rules Stan and I are sinning. But the church also preaches love. Stan and I have that. And it's a good love, as I'm sure yours was once. Now you've made it look ugly. And that's wrong and not fair to us or Willy. He may want to live with someone one day. To make sure. Is that so terrible in today's world? I mean"—I stopped to ease the knocking in my heart—"I mean, that I love Stan and I love Willy, but I can never, no matter what I do and whom I live with, take anything away from you. The memories of your marriage together stay intact, the good with the bad. You will always be Willy's mother. I can be a good friend of his, if he'll let me. There's room for both of us, Irene. "

"I love my son." Her voice was low and warm. "I want him to grow up pure of heart."

"Do you want Stan and me to get married? Will our marriage satisfy you and make Willy pure of heart?" On the submarine across the walk, a navy cruise missile sat poised for takeoff. "Good night, Irene. Thanks for listening." I held out my hand. She hid behind a curtain of golden hair. "Stan and I will be happy, married or not. We just want to be the ones to pick the date." I stopped myself from clambering down the stairs. Let Irene do the running.

Dmitri greeted me at ground level. "Ship danger-ous. Can fall down."

I looked up at the bronze statue of the sailor wav-ing good-bye, his duffel bag on his shoulder. "I don't know if I did."

When I got home, delivered safe and sound by Dmitri, an old pine dresser was waiting for me, pushed behind the bedroom door, the only available space. A note said, "We didn't charge Charlie. Yet." A Stan love note. The dresser was ugly, heavy, nothing I would ever have bought, and I loved it madly. In a spurt of wild opti-mism I gathered all the underwear I had dropped in assorted spots of the apartment and neatly put it away. I took care of sweaters, stockings, shirts. I wanted the phone to ring so that I could tell the New York Philharmonic or the Second Stage Theatre that, yes, I would subscribe, for two, please, and did they know that I had a new dresser that contained all my clothes, even my life?

Of course the phone didn't ring. Stan had an unlisted number. I called Gregory, my best friend. He congratulated me.

"It sounds like a four-carat dresser. Bring it to the office to show it off." He asked about Irene. He'd helped me prepare my little speech by calming me down. We chatted for five more minutes, then he had to go and let out his stable of cats and dogs.

I lipsticked "I love you" on the upraised toilet seat and tucked a "Ravish me" note in Stan's immaculately folded pajama shorts. I got into bed on his side so that he would have to roll me over to get in, and I would wake up and touch him, smell him, feel all right with the world.

With cold air from the half-open window making me cuddle into the blanket, I unrolled the night's program. I stared at Irene's name, remembered how beautiful she was, how she resembled Willy. I looked at my new dresser in the corner, in all its graceless heaviness, and knew she didn't matter. I was with Stan in the best time ever. Now and tomorrow.

The phone rang.

It was Anna Delgado's mother. I told her that Stan wasn't home. She started crying. She released a rush of Spanish against which my Italian was largely useless. I heard *información, importante*. Something that would free her daughter. She wanted to meet with me. Give me a piece of paper *"para lo detective Greenas."*

I said no, I would tell Greenhouse to get in touch with her.

"Por favor, Senorita Simona."

"How do you know my name?"

"Court. You with Detective Greenas." She hurried on with more Spanish, more sobs. Her raw emotion frightened me. I felt vulnerable along with her.

We hung up and my optimism was gone. I got out of bed to check the triple locks on the entrance door. I shut the bedroom window and locked it. I got into my side of the bed, folded Irene's fund-raising program, and tried to toss it in the trash can. I missed, decided to hell with it, and turned off the light. Five minutes later, I turned the bedside lamp back on and padded over to the trash can. Stan liked things neat. I leaned down, picked up the program. On the folded back page, a list of benefactors. A name caught my eye.

Happy Fu. I unfolded the program to read the rest.

Happy Futures, an adoption service.

14

I called Charlie at home. He didn't want to see me. I insisted.

"No!" he shouted. "I don't care how much Roberta is paying you. It's going to work out all right."

"Like in Happy Futures?"

Silence.

"I'll be over in fifteen, twenty minutes."

I caught Dmitri as he was depositing a couple on Fifth Avenue and Seventy-seventh Street. He'd given me the number of his cellular phone. "*I Pagliacci* with Pavarotti at the Metropolitan Opera they saw." He sang a few bars. "I would pay a kilo of hair for such a ticket."

I explained that I needed him to pay a visit to the Village with me. To pick me up all he had to do was cross Central Park. I dressed quickly and left a note for Stan. "Meeting Charlie Angelo at his place. Love the dresser!" Five minutes later Dmitri met me at the door, all in black. Mustache combed, hair slicked back, buttons bursting. A perfect bodyguard.

On the way down, he insisted that I sit in the back.

I filled him in on Charlie, on Roberta. I directed my comments to the rearview mirror. "There's a link between them that's more than professional."

"Lovers!"

"He's gay."

"Husband's lover!"

"Husband's been dead five years."

"So dead husband's lover."

"What I have to figure out is how Phyllis enters into it."

"Passion."

"In her case you're right. She was Roberta's husband's lover. Maybe she was also blackmailing Charlie or selling him information for thirty thousand dollars."

"Wife kill her. With passion, always much tension."

"It happened a long time ago."

"Passion not forget."

"What about greed? That's usually the motive these days. Love is out of fashion."

"Never! Always love. Woman love, father love, money love, hate love. Mind love. Like in *K. Brodders*. Everybody love hungry!"

I'd never gotten beyond page one hundred of that tome, so I couldn't argue. Dmitri followed me inside Charlie's building. The doorman stopped us with a worried look aimed at Dmitri's bulk. The same doorman who had seen me unlock Charlie's mailbox.

"Hi," I said. "Remember me? I'm Charlie Angelo's friend. Simona Griffo. I'm expected."

The doorman grinned, relieved. He pressed buttons, muttered into a telephone receiver. Dmitri made noise with a chewing-gum wrapper.

"He's coming down," the doorman said. I caught Dmitri eyeing the elevator.

Charlie wanted to go to Brooklyn Heights. In his own car. Without Dmitri. We'd talk there. Dmitri beamed with delight, which was understandable since it was almost midnight. I resented it. Dmitri noticed.

"You get her home," he commanded Charlie.

"As long as she doesn't live in New Jersey."

Dmitri's two-hundred-something pounds expanded into a menacing boulder about to roll. "To door. Upper West Side. City dangerous."

Charlie nodded, chewed his nails. He was wearing jeans, an Emporio Armani V-neck sweater. His chest hair was black. His face would have fit right in with the de Kooning show at the Metropolitan Museum. Abstract unhappiness. Charlie started walking toward Sixth Avenue. Dmitri stopped me from following long enough to whisper, "You woman, you safe. With him no crime of passion."

"Passion isn't the only motivator."

"Trust me." He nudged me with an arm the size of a punching bag.

I trusted him.

"I was looking to adopt," Charlie said as we approached the Brooklyn Heights Promenade from Remsen Street. Across a mottled East River, Manhattan was dressed for the night: basic black accessorized by diamond-rich glitter. "With my lover. It can be done. Even for gays. But then he left for Paris and that's the end of that. Now I got the police off my back for an hour or two." He didn't sound relieved.

"Why are they off your back?" We sat down on a bench. Behind us, lampposts hid in trees and patrician town houses looked like perfect English imports. A jack-o'-lantern swung from a porch. Mums sat in windows, proud to be the last blooms of the year.

"They must be picking on someone else," Charlie said. To the north, the Brooklyn Bridge with its double

row of sloping lights looked like a gigantic yacht ready
to party. Beyond the bridge, the tip of the Empire State
Building was dressed in yellow and orange for fall.

"Do you know who?"

"Your detective boyfriend keeps quiet?"

"About most things," I said. A tugboat glided by, its
wake swaying the reflected lights. The antenna of the
World Trade Center stretched up into the sky, a spire of
the money cathedral. A plane flickered its lights. A
sickle moon looked sharp enough to wound.

"Loving a cop must be like loving a gay man,"
Charlie said. "You never know how fast they're going to
die on you. That's why Mark left me. My lover, Mark. He
doesn't want to love anymore. He thinks he can lick
death that way."

"Whenever I get scared about Stan dying, I think
about airplane crashes, about cancer." We sat down on
a bench facing the river and the hypnotic skyline. "It's
not just cops or gays who die too early."

"Whatever fits."

"Roberta said something like that. Whatever fits our
comfort level. Why were you in the ladies' room?"

"What I told the cops a thousand times." Charlie
turned away, his face now completely in shadow. "Six
o'clock. I know the time because the flower boy had
just delivered an orchid plant and I had to sign for it
with the time. He confirmed. The bathroom door on
our floor is stuck, both ladies' and gent's. I walk down
one flight and use the bathroom to pee. There's a nail
sticking out of the doorknob. My finger gets cut as I
open it, I bleed, I leave bloody fingerprints." He
removed the turquoise and silver ring and lifted his
hand to the light to show me the cut.

"Why the ladies' room?"

"I told them it was a quirk of mine, peeing with the
girls."

"But you only left prints on the entrance door. How did you open the stall door and close it?"

"I changed my mind. My lawyer has two psychiatrists ready to swear I have a mother fixation that finds momentary relief just by being in the ladies' room."

"Charlie, I'm trying to help."

"I got a lawyer. What can you do?"

"Listen to you, to others. People might tell me things they won't share with a policeman simply because I'm not a threat."

"Come on, you live with a cop. And he's on the case. Anyone who talks to you must be crazy. I don't know why Roberta got you into this."

I thought I finally knew. She didn't want to be alone anymore. "She's not paying me, by the way. I'm doing this to keep a client happy and to satisfy a galloping curiosity about the human condition." Maybe even to needle my cop lover just a bit. A way of affirming my stubborn, independent ways at the moment of moving in with him. I'll cook dinner, even sew on a button or two, but that's all that's changing, *bello mio*.

I stood up and walked to the railing, turning to face Charlie and the yellow light of the lampposts. Underneath me, a steady line of headlights streamed north on the Brooklyn Queens Expressway. "You're not telling me the truth, but you're talking to me. Something you refused to do until I mentioned Happy Futures."

"I wanted to find out how you knew. After you called I got Roberta on the phone. She told me about you picking up the mail."

"Why didn't you want the police to know about the adoption agency?"

Charlie squirmed, shifted his weight, turned so that the light hit his profile. "Christ, it's not the adoption agency I was worried about." His knee started jerking. "It was that letter from Mark."

I asked him about Ed Mannucci. He confirmed that Ed wanted to buy out Roberta and had been after him to wear her down.

"He offered the three hundred thousand dollars for the ad campaign?"

"Yeah, Monday morning, he called me at home. Ed thought Phyllis's murder was the last straw for Roberta."

"How badly does Ed Mannucci want Riddle Solutions?"

"Not bad enough to kill, if that's what you're suggesting. He thinks Riddle Solutions is about dead in the market and he can pick up Roberta's share cheap and get his wife off his back. I was thinking I'd finally get to design."

"Roberta tells me you haven't tried to convince her to sell her share to Mannucci. How come?"

"I don't want to drape other people's ideas till I drop dead. Designing's become my life. I love everything about fashion. The smell of wool, the feel of the stitches as they curve under the armpit without a crease—God, the armpit's a bitch. That swish of silk when the model turns!

"I want John Fairchild, Suzy Menkes, Amy Spindler to splash my name across the page. 'Fall Colors from Angelo.' 'Angelo's elegant edge.' 'Charles Angelo stuns again.'" Energy, desire, hope emanated from his twenty-six-year-old face as a force I could almost touch.

"Why not?" he said. "I've got the talent. I can do it. Okay, I made a mistake when I went to FIT. I wanted to study designing, but I figured no one would hire me. I needed work right away. Everyone wants to be a designer, someone told me. I listened to bad advice and I studied to be an assistant designer. But that doesn't mean I can't design, and once I got my guts back I swore nothing would stop me from making the jump to designer."

"Something has stopped you?"

"Loyalty. I mean, I don't think it's even in the dictionary anymore, but I got it. I'm allegiance positive. Roberta. Mrs. Morewitz. They've been good to me. That doesn't happen too much. Not to Charlie. That old lady, she knew me less than three years and she gives me forty percent of the business. And she gives it to me so I'll help Roberta. I know that. She's dead, but how can I let her down?"

"Why did she pick you?"

"Why not me?" He bit a nail. He jerked his knee. Over on the next bench a couple were dissolving their marriage. She wanted children, he did not. Beneath me, the thrumming of cars. "Why not me?" Charlie repeated.

"Phyllis's murder had nothing to do with changing your mind about Ed Mannucci?"

"No! Phyllis doesn't fit into this."

"Why did you give her thirty thousand dollars?" Which was half his yearly salary.

"The cops are salivating over that one. I owed her. She helped me out a couple of years ago when I was buying my apartment. She paid me cash. Not traceable."

"You said you barely knew her."

"Christ, shut up, will you? I've had two days of questions, I've had it. You want to listen, then listen. I have my reasons for doing things, and I'm not going to share them with you or Roberta or anybody else. They're private. I don't care what evidence turns up that says I killed Phyllis. I know I didn't, and that's good enough for me. And I turned Mannucci down flat on Monday afternoon. If Riddle Solutions dies on us, we'll bring it back. That's all you're getting."

"Your desire for privacy might be protecting the real killer."

"Maybe I don't care. Maybe I'm even glad."

"To protect Roberta?"

"She didn't do it. She had reason to. But she didn't."

"Saul and Phyllis were a long time ago."

Charlie slipped down on the bench, leaning his head against the bench. The lamplight on his blond hair gave him a halo. "I always come here when the shit hits the fan. I don't know what it is about this place. Okay, it's gorgeous. The Manhattan skyline and all that, but that's not it. There's something about the smell, the sounds. It's comfortable. It makes me happy."

I sat back down on the bench. "If you're not protecting Roberta, who are you protecting?"

"No one but me." Charlie turned to look at me. "I owe you an apology." Half his face was in shadow.

"What for?"

"For acting like a smart-ass. I've been trying to impress myself on what a neat, in-control guy I was. You've got to understand our business. It's all about pretense. We're trying to sell dreams here, telling both men and women, 'If you put on our fabulous dress or our great-looking suit, you're going to be somebody different. Powerful, beautiful, whatever it is you're looking for, we're supplying it.' To be any good at this game, you've got to believe that power's yours. That the silk jersey top with the three sequined buttons you've just designed is going to make all the difference in some woman's life. And more important yet, that it's going to change your own life. Which it can. Look at Ralph Lipschitz from the Bronx. Look at his clothes. They say pedigree. WASP. The *Mayflower*. Lipschitz becomes Lauren. It's a fantasy come true. Anyway, I'm sorry. Don't trust any of us too much."

"I'm learning."

We made our way back up Remsen Street to the car, Charlie walking slowly, looking into all the lighted windows. He stopped in front of the doorway of a Franciscan

monastery and stared. Then he crossed the street and
skipped up and down the stoop of a town house. He
came back to the monastery and gave it an approving
nod.

On the Brooklyn Bridge he grinned and thanked
me for helping him.

"With what?"

"Retrieving baby memories."

So once he had lived on Remsen Street. Where did
that get me?

Dmitri was waiting for me when Charlie dropped me at
home. In a hot-pink, fifties-vintage Cadillac showing
rust and washboard fenders. I didn't get in.

"A priiesent." He opened the car door to let light hit
a photo cutout of Roberta sitting in a garden, with bell-
bottom pants, a tunic, and no hat. Standing behind her,
a man's suited torso. Her husband, Saul? In her arms a
baby.

"Where did you get this?"

"While you sit with Charlie in Brooklyn, I look in
his apartment."

"What! How did you get in?"

"Cunning." He pronounced the g. "With my face
and kilos I can smash in, but I show doorman police
badge and demand entrance. With murder case doorman is used to this, no trouble. Police come on
Tuesday. I say police need look again. I use real police
badge, gold. I find after fight in Rasputin."

A nightclub in Brighton Beach, where supposedly
the Organizatsiya, the Russian mob, liked to hang out. I
was beginning to wonder what I had gotten myself into
with Dmitri.

"Impersonating a police officer can get you into bad
trouble."

"Vodka, too. Cigarettes, sex, red meat, cheese, milk, eggs. You name it, trouble. The real badge I give back. But before I make copy. You feel better now?" I sensed a smile behind his mustache.

For some crazy reason I did, but I wasn't going to let him know it. "I didn't want you to do this."

"Naturally. Like Henry the Second and Thomas Becket. Henry doesn't want either. When Becket dead, Henry very happy."

I laughed. "Okay, I'm glad. As long as we don't get caught and you're not part of the Organizatsiya or anything like that."

"No. But if yes, I say the same, so question no good."

How reassuring.

"Photo in very interesting place. That's why I take. Nothing else good."

"Where did you find it?" I peered at the photo again. Roberta looked mystified. The baby was smiling.

"Inside patent-leather tuxedo shoe."

"How did you think to look there?"

"I got interested in shoe. Expensive. My size, I think."

He had about ninety pounds on Charlie. I tried to find Dmitri's feet underneath the dashboard.

He wriggled one out, lifting it to the light. The front seat creaked with the shift of weight. "Small feet."

Indeed. "You didn't take anything else, I hope."

"Shoe too tight." If Stan found out about Dmitri, I'd get fried in lard.

"You are never to do this again. Not for me, at least. *Patti chiari amicizia lunga.* Clear pacts, long friendship."

Dmitri's lower lip, free of hair, smiled. "I live in Rome before coming here. Ostia. I go to Rome flea market on Sunday and sell Russian coral."

"Great." I turned the photograph around. A woman's

hand had written "Southampton." Roberta and the baby had been cut out of a larger photo, and yet the writing on the back appeared in its entirety. A stroke of luck, or had someone written on it after the picture had been cut? I leaned back to get more light on the back of the photo. The fancy curlicues of the handwriting looked familiar.

"Did an envelope come with this?"

"No."

The envelope with no return address that I'd picked up in Charlie's mailbox. The curlicues were the same. I could have sworn it.

"What the hell are you doing?" That was Stan, behind me on the street. "Do you know what time it is?"

Dmitri's thick arm shot out. His hand swallowed the photo I'd been holding.

"Hi, hon." I turned around and pecked Stan's lips. Not receptive. "Meet Dmitri. He's been driving me around. Dmitri, Stan Greenhouse of the New York Police Department."

Properly forewarned, Dmitri nodded, turned on the motor, waved good-bye, and was off.

"Seven-thirty tomorrow morning," I yelled after him.

"Shh!" Stan clutched my elbow. "The neighbors."

I swung around, astounded. "The what?"

"Okay, so I'm mad. I was worried sick. I want you to move out."

15

———— ❦ ————

Stan had found out about Bryant Park. A phone call to the precinct had warned him that his work wasn't appreciated and that if he didn't keep his "mug out of an honest man's face," I, his girlfriend, would not stay around to keep him warm at night. The man had spoken quickly in a muffled, unrecognizable voice. The phone call had been recorded, as are all phone calls to the precinct, but the man hadn't stayed on the phone long enough for the police to trace the call. The voice experts were still working on the recording, trying to ferret out foreign and regional accents. So far they had found none, which was surprising.

"Do you think it's Charlie Angelo?"

"I ran the tapes of my interrogation. He's got a New York accent you'd need a bulldozer to lift. The only people who sound geographically neutral are well-trained actors. I've arrested a couple in the past. The last case, three years ago, the guy murdered his agent, but he's still in jail. I have a hunch Anna Delgado's husband's behind this. Guess what her supposed hit man does when he isn't hanging out in bars?"

"He plays a spear for Shakespeare in the Park?" I was trying to make light of the situation. Personal danger was an aspect of living with a homicide detective that I had not thought of, and I didn't like it much. In fact, I was stunned. "Who are these people?"

"Victor is a punk who rents a filthy one-room loft over on Tenth Avenue and calls it a gym. Drug dealers use it to push iron and keep up with the competition. He's got some arrests for dealing, but no convictions. Sonny Petruzzi is an actor. Clean record. Good-looking, not much personality. The follower type. Sonny reminds Raf of his neighbor's Labrador. I got Sonny's voice on tape from the Delgado case, but we don't have a match. The voice is too muffled. We'll work on the tapes some more, but I'm not getting my hopes up." The anger in his voice was palpable.

"The man who held me up in the park had an Hispanic accent."

"Probably Victor Delgado. He wants me off his back and so does Sonny, the hit man. Raf and I went to have a chat with both of them. They hang out together now, in a bar, writing their sleazy book. Thirty minutes after I left them, their lawyer was on the phone threatening a lawsuit for harassment."

Stan proceeded to show me photos of both Anna's husband and the hit man. Victor Delgado could have been the man who accosted me in Bryant Park. I hadn't noticed the bowling ball of a head, but then my assailant had worn a baseball cap and a scarf. Victor did have the same build and coloring, the same short legs, but that wasn't enough to make a positive identification in a court of law.

We went to bed and clutched tightly, physical proximity expressing love, conquering anger and fear. The curtains were drawn, the lights were out.

"I can set you up in a safe house, but I'd rather you

be with friends. Maybe Gregory in New Jersey? I want you to stop working, too. Until I bring them down. A week, two weeks at the most, a month if things go bad."

"Why not a year? Two? Did this happen to Irene? I bet this didn't happen to Irene." I slipped my hand down his back and cupped a firm, warm buttock. It wasn't a sexual move. Sex was the last thing on my mind at that moment. I was just grounding myself. "Did it happen to Irene?"

"No. This is a first." He tightened his hold on me. "I'm so sorry, Sim. I truly am. My being a cop, I don't know, maybe I should—"

"What? Quit? Not in your dreams, even. What are you talking about?"

"No, I don't want to quit. Maybe I shouldn't have you here, but I want you here."

"You just said this is a first time. It'll be the last, too." Inside I felt like someone was taking Christmas away. First Irene, now these hoodlums were conspiring to separate us.

"My job affected my marriage," Stan said, his voice muffled by my hair. "Irene was always worried. For herself, for Willy. She comes from one of those sheltering families, the kind that spends a great deal of money to isolate itself—the best neighborhoods, the best schools, the best clothes. She couldn't handle real life. At least not mine. She wanted me to quit and go to law school. I loved being a cop more than I loved her. So she left, and I found you and fell in love with you because you don't hold back, you don't care if my collar is blue or white—"

"I like it clean."

Stan shut me up with a light kiss. "Whatever happens, you just pick yourself up and throw yourself back in. It drives me crazy, but it's what I love about you, too. And now, because of me, someone wants to hurt you." I felt his chin rubbing against the top of my head. "You won't leave, will you? I mean, I want you to leave tomorrow morning, but I want you to come back. I can't promise this won't happen again."

"Where am I going to go? I love my new dresser. I put all my underwear away. I'm getting used to the pink walls, the too-soft bed. I need the reassurance of your buttock in my hand every night." I squeezed. "At least we can thank Irene for keeping Willy away. They might have picked on him."

"Someone's watching Willy."

"Good," I said. "Then someone can watch me and I can stay right here and go to work."

The buttock tightened. We argued. Stan didn't have many men to spare, not if they were going to help him find evidence against Victor Delgado and the hired killer. It was easier for everyone if I just laid low for a while. He had distant relatives who had a cottage in upstate New York. I could go there. No one would ever make the connection. He was close to getting Anna's husband, he said. He had a new lead thanks to Anna's mother. Mrs. Cordova had used her job at Nynex to pore through the hired killer's phone records. She had found calls dating back nine months between the hired killer's home number and the one-room gym Anna's husband owned. In court, the two men had denied knowing each other. The police had only looked back six months, then stopped when Anna Delgado's guilt seemed a given.

"If I can get evidence that they knew each other, I've got them."

"Isn't that a stretch? From knowing each other to collusion?"

"I'll do it. I'll get them, but first you move out."

I let go of the buttock. I don't like being told what to do. Not by my lover, certainly not by a hoodlum. Orders make me ornery and dumb. I slipped out of bed and faced him. "I'm not moving out! I've got Dmitri, recently of Moscow and Brighton Beach. He looks as mean as Stalin and he's as big as the Kremlin. And he's also part of the Organizatsiya, the Russian mob!" That last detail was pure invention. At least I hoped it was. "Dmitri will take very good care of me. Dmitri will be my shadow." As I said. Ornery and dumb. "Now I want to know why you've let up on Charlie. Do you have another suspect?"

Stan's head hit the pillows with a lamenting *whoosh*. How was I going to tell him about Dmitri snitching that photo of Roberta with a baby? Did he need to know? Maybe it wasn't important. "It's Phyllis's accident. You're looking into the accident, aren't you?" I slung a robe over me, my signal that I was being serious.

"Sim, you're relentless!"

"*You* don't give up. You're willing to risk your life to get the rightful killer in the Delgado ca—"

"Sim, I'm a cop, I can't—"

"I'm not criticizing. I'm just asking why I can't be like you. Stubborn and impossible." *Dio*, he looked sweet and delectable with mussed hair and worry hunched on his face.

Stan sat up, leaning on an elbow. "Why not? I love you for it." He smiled. Worry took a walk. I slipped back into bed. We do everything best there. Conversations, too.

"We looked into the accident," Stan said, hooking his toes under my ankle. "It's a dead end. A young woman died. No boyfriend. Parents have been dead over ten years. Most of the relatives live in Utah and California and barely remember the dead woman or care about the accident. Raf looked into it, and he thinks these people didn't like the victim too much. A second cousin in Utah said the victim boozed it up and ran around a lot."

"So who cares if she's dead, right?"

"That's what it sounds like."

My fingers rubbed the curve of his shoulder. "Didn't a baby die with her?" His skin was hot. Tomorrow, I'd get the photo from Dmitri and show it to Stan.

"No baby died. Just the woman. The one cousin who's still in Port Washington was only ten years old at the time. She remembers the mother crying a lot after it happened. She never heard anyone scream revenge."

"So who is your new suspect? Roberta?" It had to be her.

"No one."

"My, your nose grows long when you lie."

"I'm not lying. This afternoon Ernest Gold, Mr. Nite, reported a hundred and eighteen thousand dollars missing from his safe. He thinks Phyllis might have seen the thief and been killed for it. We've got to cover that angle first."

"You don't think Charlie's the thief?"

"Could be, but there was another theft in the building a month ago. Also on a weekend. Probably they're connected. That weekend Charlie was down in New Orleans and Atlanta doing a fashion show with the head salesman. Trunk shows, I think they call them. He's got an alibi for five days. We're following other leads. An old boyfriend of Phyllis's. Disgruntled employees. Newly hired ones. The maintenance staff."

"That's right. Blame it on the servants." I snuggled into his armpit. I like heat. "Why did Mr. Nite wait three days to tell you about the theft?"

Stan bent down to kiss me. "Claims he didn't open the safe until this afternoon."

"Are you telling me the truth? Is Charlie out of arrest danger?" Where did my loyalties lie in this case? With Stan or my client Roberta?

Stan gave me another kiss, confusing me even further. "I am telling you the truth, Sim. No one is out of arrest danger until the case is closed, and that's all I'm going to say about it. We have to keep this case out of our lives. That's what we agreed upon when you said you wanted to help Roberta out. You do your bit, I do mine. Remember?"

"I do, but divided loyalties feel funny."

"It was your decision, and as for you and Dmitri, let's continue that discussion in the morning." He dropped back down on the pillows, taking me with him, and we made love. To invert a Dmitri maxim—with tension, always much passion.

"Good morning, Sim," Stan yelled from down the hall as I fumbled out of bed. He has an animal's knack of hearing my first morning movement no matter how silent it is. "We've got company."

Willy! Irene had listened to reason and let him come. I dug up one of Stan's T-shirts for cover, then wrapped my bathrobe, a chaste striped cotton affair, tightly around me. I ran fingers through my hair, checked for telltale marks of love on my neck, and pinched my cheeks to look alive. I even put on slippers.

"Great to see you—" I stopped at the kitchen door.

Dmitri, in black from head to foot, looked up from the fashion page of the *New York Times*, a coffee mug disappearing in his fist. The buttery-soft double-breasted jacket draped over his vastness must have cost all the tresses of Uzbekistan. The slacks were waiters' specials, the shoes black high-tops. Everything black, to match his hair and mustache.

Stan stood behind him, drinking coffee, looking pure early morning Brooks Brothers: damp hair and a fresh shave accessorized by a gray suit, blue shirt, and rep tie. He should have been a lawyer.

"*Buon giorno.*" I didn't kiss or grin.

"Amy Spindler's headline is 'Two Magical Mystery Tours,'" Stan said as his Old Spice and cinnamon wafted my way. He looked pleased with the world.

"Fascinating. What's Dmitri doing in my . . . your kitchen?"

"Erotic zones!" Dmitri said gravely before chomping on an onion bagel.

"Our," Stan chimed in. "I think the headline's funny given the fact that I'm working two cases at once."

"*We're* working. The Delgado people are after me, remember?" I sat down opposite Dmitri. "And I wouldn't call them magical. What about erotic zones, Dmitri?"

He tapped his half-eaten bagel at the paper. "Even in dress, passion!"

I swiveled the page around and read. "Erotic Zones" was the title of Vivienne Westwood's Paris fashion show.

"I read fashion to see the wigs," Dmitri added. "For window of opportunity. Last year many ponytails. This year not good." He took a bite of the bagel, leaving only the hole. "Thank God for Broadway. *Sunset Boulevard* got a hundred and thirty-two wigs. *Phantom of the Opera,* a hundred and thirty. *Beauty and the Beast,* two hundred and thirty-four!"

I turned to Stan. "Does Dmitri pass the test?"

"What test?" Dmitri asked. The flecks of burned onion sticking to his mustache trembled. "Stan jealous?"

"No, he's a control freak. He doesn't want me killed." I explained about the specific threat to my future breathing while Stan offered me decaf coffee the way I liked it. In a cup, not a mug. "Stan's probably already checked up on you, and he invited you in so that he can get your prints off that mug. He's a homicide detective, by the way."

Dmitri laughed. "Next to KGB, NYPD nothing." He put his mug on a plate and handed it to Stan.

Doubt tiptoed across Stan's eyes. Dmitri saw it, too. "I take good care of your love lady. I got long security experience. Russian imperative."

"Who did you guard?" Stan asked.

"Me." Dmitri held out a hand.

Stan shook it, doubt giving way to a friendly caution. "Dmitri and I have already exchanged views on how best to protect you. He's got a gun permit and a gun. And"—Stan patted my shoulder, a sure sign that I was getting a comeuppance—"we have no record of him being in the Organizatsiya."

"As yet." I would, under normal circumstances, not want to be anywhere near a member of organized crime of any country. But I felt that my life had taken on a cartoon quality. Part of a Garry Trudeau comic strip. He'd draw me as a patsy.

Bringing the bodyguard of my own choosing into the house, questioning him, checking his fingerprints was perfectly reasonable behavior for a man who felt responsible for the danger I was in, a man who loved me, a policeman. And yet I was annoyed. The single life had spoiled me. I was not used to deliberating my actions. I was uncomfortable with protection. Except Dmitri's. He was being paid. There were no emotional losses or gains involved.

"I'm counting on Dmitri scaring off those two hoodlums," Stan said, "but, Sim, one more incident, however small, and off to New Jersey or upstate New York you go."

"I'm glad I get a choice. And I'm paying for Dmitri, not you." I couldn't ask Roberta to foot the bill. My being in danger had nothing to do with her.

"It would be cheaper to go to New Jersey," Stan said.

"Thrills are expensive."

"I lower my price," Dmitri offered. "Twenty-five dollars for hour."

"We agreed on twenty!"

Dmitri tried to look contrite. "I forget."

"We'll share the expense." Stan kissed me goodbye. "It's your stubbornness, but my case. Be careful, honey."

"Okay, we'll share." I finished my coffee and gave Stan another kiss at the doorway. "And you be careful, too." I left Dmitri in the kitchen with the fashion page while I showered and got dressed.

The office was the first stop. No one followed us except the Fifth Avenue bus.

Jonathan's secretary had come through. She'd messengered over a manila folder, which was sitting on my desk. It held copies of newspaper articles regarding Phyllis's accident and Roberta Riddle's career. I also found a dozen pink roses in a basket. I tore open the card:

I apologize from the depth of my heart. I was not a gentleman. Ernest Gold.

I called him. I wanted to thank Mr. Nite for the roses, but I also wanted to ask about the theft of the $118,000 he had only discovered yesterday. The receptionist told me that he didn't come to work until ten. I left a message that I wanted to take him to lunch. One P.M., 44 at the Royalton, where the fashion crowd hangs out. I'd check back later to see if it was all right.

I called Annie at Elite Model Management and begged her to confirm Margo, the Nadja Auermann look-alike, for the Monday after fashion week. Margo was in demand, and I had only managed to get a "tentative" booking on her. We bargained. I released a "confirmed" I had on a model for a wine shoot, knowing I could easily replace her. Annie and I thanked each other, I marked a big check mark by Margo's name on my photo-shooting schedule, and dialed Roberta's number. I wanted to give her the good news on our model and ask for a hundred-dollar check as payment for whatever "help" I was going to give her. A check would establish a client-detective relationship and solve the loyalty question. I also didn't want to assume that she would spring for lunch for two at the Royalton, where a plate of chicken costs twenty-one dollars. Her number was busy. I was late for my appointment with Jerry Sarnowski in Chinatown. Roberta and the check could wait. If she wouldn't pay for lunch, I would. A dose of fancy is necessary when a hit man's after you. I couldn't quite picture him coming after me at the tony Royalton while Dmitri gulped Stoli and *Vogue* editor Anna Wintour exchanged fashion gossip with Bill Blass.

I pattered down to Gregory's office. He's always the first one in. I kissed him good morning on his cheek and told him about the threat. If I had to, could I hide at his house with the dogs and the cats? The panic in my voice was as welcome as morning breath.

Gregory smiled his slow smile and looked at my hand, "Where's the four-carat dresser?" Then he demanded pictures and offered espresso, a Gregory office specialty I depend on. I declined. I was late. Dmitri was huffing by the elevator. Yes, I could stay at his place he said with his usual even-keeled tone, as if I'd asked to come for a lovely weekend instead of possibly hiding for my life. Maybe he didn't believe me. Hyperbole and I are often close friends, he's told me.

"I won't need to come, I'm sure, but thanks." I walked back to my office and left a note for Linda saying that I was taking the rest of the day off, to confirm the photographer and the rest of the crew for Roberta's shoot, I'd call later. I stuffed the manila folder with its articles into a tote bag. The photo Dmitri had shown me had given me lots of ideas. As I rushed down the corridor toward Dmitri and the open elevator, Gregory yelled, "No radio can replace you, Simona. Not even Carnegie Hall!"

Gregory, my best friend.

Dmitri had set up his office in the Cadillac. Files, a Rolodex, fashion and hair magazines flowed over the front seat. A blond wig Mae West would have been proud of sat on the dashboard. I got in back, hunching down so that my head didn't make a moving target. As we headed downtown to Chinatown, I checked the articles. It was hard going. Dmitri was having fun swaying in and out of avenues. I kept banging my head.

"Dmitri! Do we have to?"

"Like film noir. We shake tail."

"It might be easier if we got rid of the pink car."

"No, pink for panache! Confuses enemy. KGB method."

"That's absurd!"

"Correct. I never know anyone in KGB, but secret police always sound good to Americans. Gives them cold in stomach. Americans like cold everything. Even in vodka. Obnoxious!"

I dug my heels under the front seat, my shoulders against the backseat and, holding the Xeroxed articles firmly in both hands, tried again. The accident got a few paragraphs in the *News* and the *Post*. The date was February 24, 1967, the same day the Boston Strangler escaped from a mental ward in Lynn, Massachusetts.

The accident victim was eighteen-year-old Gloria Hernandez of Manorhaven, Long Island, which is a forty-five-minute drive from the city. The first report, which made the papers the next day, simply stated that Gloria had been found dead at one-twenty A.M.

on the beach off Lighthouse Road in nearby Sands Point, killed instantly by a hit-and-run driver. Gloria, the only daughter of a gardener and a housekeeper, had plans to go to college in the fall. Her parents were devastated. Phyllis's name came up the following day. According to that article, after ascertaining that the girl was dead, Phyllis Cirni had gotten back into her rented car and driven to the city despite the fact that she had sustained various abrasions and a deep cut where her jaw had hit the windshield. At St. Vincent's in Greenwich Village, the ER doctor was quoted as saying, "She must be one hell of a determined woman to get from Sands Point to Manhattan with that wound."

Phyllis had not told the details of her accident to the hospital staff until four hours after her arrival. The Manorhaven police were notified right away.

I wondered why Phyllis had picked St. Vincent's. There were hospitals along her route, one not fifteen minutes from the site of the accident. She was probably running away, but why St. Vincent's? At the time of the accident, according to the papers, she lived on Eighty-fifth and First Avenue. St. Vincent's was not on the way.

I told Dmitri about the accident. I filled him in on what little I knew about the murder case. Charlie's fingerprints being in the ladies' room where Phyllis was found, the $30,000 Charlie had paid Phyllis. My feeling that Roberta knew a lot more than she was telling me. That she cared for Charlie even though she wouldn't admit it. My feeling that Charlie was lying about what it was that he wanted kept from the police when he asked Roberta to pick up his mail for him. I also told him about Charlie inheriting 40 percent of Riddle Solutions and claiming that he didn't know why. About Mr. Nite, who took his time to discover a theft and who may have been the reason Charlie was in the ladies' room in the first place.

Dmitri hit the brakes for a red light on Canal Street. The Cadillac gulped. I swooped forward, my nose bumping into the back of the front seat. The manila folder fell out of my hands. Dmitri's bulk stood still. Sitting on a stoop, a Chinese woman looked up at us, foreigners in her land, then went back to slamming a hammer into a conch as if she were still sitting on a far-distant shore. Mulberry Street, once the reigning street of Little Italy, was at this point crowded by vegetable and fish stands owned by Chinese. One vendor sold dried fish the size of a child's little finger. The silver heads had the sheen of jewelry. The smell was heavy with salt, and my senses flashed back to my childhood. Friday mornings and my good Catholic mother soaking salted codfish for that day's lunch.

Dmitri picked up the sheets that had slipped out of the folder. He handed me an article with a picture of Roberta, young and hatless, smiling into the camera, after her first fall show. "Elegance with Verve," Bernadine Morris of the *New York Times* had decreed.

"This Roberta and Charles, and Mr. Nite"—Dmitri started the motor again—"you think of them too much maybe. No other murderer possible?"

"There are other players. Ed Mannucci, Roberta's neighbor at 530 Seventh Avenue, who wants to buy her out. Flossie, the sample maker, who makes great French toast. Jerry, the production manager, who, according to his mother, Flossie, was not at the scene of the crime, but mothers have been known to lie. Kathy, the cleaning lady, who found Phyllis's body and who may have overheard something she didn't tell me or the police. The light's green, by the way." The morning sun whacked us as we crossed Canal Street in a spurt.

"Lourdes Montalvo," I said after straightening myself out again, "the new seamstress. Phyllis got her hired, and she claims she knows plenty. She was also afraid Roberta would be arrested for the murder. Mario Lionello, the tailor. He's been with Roberta from the beginning. He made strange statements about good people doing bad things but wouldn't elaborate. And there is that photograph you snitched from Charlie's patent-leather shoe. You have it with you?"

Dmitri cajoled the pink Cadillac into a tight spot in front of a rusted fire hydrant, then with a grunt of satisfaction slipped the photo out of his breast pocket.

"When do you think this picture was taken?" I asked. Who was that baby Roberta was holding?

"Sixty-six."

"There's no date anywhere. How can you be so sure?"

"Hairdo. Sharp cut. That year futuristic look famous."

"You knew this in Russia?"

"Hair my business. I know also from this." He rummaged in my manila folder and produced an article on Roberta after the spring show given in October 1966. The hairdo was identical. Then he showed me an article dated September 1967 in which Roberta had received the Coty Award for best American designer. Her hair, now grown out into soft romantic curls, fell out of a sequined beret. "That could be a wig," I said.

"Hair too skimpy for wig." Dmitri patted the gun strapped to his waist and got out of the car to check the street. He scanned the laundry drying on the fire escapes, pajamas being perfect hiding places for kidnappers and killers. I called Stan's precinct as agreed, and left the message that I was still alive. I sifted through the articles regarding Roberta's career. She had won the Coty three times. WWD had showered praises on her. Harper's Bazaar had featured an interview and her fall 1971 collection in its editorial pages. "Welcome back, RR!" the headline read under a close-up shot of Roberta with her romantic curls dropping out of a red velvet cloche. Welcome back from where, I wondered and read on:

After closing her studio for two seasons, Roberta Riddle is back with a renewed, refreshing take on classic elegance, striking a much-wanted chord in this year's fashion anarchy.

Roberta had closed the studio in 1970 then, right around the time Phyllis had gotten out of jail. Lourdes had mentioned a nervous breakdown, I remembered. Mario had denied it.

"There was a lot of speculation about your disappearance from the fashion and social scene at a moment when your designs had reached a new high," the interviewer said. "Can you tell us what happened?"

"Exhaustion. The fear that I couldn't keep it up. I hid in a house up in Maine for a year. Success is terrifying."

"You're being very honest."

"I have to be. That's what my clothes are about. Bringing out the best in a woman without subterfuge. Offering solutions."

She hadn't offered me any. I looked back at the photo of Roberta with a baby.

Why did this image end up in Charlie's shoe?

16

"I know plenty," Lourdes Montalvo answered as we settled down on the narrow steps. We were on the fifth floor of Mr. Hsu's clothes-manufacturing company. I had come to see Jerry. Lourdes was an added bonus. She had just delivered two samples to Roberta's contractor, to have the bodices beaded. In my mind I dredged up the bio Roberta had sent me. Lourdes was twenty-nine years old, married to a cutter who worked for Oscar de la Renta. She had a two-year-old child, lived in Glen Cove, Long Island, and had been working for Roberta for only three months. "She's an eager worker," Roberta had written.

"What exactly do you know?" I'd run into Lourdes just as Dmitri and I were trying to get out of one of those creaky metal cages that can sleep a family of four—what New York City warehouses pass off as elevators.

Lourdes sat on the stairs and clasped her knees. A grimy, chicken-wired window, half-covered by a steam pipe, washed her quiet, moon-shaped face with meager light. She had large, dark eyes, a small, tapered nose, and full, uncreased lips. Her thick black hair was held back with a sunflower clasp. She was a pretty woman. "I'm new at Riddle Solutions, so I see things with clean eyes."

"Go on," I said, sitting two steps below her. Dmitri stood on the landing, a protective monolith. When I introduced him as a friend, Lourdes smiled and offered a hand. She struck me as the kind of woman who would pet a stray pit bull without a moment's hesitation. As I would. Which made me like her. "Go on, what do your clean eyes see?"

"Right away I notice Roberta does not like Phyllis. No one likes Phyllis, but Roberta, she hates her. I see it in the eyes. Brrr. Makes me shiver. Both of them, they hate each other, but Roberta hates more."

"Why, do you think?"

"Everyone says the husband, but I ask, why does she keep Phyllis if there is so much hate?" Her eyes beamed with information.

"You know?"

Lourdes nodded and whispered, "It has something to do with a baby."

I pushed myself up a step. Dmitri leaned down. "A baby?" we echoed.

"When I first come to Mrs. Roberta—I am there two, three days—you know Phyllis get me the job, so I am grateful, I was only working part-time at 480 Broadway. Now this is a good job, I say to myself, and Flossie is teaching me more. I will become a sample maker like her—"

"Tell me about the baby."

"Tell us," Dmitri corrected.

"I am trying to explain why I don't say anything to police. I don't want to get Mrs. Roberta in trouble, but she tells me I must talk to you. You will help."

"We'll try. Go on."

Lourdes smiled. "That day, I am in the shipping

room calling my mother—she keeps my son—and the door to the design room is open. I hear Phyllis, she turns on the high voice, like a switchblade." Lourdes clasped her ears. "First she talks about me and how Mrs. Roberta should be happy Phyllis has found me. That I am such a good worker. I am happy, and want to listen more, but my son comes to the phone and I talk to him and sing a little, too—he likes that—and so I miss what they say next. But when I hang up, I hear Miss Roberta's voice. It sounds like soup boiling out of the pot. Jalapeño soup." Lourdes's cheeks had gotten red, her eyes eager. She was enjoying the telling.

"What did Roberta say?"

"'I don't owe anything,' she said. 'I've paid enough.'"

Dmitri crouched down. "What Phyllis say?"

Lourdes hesitated, looking back at Dmitri, then at me. I sensed she was afraid that she was stepping over some forbidden boundary.

"We help," Dmitri said, his voice suddenly caviar-rich. "Trust us."

Lourdes aimed her face back at the window, as if looking for a shaft of sunlight to absolve her of her indiscretion. She got jets of steam instead. "'You and I have been together all these years,' Phyllis said, 'because we both know, when there's a baby, there's always more to pay.'"

That's when I made a mistake. When *we* made a mistake, since Dmitri had elected to become a partner in this muddled investigation. Our mistake was to let Lourdes rush down the four flights of stairs and back to Roberta's studio, regret biting at her heels. Her information was brimming with possibilities, and we never thought to ask why Phyllis found Lourdes her job with Roberta. Phyllis, who, by all accounts, never did anything out of generosity. Lourdes might not have known the answer, but we should have asked, or at least thought of it.

Instead, Dmitri and I huddled on the landing and came up with a theory:

Roberta had closed her studio in 1970 to have a baby. For some reason, she had wanted that birth kept a secret. She had given the baby away for adoption. Phyllis had found out and had blackmailed her.

The theory explained the photo of Roberta and the baby. It explained why Roberta had put up with her fitting model, even though she knew Phyllis was her husband's lover. It also gave Roberta a good motive for murder. Not something either of us enjoyed. I liked and respected Roberta. Dmitri had the fixed notion that Roberta was the heroine of the story. Heroines can't be murderers.

The clothes factory was impressive. I had introduced myself as Roberta's ad exec, leaving Dmitri's presence unexplained. He kept his eyes on the freight elevator and the fire door while Mr. Hsu, the owner, showed me a fifty-foot-long room with four rows of sewing machines, each operated by a Chinese woman. Young, old, thin, they flowed forward and back like a quick-turning tide, feeding the garments to the pulsing needles. At the foot of each machine a plastic basket with the pieces to be sewn. Fluorescent light streamed down from a patterned tin ceiling washed in white paint. No one looked up.

Mr. Hsu worked for many Seventh Avenue firms, he assured me. Designer and better dresses only. "I am state of the art," he said, and bowed.

"I can see that," I said, and bowed back. He was surprisingly tall, with a handsome face, and was dressed in a red-wool knit tunic with sleeves pushed above his elbows, black slacks, and embroidered Chinese slippers. Next to his muffled footsteps, mine sounded vulgar.

"How do you keep one designer from seeing the work of another?" I asked.

"They are all honorable persons. I make appointments carefully. If not, I go out of business quickly. What you see here is only Riddle Solutions designs."

I doubted that Roberta would claim the purple-striped-and-chartreuse-flowered suit over in row three as her own, but I wasn't there to ferret out a possible design thief. Knockoffs in the garment trade, I had discovered, weren't strong motives for murder.

"You have solved the problem with the zippers?" I asked.

Mr. Hsu pushed up his sweater sleeves and seemed not to understand. Behind him, on the walls, hung stiff paper cutouts of left-front jacket, right-front jacket, left sleeve, right sleeve, each group hooked together under a number, a cutter's must sheet giving precise instructions.

"The holiday line," I reminded him. "One style turned up with zippers that didn't zip." Over the tall loft windows, Mr. Hsu had placed leftovers from his cutting machines to protect his workers and the clothes from the morning sun. Red and white polka dots covered the last four windows. Three windows burned with an orange-cotton glow. The first window, where the supervisor sat, shimmered a watery turquoise. The floor was covered with thread balls. No dust anywhere. Past the elevator, from another room equally as long, came the hiss of steam from the pressers. The two rooms on the floor below had been filled, in military order, with machines that could cut through three feet of thick wool.

"Jerry had to go back and forth between here and the showroom last Sunday," I said. "Remember?"

Mr. Hsu pulled down one sweater sleeve. "Supplier mistake. By noon, everything solved. Jerry was very pleased."

"By noon. That's good."

Mr. Hsu saw me notice the air-conditioning units as Dmitri and I prepared to leave. Jerry was waiting for me across the street. "State of the art," Mr. Hsu said. "Not a sweatshop." I left him padding across his realm, a lopsided king. One red sleeve up, the other down.

"You know why the air-conditioning?" Jerry asked. We were sitting in the Excellent Noodle Shop. "Hsu's girls handle silk. Sweat stains silk."

Jerry Sarnowski. Flossie's son, Roberta's duplicate pattern maker turned production manager. He was forty-two years old, lived in Queens, and had never married. "Flossie brought him in," Roberta had written in his bio. "He drops all his money on horse racing, he's pushy and resentful, but he does a good enough job. And Flossie's happy."

"Did you introduce Charlie to Roberta?" I asked Jerry. A plucked duck, neck folded neatly through a meat hook, was staring at me with honey-glazed eyes. Better than a gunman, but still not my favorite sight at nine-forty-seven A.M. On the walls of the narrow space hung red and green back-lit photos of noodles. Noodles with chicken, noodles with pork, beef. Fried noodles. Steamed. Pasta by any other name . . .

"Hell, no, I didn't introduce him to nobody." Jerry drowned his rice noodles with hot sauce. Behind him, a lobster waved from a large tank, the rubber bands on each claw a different color. Blue and pink, to cover both sexes. From the other side of the table, Dmitri eyed the plate-glass window facing Lafayette Street and snuck McDonald's fries under his mustache. He had checked the back door and the waiters. We were the only customers at that hour.

"Roberta went looking for him," Jerry said. "She even had me asking around. Right after her husband died. Our assistant designer was in and out of the hospital by then." He fingered chopsticks with short, stubby fingers. His gold signet ring could pass for a nose mangler. "She wanted another gay."

"Is Charlie that talented?" I moved out of the duck's sight.

"I think he sucks." Jerry had his mother's broad cheekbones, a potato nose, small brown eyes that looked as dead as the duck's. His lips, wide and thin, tried for a sweet smile and settled on sour. The rest of him was squat. "Look, you can't believe everything Roberta tells you. She's an artist. *And* she's a salesman. She's been selling Roberta Riddle all her life, know what I mean? Fashion is hype. So are the people in fashion. Fakes. Liars. Hiding behind fancy rags, thinking they've got something over all of us. Dress for what you wanna be, not what you are, that's the shit we sell. If it wasn't for Flossie, I wouldn't be in this sissy business. I hate it."

"Walk."

"Yeah, sure. Look, what I'm trying to say is, don't believe everything you hear." A white noodle slicked across his chin. "Roberta Riddle, fashion designer, everyone's going to come to her, right? She's proud."

"She's had her bad moments."

"Yeah, Saul. She shouldn't take it out on us."

"What business was her husband in?"

"Salesman for a *clochmacher*. Moderate coats. Except Saul couldn't sell matzoh at Passover."

Dmitri let out a roar that sent the lobster scuttling to a far corner of the tank. "Good joke!"

Jerry wiped a paper napkin across his chin. "What's Gorky Park doing here?"

"His name is Dmitri. I'm in a rush, he gets me places fast. Why don't you like Charlie?"

"That's no name for a Jew. Dmitri's gotta be a saint."

"How do you know he's Jewish? I didn't know he was Jewish."

"You're Italian, that's why. We Jews got an instinct, developed back in Egypt. Along with matzoh."

"I am also Yakov." Dmitri licked mustard from his finger. "Dmitri business name. Like Karamazov brodder. More sophisticated flavor." He handed Jerry two business cards. One black with silver lettering, one silver with black lettering. "I got wholesale fashion operation. Hair for wigs. Big business. Hollywood give Oscar now for hair. For Orthodox women, my name Yakov. For others, Dmitri. If your girlfriend cut hair, let me know. Dmitri pays good price. Yakov pays better."

"Why don't you like Charlie?" I asked Jerry again.

"Because he's ready to sell us out to Mannucci." Jerry dropped the business cards in the ashtray. "I warned Roberta, but she doesn't listen. You saw that rat on a spit? Who do you think put it there? It's part of a strategy to get her down, to get her to let go of the business so he and Mannucci can take over. Charlie's a mean bitch. We had it good before he sashayed in."

"If he's not good at his job and if he doesn't get along with the rest of you, why doesn't Roberta fire him?"

"I never figured out why she hired him in the first place. Then Elsa, that's Mrs. Morewitz, she goes and leaves him the forty percent."

"What was Elsa like?"

"Big woman with even bigger bank account. She didn't come around much. Just to the shows. We used to do them in-house. If I was to say what she was like, I'd say mean. She died and didn't leave us nothing even though some of us worked for her for thirty years. Mario, for one. Me, I've been breaking my back for almost twenty years for both those ladies." He sucked air through his teeth. "You know what I'm deciding right now?" He jerked his head back. "I'm deciding I'm getting out. I've had it with Riddle Solutions."

"Any idea why Charlie got that forty percent?"

"Sure. He must have played the walker. You know, escorting her around. Old women get sentimental."

Dmitri banged a fist on his table. "Generosity of passion!"

I blinked at Jerry. "Must have?"

"I never saw him do it, but that don't mean it didn't happen."

"What alibi do you have for Sunday night?"

"I can't believe this! Roberta's trying to pin this on me?" Jerry bobbed his head at the waiters who stood in the back. They continued to fold napkins for the lunch crowd. "To save her neck? Or maybe so Charlie can get off? Which is it?"

"Neither. The zipper problem was solved by noon."

"I could have been in the building with the rest of them. Doorman saw me come in, saw me go out so many times he's not going to remember which way I was facing the last time. I could have killed Phyllis, except you're not going to find a motive. I liked her. Tough lady who knew how to defend herself. I told Roberta I was still working with Hsu Sunday night. The police know the truth. I was winning two hundred bucks at Meadowlands, on Zipping By." He leaned forward, neck craning, his nose two inches from mine. "I got betting stubs to prove it."

I didn't budge. "You and Phyllis were friendly?"

"That's right. We hit a couple of bars together after work. Sometimes we'd end up at her place. Once I made the mistake of getting soppy. 'Tootsie, I love you,' I told her. She liked to be called that when . . ." Dmitri smacked his lips.

". . . it was a turn-on. Except she didn't like the 'I

love you' part. She slid off me like a seal off a rock and locked me out for months."

"Were you two meeting while she was seeing Roberta's husband?"

"Yeah, she was in love with him. I didn't like that. Not for me. I'm not the jealous type." I thought I heard a snort. I glanced at Dmitri. He pointed to the lobster.

"Got Roberta all twisted up," Jerry added. "Bad for business."

"Saul and Roberta had no children?"

Jerry's face scrunched up. "Roberta, kids?"

"We hear she get pregnant," Dmitri said. "She get pregnant?"

"Yeah, with mother-of-pearl buttons. You know what Roberta would see in a nursery? That the wallpaper would make a nice dress."

I took out Roberta's photo, holding it so that Jerry could only see the back. "Do you recognize this handwriting?" A distinctive hand, slanted heavily to the right and embellished with curlicues. The same hand that had sent Charlie a letter that I happened to remove from his mailbox before the police got there.

Jerry squinted, too vain to wear glasses. "Southampton. That's where Roberta used to have a place."

"Do the curlicues ring any bells?"

"Sure. Phyllis. She thought they were classy."

Charlie had lied. The letter I had picked up from his mailbox had been written by Phyllis, not his lover.

"Where'd you get that?" Jerry clutched my wrist. "What are you doing?"

Jerry held fast, grabbing the photo with his other hand. "Hey, you don't ask questions and not answer mine."

I glared at Dmitri, who held my gaze and pocketed his rejected cards.

"Let me see." Jerry studied the photo. "Roberta a while back. Hey, maybe this is why you thought she had a kid. Well, she didn't, you can take that from me." He waved the photo. "This was probably taken at a bris. That's when they get a man's foreskin."

I rubbed my wrist. "I know!"

"Where'd you get it?"

"I found it on the floor at the studio. I knew it wasn't Roberta's handwriting."

Jerry threw the picture down on the Formica table. He seemed to accept my lie.

I swept the photo into my purse. Dmitri, mustache twitching, dug into my pineapple roll. Our theory on Roberta's baby had suffered a setback. But now we had new possibilities. Why had Phyllis written to Charlie? Did it have anything to do with the $30,000 he'd given her? And which letter was Charlie trying to hide from the police? The one from the adoption agency or the one from Phyllis?

"Did Phyllis ever talk to you about the accident?"

"Sometimes when she was boozed up, she'd go on about Elsa Morewitz and what a bitch she was. She blamed Elsa for the accident."

"Why?"

"You should ask Mario. He was there. All I know is that Elsa gave a party out at her place in Sands Point to celebrate how good things were going with the business. Everybody got invited. Phyllis took her camera. She was supposed to be the unofficial photographer for the great event. Then I don't know what happened, and Elsa kicked her out of the house. So Phyllis got in her rented car, a little drunk, and smashed into the girl. No more parties after that."

"Maybe that's why Roberta put up with Phyllis all these years," I said. "To make it up to her."

"I asked Phyl once. I mean, she wasn't the only

good fitting model out there. 'Why's she taking your crap lyin' down? What's with Roberta?'"

Dmitri stood up, blocking out the ducks, the lobster tank, the light. "What Phyl say?" His expression was transfixed. Anyone could have walked in and shot me full of holes.

Jeryy sipped green tea. I moved behind Dmitri's back, an eye to the door. "What *did* Phyllis say?"

Jerry threw money on the table. "'I've been real good to little Berta Pbrzybyczski. Real good.'"

It was too glorious a day not to stay outside. Using the Cadillac as an office—I seemed destined to be stuck within pink walls—I called Mr. Nite on Dmitri's cellular phone. Outside, Dmitri scanned the street and the parking ticket on his windshield. I offered Mr. Nite a choice of eating places: 44 at the Royalton, elegant but dark, or the Thompson Street playground in Greenwich Village—full of sunlight, children, and pigeons. He chose the sun.

"This crazy," Dmitri shouted on the way. He was getting proprietary. "Playground too dangerous. Head down!" His hefty arm dunked me below viewing range.

"You could have helped with Jerry!"

"Jerry no big deal."

"He could be the killer. He had the means and opportunity. Anyone could have placed the bets at Meadowlands and handed over the stubs the next day. But where's the motive? No, don't tell me. He loved Phyllis, she spurned him." I stretched out in the backseat. "Let's go back to Roberta and our blackmail theory. First of all, remember that Roberta's my client. You can't go telling people you heard she was pregnant. It'll be all over Fashion Avenue by this afternoon."

"Direct approach best. Detective ruthless job."

I ignored that. He was right. "If Roberta didn't have a baby, Phyllis had no reason to blackmail her. How was Phyllis real good to her?"

"I not speak till you put smarts in head."

"Stop worrying. No one's coming after me today."

"Pshaw!"

"Delgado and his hit man have delivered the threat. Now they have to wait to see if Stan buys it. They're going to wait at least twenty-four hours." I called Roberta and waited five minutes for her to come to the phone. From the shouts coming across the phone line, the day was an even bigger fiasco than Robert Altman's film *Ready-to-Wear*.

"I'm losing my mind!" Roberta shouted over the din. I realized that booming man's voice was Charlie's.

"Roberta, we've got our model," I said. "Everything's set for the Monday after the shows. I need a hundred-dollar check from you to establish a client-detective privileged relationship, which means I can lie for you and not feel guilty."

"I can't manage it anymore. The show. The models, every one of them making demands. The minute you put a dress on them, they get attitude. They don't like the color, 'Couldn't I trade with Tanya, who looks awful in red, purple.' Nothing fits! The backdrop is terrible. The music worse. I don't have an idea left in my brain. Nothing! I'm taking dictation from Charlie! He has this crazy idea . . . I won't survive this."

"Roberta, it's preshow jitters."

"I know it's my last show. At night I can hear the critics sharpening their teeth. Please, Simona, let everything stand as is, Charlie's safe now. Phyllis was killed by a thief. There's no point anymore. I will send you a check, but there's no point."

"Don't you want to know what happened?"

"In fashion, there is no truth. Only entertainment!"
Roberta hung up. Exclamation-point time at Riddle
Solutions.

"Dmitri, I have just lost my lunch money."

"*Our* lunch money. We go home."

"We go to the playground." I leaned forward, tuck-
ing my feet under the front seat. One foot dislodged some
books from under the seat. "I have a revised theory."

"Me, too."

"Tell me." I picked up one of the books.

"No, woman first."

"That's politically incorrect." The thick paperback
had curled pages and a half-torn cover. *Aching Passion* in
raised gold letters arched over a breast-popping bodice.

"Politics always incorrect!"

I held up the book. There were at least five more
where that came from. "Your cousin's wife is an avid
reader."

"No, me. To learn English. 'At his touch, her heart
throbbed underneath the whiteness of her breast.' Good
English sentence."

"Not very useful."

"Give theory."

How could I resist a Stalin look-alike hooked on
romances? "Jerry reinforced our original theory. Roberta
isn't the motherly type. That's why she gave the baby
away. But now there's a new twist. Jerry identified Phyllis's
handwriting on the photograph. Which happens to be the
same handwriting on the envelope I took out of Charlie's
mailbox on Monday. I think the photo was inside."

Dmitri's eyes glittered. "Police not find Charlie's
photograph because Roberta keep it."

"After the police searched his apartment, Charlie
asked for the envelope. Roberta gave it back, not knowing what was inside."

"He hides photo in shoe for safety."

I stuck my head over the front seat. "Charlie wanted Roberta to sell out to Ed Mannucci." I was excited. We were turning major lights onto the case. "What better way to convince Roberta to sell than to gather information that she doesn't want revealed? Charlie figures out that Phyllis must have something on Roberta or else she would have been fired years ago. He asks Phyllis to share the information for thirty thousand dollars."

"Phyllis got money passion," Dmitri added, impatiently slapping a hand on the steering wheel. We had by now gone around the block four times, looking for a parking space. "She sells picture. Not negative. Picture enough."

"In the meantime, he's nosed around some adoption agencies."

"Aha!"

Ahead of us, across the street from the playground, a pickup truck was pulling out. Dmitri accelerated and swung in, missing the truck's rear fender by millimeters. He switched off the motor, gave the street the once-over, and turned to face me. "I don't like this lunch idea."

There was no sign of Mr. Nite. "I'll be perfectly safe. The hit men, hoodlums, whatever you want to call them, they haven't been very good at their job. Rollerblades ran the minute he saw you."

"I am fearsome personality." The driver's seat swelled.

"Indeed you are. That's why I hired you. Now don't hover over me. Mr. Nite has had some bad experiences in the past and your fearsome personality might make him uncomfortable. Try to blend in with the woodwork."

17

———— ⊙✦⊙ ————

Dmitri perched on top of the jungle gym, a black-clad Humpty Dumpty. Hawk eyes scoured the low-lying Village horizon while chunks of salami and provolone sandwich periodically disappeared into his mouth.

Below, Mr. Nite and I settled on stone benches, a stone chess table between us. Graffiti added a rococo feel to the asphalt and concrete. My back was protected by a twenty-foot wall. The sides of me were wide open to guns, knives, poisoned darts, and pigeon droppings. As I'd told Dmitri, I was confident that Mr. Delgado and Company wouldn't try anything that day. I have a way of taking broad jumps over unpleasant realities.

I unwrapped my "Julie" sandwich—smoked mozzarella, sun-dried tomatoes, and marinated artichokes on a *ciabatta*, a large round slipper of bread. I had treated Mr. Nite, Dmitri, and myself at Melampo, a narrow scrap of a store on Sullivan Street owned by Alessandro, a grouchy Florentine who makes the best sandwiches in the city.

"The flowers were beautiful, but unnecessary," I said.

Mr. Nite fingered his "Max Special"—sardines, Bel Paese cheese, and sun-dried tomatoes. He'd opted for a roll. "Lately, my flowers seem to be unnecessary. Like Maurice Chevalier, I ask, 'Am I getting old?'"

"Never."

He was wearing a navy suit, white shirt, and yellow tie. No camel-hair coat, no fedora—the day was that warm—but his blue scarf wrapped his throat and a black knit yarmulke rested on his silver hair. I wanted to hug him. Behind Mr. Nite, two mailmen parked their carts and sat down to eat lunch.

New York with its enclaves, each one different from the next, makes you forget you are in one of the largest, most renowned cities in the world. The enclave south of Houston Street, now known as SoHo, is legally still part of the Village. It is, in itself, as varied as the city. West Broadway acts as a divider between the trendy eastern section, with its expensive shops and galleries, and the more modest western section. The playground spans the space between Sullivan and Thompson, streets with low tenement buildings where bathtubs are found by lifting a counter in the kitchen and fire escapes cling to the red, yellow, white brick facades. The streets offer off-beat clothing, chess sets, baseball cards. Always food. Only a few tourists mingle with the old people and the children who dominate the sidewalk. If I sit on a bench and listen to the men whiling away the day, I'm likely to hear Italian. Not from the tourist in his newly bought Timberlands, but from the old-timers who, like Roberta's tailor, came over fifty or sixty years ago to sew, to sell vegetables, to knead dough. It is here that I truly feel I'm in a village.

I poured seltzer for Mr. Nite. "Tell me about the theft. When did it happen?"

"The money was in the safe Sunday morning. Yesterday it was gone."

A grade-school boy threw a basketball at Dmitri. Dmitri reluctantly threw it back.

"Why was it in your office safe and not in a bank?"

"I thought I would need it." The ball went back to Dmitri.

"On a Sunday?"

Mr. Nite leaned over to bite into his sandwich. Oil dribbled down on the table. He chewed slowly, swallowed. Up on the jungle gym Dmitri had hooked the basketball under his arm and wouldn't give it up. The boy was walking the bar behind him, arms flapping for balance, a determined look on his face.

"Knishes are neater," Mr. Nite said, averting his face from the boy and his tightrope performance.

"Much neater," I said. "Dmitri, give the boy the ball before he falls. You're Roberta's missing backer, aren't you?"

"I wanted to be."

"What happened?"

The basketball flew past us and hit the cyclone fence. "Dmitri!"

My romance-struck bodyguard grinned. "Fearsome!"

Mr. Nite picked up the ball and tossed it to the boy, who had scrambled down from the jungle gym. The boy threw it at Dmitri again. I stopped looking. I can't fathom boys. Of any age. "What changed your mind about backing Roberta?"

Mr. Nite sat back down and took a sip of his seltzer. "I have known Roberta since 1971 when I moved into 530 Broadway. She has worked hard under difficult circumstances. These past years have been bad for everyone. I have been a little luckier than most. I moved my business to China just in time. I have less expensive suppliers. Faster, cheaper workers. I am not in the designer business. I can cut corners with quality.

Roberta cannot. She has also perhaps not kept up with the times. She has allowed her designs to be stolen. She has, according to rumor, 'lost her grip.' Above all, the death of her husband has been tragic to her."

"He was not the best of husbands."

"Maybe. But in these past five years Roberta has changed. Something has pierced her heart. I can only imagine it is the death of Saul."

"When did you decide to be her backer?"

"We have talked these past three months. I hesitated. I am a great admirer, but I do not want to find myself poor again, like a new immigrant. Sometimes I think I have traded my shadow for fear, and I am ashamed. But with Roberta, after a luncheon at her beautiful home overlooking the Central Park trees changing colors, I remember I am seventy-two years old, and winter is almost here, and what am I waiting for to give this wonderful woman some help? I offer a sum in exchange for five percent of her business. It is double what I should be paying, but the orange and the yellow of the trees was very bright." He shook his head with a smile.

"Bright," Dmitri repeated, sitting down next to me, a rapt expression on his face. The boy had left with his ball.

"I became a little blind," Mr. Nite said. Dmitri's presence did not affect him. "You understand."

Dmitri nodded. I nodded. After much hesitation I'd said yes to moving in with Greenhouse in the spring, with the azaleas blooming and the thought of summer ahead. "But the blinding moment didn't last?"

Mr. Nite took another bite of his Max Special. He chewed slowly, drawing out our meeting as if he had nowhere else to go. A squirrel on a ginkgo branch held up his paws in prayer, waiting. I had long ago finished my Julie.

"The orchids you saw in my showroom?"

"The ones you sent to Roberta."

Mr. Nite wagged a finger. "The ones Roberta sent to me." He enjoyed my surprised look. "She ordered the orchids to celebrate our agreement. I was to give her part of the money on Sunday. One hundred and twenty-five thousand dollars."

"Why in cash?"

"Not to trace," Dmitri said. "So Charlie not know."

"It does not matter," Mr. Nite said. "The orchids came too late, you see. I had left the office by then. They were sent up to Roberta."

"Why did you renege on the deal?"

"Because the young man whom Roberta has helped a great deal, Charlie, he is going to sell his forty percent to Ed Mannucci."

"He told me the exact opposite!"

Mr. Nite wasn't listening. Pink spots of anger livened his cheeks, words untangled from his mouth. "Ed Mannucci does not belong in our building. His garments are terrible. He cheats his workers, he has sent one supplier into bankruptcy. On Sunday, in my showroom, I told Roberta, 'I will not work with that man. The deal is off!'" He swept his sandwich aside, the gesture frightening the squirrel. Sardines and cheese slapped the asphalt. "The next morning she sent me down the orchids anyway. Roberta is a lady always. But now I think her heart is a little more pierced, and it is I who have done this."

"I can't believe Charlie told you he was selling his share. If anything, he wanted Roberta to sell."

Mr. Nite looked bewildered. "Charlie told me nothing."

"How do you know, then?"

"On Sunday afternoon, a few hours before she was killed, Phyllis showed me a draft of the agreement."

It turned out that the draft was a simple typewritten sheet on Mannucci Sportswear letterhead. No identifiable handwriting or signatures.

"According to Flossie," I said, "Phyllis was always going next door to Mannucci's. She could have swiped a sheet and typed it herself. Do you know of any reason why she would want to hurt Roberta in that way?"

Mr. Nite widened his blue eyes. "No."

Dmitri nodded solemnly. "Other way around should be."

"If Phyllis presented you with the draft on Sunday," I said, "she must have known the deal was about to go through, and maybe she even knew you had a hundred and twenty-five thousand in your safe. How was the safe broken into?"

"The thief knew the combination. The safe is easy to find. I keep it in my office behind a map of Hungary. I always forget the combination, so I wrote it out on a strip of paper that I hide in the band of a hat. It is not a good hiding place, but it is one I can remember. A man of my generation does not forget his hat."

"Isn't the hat always on your head?"

"In the showroom my yarmulke is enough. After I discover the theft, I get so angry at my stupidity, I don't want to wear my hat anymore. I *am* getting old."

Dmitri slapped his hand on the stone table. A pigeon scuttled away. "Phyllis steal money! Get killed for it!"

I looked at Mr. Nite. His face had turned red. "You should always wear your hat. The sun is still strong." Mr. Nite pressed white hands against his cheeks. He looked tired and confused.

"Could Phyllis have stolen the money?" I asked.

"Maybe. I leave her for a few minutes in my office. I don't know anymore. Roberta, I must call her. I denied her the money. If the draft is false . . . it is terrible." He stood up, felt his head as if looking for his hat, tugged at his scarf. "This whole story is terrible. And I am making it worse." He thanked me for lunch, he wished us luck in our lives as if Dmitri and I were going off to get married. We offered to take him back to his office. He waved us away with one hand and hailed a cab with the other.

I held the door open for him. "One last question. How well did you know Roberta's partner, Elsa Morewitz?"

He doubled into the cab. "Well enough. We used to play bridge together."

"Do you see her as sentimental? The kind of woman who would leave money for kindnesses received?"

"Elsa Morewitz had only one friend in her life. That was Roberta Riddle, who has the patience of a rabbi."

I closed the door and leaned down into the window. "Mrs. Morewitz was that bad?"

"With the steel in Elsa's heart, we would have won the war without the Allies."

"Nice old man," Dmitri said after the cab retreated. "Like Uncle Vanya. A man works a life and got nothing on his plate."

"He has money."

"No love."

"I wouldn't rule that out yet." A squirrel ran down the tree, beady eyes on what was left of Mr. Nite's Max Special. A pigeon waddled into view. "On Sunday Mr. Nite met Roberta in his office. Charlie probably followed her down there and watched from the ladies' bathroom, where he had a good view of the showroom. That would explain those prints."

"Why go down?"

"To see if the deal was going through. If Mr. Nite backed Roberta, she'd never sell her share of Riddle Solutions to Mr. Mannucci and Charlie wouldn't fulfill his dream of becoming a designer. Remember, he still didn't have the photo in his hand."

"Deal off, but Charlie tells Mannucci no. Why?"

"Loyalty is what he said."

Dmitri nodded, pleased. "Romance books got passion *and* loyalty."

"But why is Charlie loyal all of a sudden? Does it have something to do with Phyllis being dead? And if the safe held a hundred and twenty-five thousand, why did the thief only take a hundred and eighteen?"

The squirrel grabbed the cheese, the pigeon picked at the bread. Maybe the ants would line up for the sardines.

"New York State adoption law 421.16H states there can be no discrimination based on race, ethnic group, religion, marital status, or sexual preference." Faith Pace, social worker of Happy Futures, gave us a bureaucratic smile. Dmitri had insisted on not leaving my side. Not to protect me better, I suspected, but because he was hooked by the possibility of another bend in the story. I didn't try to explain his presence. Driver, lover, husband, bosom buddy, bodyguard—he could be one or all of these.

I twirled my freshly sharpened pencil, flicked through pages of my steno pad, playing the role of a freelance journalist doing a story on parenthood in the nineties. "You have had requests from gay couples?"

Faith looked at the bare yellow wall behind us, trying to come up with another state law to reel off.

We were sitting in a small, square interview room, with a paned window that overlooked the airshaft. At the top of the window a wedge of blue sky dropped light on the ledge, where a cyclamen drooped from thirst. Dmitri and I sat on a navy and red plaid sofa. Faith surveyed us warily from a green rocking chair that had seen too many coats of paint. The room smelled of doughnuts.

"You would not be betraying anyone's confidence," I said.

Faith nodded, her eyes on my pencil. I stopped twirling. She was somewhere in her late forties, early fifties, with a long, bony face clean of any makeup, watery blue eyes, and gray hair worn loose below her shoulders. She had once made a handsome hippie, I thought. Her face was now smudged by disappointment.

"How does the adoption procedure work, Ms. Pace?" I lowered the intimidating pencil. On the teak coffee table, someone, in a bout of black humor, had scratched, "If you lived here, you'd be home."

"The birth mother voluntarily signs a legal document surrendering her parental rights. If the birth father is known, he signs a consent for adoption. We look through our files or wait until we identify a family who wants to parent the child. That family then signs a placement affidavit accepting that child as their own."

"You got two entrances to building," Dmitri said.

"We like to assure that the birth parents and the adoptive parents have some privacy. We also have two elevators."

"You make the process sound fairly easy," I said.

A real smile. "That's my job."

"What if I were adopted and wanted to find out who my parents were?"

"New York's a closed-record state. The adopted child has no civil rights to have any knowledge of who his parents are, not that the law stops anyone from trying. We get a deluge of people begging us to open the files."

"It doesn't seem fair."

Faith gave her head a sad tilt, as if to tell me she agreed. "We do give out the mother's first name, and if the adopted parents elect not to change the child's first name and birth date, there is a chance that the child will be able to discover who his mother is."

"How?"

"The last four numbers of the amended birth certificate stay the same as the original one. So with a little patience . . ." She shrugged and righted her head.

"Have any gay couples asked to adopt children from your agency? In the past two years, for example."

"I told you, New York State adoption law says—"

"I know. No discrimination. Have no gay couples asked, then?"

"I would have to search my files, and right now, with all the work I have to do . . ." Her eyes searched for the door.

Dmitri scowled. "You don't tell because agency discriminates. You no better—"

"Dmitri, please—" I tugged at his jacket.

"—than Communist regime!"

"Communist regime!" Rage crossed Faith's face. "We have an unblemished record on every count of every law in New York State. If birth parents don't want to give up their babies to single-sex families, we can't coerce them."

Dmitri bore all his weight forward, a crafty look replacing the scowl. "My friend, Charlie Angelo, he asked for baby. What you write last week to him? You write no. He is queer, he cannot have baby. That is what you write."

"Charlie Angelo said we discriminate? Charlie Angelo?" Her fury was unblinking. "Charlie Angelo isn't looking for a baby. Charlie Angelo—" Faith clasped her mouth. Repressed anger bloated her face. "I would never call anyone queer!"

Dmitri stood up, towering over her. "Charlie Angelo what?"

I started apologizing. Faith Pace wouldn't tell us anything after that. She had nearly broken the rules and bared a secret we had no right to know. Dmitri was smug. I felt guilty. I assured her that I wouldn't print a word she had told me, I would scrap the article. That was easy, since I had never planned to write one in the first place. She kicked us out.

Back in the office on wheels, I called 1-800-FLOWERS, ordered a fresh batch of cyclamens for Faith, left word with Stan's precinct as to where he could find me, and then proceeded to have a fight with Dmitri.

"This is America. We don't intimidate people!"

"We got information. Charlie looking for baby. Roberta's baby."

"You are no better than the KGB."

"You as bad as CIA. He cannot blackmail with picture of baby. But real baby grown up? That is evidence!"

It hit me then. "No! *Tutto sbagliato!* All wrong. Dmitri! I finally got it. Listen to this." I scrambled out of the backseat of the Cadillac, slammed the back door, opened the front door, threw Dmitri's files on the floor, and plopped down.

Dmitri eyed the mess I'd made of his precious work records. "This better be excellent."

"Excellentissimo. Charlie is Roberta's son."

"No."

"It's perfect. Roberta closed up the studio in 1970 because she was pregnant. We assume Saul was the father, but who knows? I don't think it's important at this time. She has the baby, she gets rid of it—"

"I give my eyes to have beautiful baby with woman I love. I never give baby away."

"Stop interrupting. Roberta has the baby—remember, she could have had an abortion and didn't—and gives it up for adoption. All Roberta wants to think about is work. Or maybe Saul is the father and she wants to punish him. She gives the baby away and then her husband dies and she wants to find this baby or maybe she's kept an eye on him all along. Remember, she went looking for Charlie. Jerry confirmed that. Roberta brings him into the company and gets Elsa Morewitz to leave him her forty percent. That way Charlie inherits indirectly, without Roberta being exposed."

"Stupid."

"Desperate people can be extremely naive."

"Why not let him be designer if she loves him?"

"Because emotions are not clear-cut, as Roberta herself has pointed out. She probably resents him, too."

"Charlie inherits. Asks why. Thinks adoption." Dmitri knitted fingers across his chest, his hands mounding into rocks that would break a windshield. "He goes to Happy Futures for answer. If Roberta his mother, Mannucci out. Is this story you propose?" His voice was not convinced.

"Phyllis knew about Charlie all these years. That's why Roberta put up with her. Phyllis told Charlie after he paid her the thirty thousand. For proof she sent him a picture of Roberta with Charlie as a baby. That's what I picked up from Charlie's mailbox. Phyllis's envelope with the photo in it. Along with a letter from Happy Futures probably telling him they couldn't help. New York is a closed-record state."

"Why keep baby secret? No big deal."

"Image. That's what fashion is all about. Roberta had been surrounded by enough gossip about her husband sleeping with her fitting model, who then kills a girl while in a drunken stupor. Roberta's image has always been that of a woman above the fray. Strong, unflappable, more creative work machine than flesh and blood woman. She might also be ashamed of not having kept the baby."

Dmitri released his fingers. "What proof for all this?"

"None. Hand me the phone."

The operator laughed. There were thousands of

Angelos in Brooklyn. Without a first name or a street, she couldn't help.

I called Stan.

"What do you need her address for?"

"I thought I'd pay a visit and reassure her about her son's innocence."

"You're lying."

"Pinocchio's my soul mate."

"That's right, hollowed-out wood. Dmitri's with you?"

"My shadow, my wall, my umbrella."

"I'm going to regret this."

"I'll solve the case and give you the credit. Promise."

A pause. Stan is slow on decisions. I've often wondered why he's still alive given the job he's in. He assures me that criminals don't raise the doubts I do. Which flatters me, but this time he was taking too long.

"I can always call Riddle Solutions and ask someone there, but they're going crazy right now. Besides, I wanted to tell you how much I love you and how I hunger for your thighs."

"You're being recorded."

I gave my best throaty laugh. "I know, hot lips. Shall I go on?"

I got my address and a telephone number. Charlie's mother lived in Bensonhurst, the Little Italy of Brooklyn. My first September in the States I'd gone to the Santa Rosalia festival to soak up homesickness with fried sausage sandwiches.

Mrs. Angelo didn't answer.

On our way uptown to Roberta's studio, no one followed us.

18

Roberta was sitting in a spacious, windowless room. The furniture was sparse. A long, pale peach sofa at the center. A six-foot blond-wood table behind it. A couple of cane chairs. An eggshell-leather armchair. This was the design room, the sanctum in which ideas first came. To design a new collection, Roberta would fill the room with the new fabrics she had spotted at the fabric shows and lock herself in. She would spread the samples on the thick, flesh-colored carpet and weave through the maze, picking first one square, then another. Ideas would spin from the feel of the texture, the fall of the cloth, the mood of the color.

On that Thursday evening, with four and a half days left before the show, the place was bedlam.

Stravinsky blasted from a CD player perched on a precarious stack of lingerie boxes. Behind the CD a willowy young man fingered the three silver hoops in his ear and shook disapproval from his ponytail.

Two young assistants, straight out of fashion-design school, stuffed Ziploc bags with shoes and marked each with tape. Selected models' names, black Magic Marker scrawls on white tape, covered the walls. Under each name, more tape held up Polaroids of the designs each model would wear. Sketches of makeup and nail color accompanied each photo.

A Japanese woman in black tights and an oversized black turtleneck sat cross-legged on the carpet, in front of her a tumbling collection of blue velvet trays brimming with costume jewelry. An expectant, patient gaze filtered through her black bangs as she held a rhinestone butterfly brooch with the tips of two fingers. She was waiting for Roberta.

A third, snake-thin assistant, with less patience, waved stockings in Roberta's direction.

"Naked!" Charlie shouted as he brushed past me in the corridor, giving me a quick smile. "Stacia, the legs have to look naked!"

The snake-thin assistant showed her pique by lengthening her extremely elegant neck. "Naked how? Nude? Blush? Barely There? Second Skin?"

Charlie picked a stocking and held it against his wine-red shantung silk slacks. He had on his signature alligator boots that added three inches to his height. An open knit vest covered his white T-shirt. "Second Skin. Right, Roberta? Second Skin. Miko, honey, that butterfly's exquisite." Charlie got down on his knees and took the pin.

Miko, the jeweler, smiled.

From the sofa, Roberta fluttered a pale hand. "Perfect, darling!" She was dressed in a forest-green suit and a bark-brown turban. Fabric rolls leaned on the wall behind her.

My eye caught a long rack of clothes in the near corner. The Riddle Nothings knits. They were sheathed in transparent plastic garment bags. I recognized the primary colors Roberta had talked about. The knits had come out of hiding. Roberta no longer feared that they would be copied. Phyllis had died and Charlie was on her side.

"The theme of my spring collection is renewal!" Roberta addressed herself to the *Vanity Fair* editor sitting next to her on the sofa. A minute tape recorder sat on the young editor's lap. *Vanity Fair* was all dove gray, with no makeup or jewelry, a perfect example of the monastic look that is de rigueur for fashion arbiters.

"I am shedding fossilized concepts, old skin. I want women to come out of their cocoons." Roberta's voice rang above Stravinsky's plucking of violins. She glowed with electric energy. "Spring, that's what my clothes are about. Persephone leaving Hades to go back to Demeter."

The willowy young man lashed out with his ponytail. "*The Rites of Spring* is too drastic! You're paying me to advise you on the music for the show, and I say no way." His shoulder slumped and his long body formed a languid *S*. "The sacrifice of a virgin is *not* the fashion statement you want to make! Fashion and irony don't mix."

Roberta shook her head. "Think of Vivienne Westwood, Moschino, even Gianni Versace. Pure irony!" She looked like a fir tree no one was going to cut down. The editor leaned forward and murmured something.

"You don't know Demeter and Persephone?" Roberta looked surprised. "It's a wonderful, sentimental myth about how the seasons came to be. About a mother getting her kidnapped daughter back and in her happiness giving us spring and summer. What, darling? Certainly. That's *P* as in Peter, *E*, *R*—"

I walked away. I wanted confirmation from Roberta. "Are you a mother?" "Is Charlie your son?" I let it be. Too many people, too much going on. These were questions that needed a white space of time and the intimacy of a room emptied of everyone but the two of us.

When I had spoken to Roberta on the phone that morning she'd told me my sleuthing job was over. Charlie was safe, she'd said. Maybe he was. But now I was hooked. I wanted to know how this story ended. I knew Stan would find out, and once the killer was tried, he would tell me all the details. But the justice system being what it is, that was a long time away. I wasn't simply being impatient. I wanted my hand to turn the page.

The hundred-dollar check Roberta had left with the receptionist was safely in my pocket. I was now Roberta's employee. Loyal and eager, whether she wanted it or not.

I checked in at the reception desk. Dmitri was still flirting with Beverly, the receptionist. She was good-looking, but her greatest asset was blond hair that reached her belt. They both ignored me. I plucked the phone out of his back pocket and went out to the end of the corridor, by the fire stairs, where no one could hear me.

Mrs. Angelo still didn't answer. This time the answering machine was on. Was she home, screening calls? I introduced myself by telling her that I'd been hired by Roberta to help clear Charlie's name. I needed to talk to her about something extremely private. I left my work number, my home phone number. "Call me any-time," I urged her. "I will call again." I waited, hoping she'd pick up. "Please," I added. Nothing. I hung up.

On my way back to the studio, I passed Mannucci Sportswear. Ed had his back to the glass door, one arm waving a hanger with a pink-and-red-flowered running outfit. The buyers—the showroom was full of them—looked ecstatic. If only Roberta would be equally blessed with Riddle Nothings.

Dmitri was exactly where I had left him, flipping through magazines with Beverly. I stuffed the phone back into his pocket and went looking for Mario. He was the only person who had been with Roberta from the beginning of her career.

"Thirty-two years I work for that woman," Mario said. He was taking a cigarette break in the shipping room. Empty cardboard boxes lined one wall. The fall style with the faulty zipper—from sizes two to twelve—was sheathed in vinyl garment bags and filled the length of one rack, ready to be shipped. The other racks held a few leftovers from the holiday line.

"I tell you she is like glass that has been blown too thin." He had lost the belligerence I had heard over the phone. Now he looked worried and tired. He was thin, with rounded shoulders, sallow skin that fell from his face, and a mournful expression in his large, dark eyes. His glasses sat on his head, over the tight cap of tar-black hair. Dying his hair was an odd vanity for a man who seemed so spent.

"What happened in 1970 that made Roberta close up shop?" Now that I was convinced she had given birth to a baby, I couldn't bring myself to ask outright, "Was she pregnant?" Roberta had spent too much time and energy to hide that fact. Who was I to start the rumor mills? I could hear Dmitri's eyes rolling in disbelief.

Mario narrowed his eyes against the smoke. "That was a long time ago. I didn't have to wear glasses then."

"I bet you remember."

He sighed. "I had to go looking for work, and my wife took Rino, Rino's my son, back to Italy with her. I remember, and what I remember isn't good." He was wearing his blue duster, spotless, ironed, with straight pins neatly lined up along the breast pocket. Another vanity, or was it simply a lifetime of habit?

"Roberta took a break," Mario said.

"That's it?"

"That's it."

Mario walked over to the burner sitting on top of a file cabinet and lifted a mug from a hook on the wall. "Want some?" He poured coffee. The silver thimble was still on his finger. "It's been brewing since this morning, which for some means you can pack it on your face and get a lift out of it. For me it's just right."

I declined. Although my face could have used some help.

"Come on, sit down." Mario kicked out two metal stools. We sat facing each other. "What do you want to know? Who killed Phyllis? And you think maybe the why is connected with Roberta closing down the studio twenty-five years ago? Does that make sense to you?" He waved his mug. "To me it doesn't make sense. That's a good woman I work for. We used to be one big happy family."

"Did you hear Roberta fire Phyllis Sunday night? There was quite a fight apparently."

"I fill my ears with good music, that's what I do, to keep out the filth." He pointed his thimble at me and his eyes went hard. "You know where my family is? In a beautiful Sicilian town smack in front of the sea with the best sun God's got to give. Every month, like the full moon, my money order shows up in Acitrezza. My wife, she cashes it. But she won't see me." He flashed his left hand. There was no wedding ring on it. "I have a thirty-four-year-old son I last saw in the flesh when he was seven, and a wife who thinks she's holy water and I'm the devil. So I don't go back. What's the point of going back? That's *finito*, over. My life is here in this studio, so I like it when work goes good. It makes up for things." Mario finished his coffee.

"Roberta's a good woman," he said. "When she

closed up the studio, she didn't leave us without money. Half pay she gave us until we found jobs. I got work with Jonathan Logan. Big, real big outfit. They paid better, but when Mrs. Riddle reopened, I was the first one back." He lit another cigarette. "At Logan, I was one of a dozen tailors. Here, I work harder, but I'm king. A man needs to feel important, that he counts."

"You've become very talkative all of a sudden."

He smiled thinly. "Beats hanging up on you the other day. You ever notice? You ask people a question about anything and if they get half a chance, they're going to twist it around and think it's about them you want to know. So they tell you their life story and maybe all you wanted to know was the time." He stubbed out his cigarette on the bottom of his shoe and dropped the stub in the metal pin box he'd been using as an ashtray. "It's got nothing to do with age. A sad sack like me, no one thinks I got anything but fingers and eyes to cut and sew with. But I got ego, too. You're asking why Roberta closed up the studio for a year? A broken heart, that's what."

"Because of Saul and Phyllis?"

"After two years Phyllis got out of jail and nothing changed. She was still after Saul, and he was still liking it. It's bad stuff. Leave it alone."

"It's a shame Roberta never had any children," I said, my eyes on Mario's face, on the lookout for a flicker of discomfort. A revelation of knowledge.

Mario did flinch. "Kids can break your heart." He was remembering his own.

"She's worked so hard," I said. "Who's she going to leave the company to? Charlie?"

"He's got his share, and he didn't do anything to get it." His resentment dripped as black as the coffee he'd been drinking. "I've worked hard. We all have." He smiled to dispel the bad feeling he'd exposed. "Can you see Roberta with a kid? She'd hang him up on a hook with the patterns or roll him up in the fabric just to keep him out of the way." He shook his head. "I'm not saying she didn't want a kid. I don't know about that, but I'm saying it's a good thing she didn't have one. Phyllis liked to needle her about not having children. The others must have told you about it."

I made a noncommittal sound. "How did you get along with Phyllis?"

"Bad. Like everyone else."

"Jerry liked her."

"Don't believe it. Jerry likes his racing form. He's gone. Quit an hour ago. You should have seen Roberta's face."

"She was upset?"

"Relief! Even his mother. She grew two inches."

"Why?"

"The nasty tricks against Roberta? Who do you think did it?"

"You told me Ed Mannucci."

"I wouldn't put it past him, but I was wrong. Jerry, that's who it was. Ever since Charlie come in here. Charlie thinks too much of himself, but he's got good eyes and a forty percent investment to protect. He caught on to Jerry right away."

"Caught on to what? The tricks?"

"Those came later. Jerry's always losing at the races. He's got to add to his income, so he knocks off a few designs each season. Not too many so as to really hurt, but enough to pay his debts. Yesterday Charlie gave him twenty-four hours to leave. If he didn't, Charlie was going to spread the word. No one in the trade would touch Jerry. He left without a fuss."

"Why the dead rat and the roaches?"

"To put the blame on Charlie, to get him fired. Jerry knew Charlie was bad news the minute he laid

eyes on him. There's no morality in the world which-
ever way you look at it."

"Did you know Jerry was stealing Roberta's
designs?"

"I thought maybe he was the one," Mario said. "But
I had no proof. Roberta was pretending nothing happened. If Flossie knew, well, her boy comes first.
Flossie's a good woman. I said nothing. Roberta pays
me to cut and sew her suit jackets, no more."

"Was Phyllis involved?"

"I think she caught him at it."

"How?"

"She brought Jerry a knockoff once, of a suit I'd
gone blind on. She threw it at him. Right in front of me.
She told him she knew where the knockoff came from
and that Jerry better put a stop to it."

"That sounds like a perfectly logical statement
under the circumstances."

"She was smiling. I was thinking then she was giving him a come-on. I think different now. She knew,
but kept her mouth shut."

"I hear Phyllis liked to leverage what she knew."
Mario had just given Jerry a possible motive for murder.
"Did she have anything on you?"

Mario walked over to a shelf with a flat-footed shuf-
fle. He wore felt slippers on his feet. "Did I kill her?
That's what you're really asking." He used a couple of
napkins to wipe the inside of his mug. "If I did, I
wouldn't be telling you, so what good is my answer?" As
he spoke, he looked down the corridor. At the far end,
the design-room door was open.

Roberta was showing her Riddle Nothings designs
to the *Vanity Fair* editor, hoping the magazine would
include them in the next issue. She mixed and matched
the knits against an assistant's tall, thin body, spilling
the magic words of the fashion moment. "Heightened

glamour." "It's all about shape." "Rediscovering female sexuality." "The body as icon." She was laughing as she spoke, as if aware that it was nonsense.

"You think she's having a good time, right? She's all happy. The collection's good, the best she's done in years. Phyllis is dead. Charlie is turning out all right. So why not be happy? But you know what she's going to say when that editor walks out of here? She's going to say, 'I feel like an emptied perfume bottle, all scent, no substance.' She says it every time after she shows to an editor. Every single time. And she's not happy. That's how well I know her."

"How well do you remember the night Phyllis killed that girl with her car?"

Mario kept his eyes locked on that rectangle of light down the corridor. Roberta moved in and out of frame, each time with a new outfit.

"That's her favorite hat," he finally said with a voice so filled with softness that I realized he was in love with her. He caught the new knowledge on my face and started coughing. A long, racking bout that brought tears to his eyes. I offered water. He hung up his mug and took out a handkerchief to wipe his mouth.

"February twenty-fourth, 1967," I said to jog his memory. "Elsa Morewitz gave a party at her house in Sands Point. Everyone was invited."

"Rich, big house. You could see Manhasset Bay from the kitchen even. Mrs. Morewitz rented a van for everybody. I took my car. Phyllis rented one. That was her mistake. We'd had a great fall season. All the magazines were raving about Roberta, the stores couldn't get enough of Riddle Solutions. I had my son at home with me. Roberta thought she had Saul. We were on top of the world." His eyes stayed teary.

"Why did Elsa kick Phyllis out of her house?"

"Roberta walked in on Phyllis and Saul. They were

making love in a walk-in closet. The whole garment center knew about Saul and Phyllis, but not Roberta. She didn't want to see it. She just stood in front of that closet and started shaking, with those two half-undressed, looking like rats stuck on a track with the train coming. I was right behind her, trying to get to the bathroom. I tried to pull her away. She ran upstairs and locked herself in one of the bedrooms. Mrs. Morewitz grabbed Phyllis by the arm and pushed her out the front door."

"Why didn't she kick Saul out, too?"

"He's the husband. If Mrs. Morewitz kicked him out, too, how was he going to come back? You got to leave a man some pride. You push him against a corner and you've lost him for good." Mario looked down at his hand and started twisting the thimble on his finger. "I got rid of the wedding ring, but I don't take this off. If I did, I might forget who I am."

"You're a tailor, son of tailors," Roberta said from the doorway. "The best, but if we don't get back to work, darling, I don't have a collection."

We both stood up. "Roberta, I need to talk to you."

"I'm sure you do, darling." Roberta stepped into the room and took Mario under her arm. "Later. Right now we've got a big problem with the blue linen sundress." She turned around, and I let her walk away with Mario by her side. "You wouldn't believe how I feel, Mario," she said, her voice wafting down the corridor. "Like an emptied perfume bottle. All scent, no substance."

19

━━━━━━━ ⌑ ━━━━━━━

We rode the elevator, racing each other for who would punch the buttons first, getting out on every floor to look for Kathy, the cleaning lady. I had tried Mrs. Angelo again and had left another message. Now I relayed to Dmitri what Mario had told me about Jerry. Dmitri happily confirmed it. Beverly the receptionist had filled him in. Jerry was gone. He hadn't admitted to stealing Roberta's designs, but he hadn't threatened to sue her for libel either.

Dmitri preened with pride at knowing as much as I did.

"Well, I have more news." I told him about the night of the accident, adding the newly discovered romantic twist.

"Fantastic! Phyllis destroy Roberta, Mario destroy Phyllis."

"Why did he wait twenty-five years to do the job? And what about Jerry?" We got off on the third floor. "Phyllis threatens to expose him as the design thief and he kills her to shut her up, keep his job, and go on stealing to pay for his racing debts. Or as you would have it, Phyllis spurns him, he seethes with jealousy, and at the first opportunity kills the object of his thwarted desire."

Dmitri's chest rose again, this time with suspicion. "You make fun of me."

"A little." We walked the corridors, Dmitri craning his neck around corners to check for possible kidnappers, a gloating expression on his face. Two pastel-clad buyers from the South came out of a showroom, eyed Dmitri's Cossack looks, and scurried to the elevator.

"He's an actor," I yelled after them. Their footsteps slowed.

"I have news!" Dmitri announced, a bulldog spitting out the beloved cat. "Important news. Revelatory." He checked the men's room.

I checked the ladies'. No Kathy. We waited for the elevator. "What's the news?"

"Three important informations. First. I have list of old employees. Old from thirty years. To check Mario story." He extracted a crumpled list from his pants pocket. "Receptionist Beverly get for me. She got hair like the river Don."

There were ten names on the list, with addresses and phone numbers. They were probably not updated, but maybe one or two of them had not moved. "You didn't show Beverly that phony police badge, I hope."

Dmitri took a deep breath and nearly popped three buttons. "I show her charm."

"I forgot. You were after her hair. Seriously, though, thanks. I appreciate you and your charm." I dropped the list in my purse. "What else?"

"I show Beverly fashion magazines, I see her desk." We stepped into the elevator. Dmitri pressed two, beating me to the punch. He was now winning by one floor. "I see check from Riddle Solutions to managing agent. Eight thousand dollars for one month's rent! I could get Winter Palace in St. Petersburg for so much money. Long hair no longer chic, I show Beverly models and their haircuts. She will sell me hair if boyfriend okay. He will not okay, so I work for nothing, but I find out about rent."

The elevator door opened on two. Dmitri stepped out. I didn't. "I get it," I said. He stepped back in, the elevator door closed, and we descended before either of us reached the floor buttons. "At the Union Square Cafe Roberta said the rent was due Monday. You won, by the way. Fifteen floors to thirteen."

"Sixteen to twelve."

I didn't argue. As Mario said, don't corner a man. At least not the one responsible for your safety. "Mr. Nite had a hundred and twenty-five thousand dollars in the safe, but the thief stole only a hundred and eighteen. That conveniently leaves seven thousand dollars with which to pay the rent, assuming he pays the rent in cash."

"Always cash. Everything he pay cash—fear from war. Beverly call for me managing agent to ask if Mr. Nite pay rent this month. I explain my accent is too strong. Not trust making. She does this because she likes me, I think. Her lips are moist with desire. My heart takes notice. Maybe she breaks up with boyfriend."

"What did the managing agent say?"

"Now I joke. My heart spoken for." Dmitri's sigh was a sudden hair-ruffling breeze. "My heart also breaking."

"What did the agent say?"

"On Monday Mr. Nite paid! Seven thousand dollars, as you say. One thousand dollars less than Roberta's rent because he is one floor lower."

"If the money was taken from his safe, that means he would have known about the theft of the hundred and eighteen thousand on Monday, not on Wednesday as he claims."

We reached the first floor. A baseball-capped boy waited. Dmitri stepped in front of me, his girth my protection.

I stepped out from behind. I could tell at a glance that the boy was a good guy. He was carrying pizza.

"So what do we think?" I asked Dmitri.

"We think man lies." With that, he pushed me right into Kathy's pail.

She hustled us into the lobby's barbershop at the sight of Dmitri fanning out five twenty-dollar bills. In the breadth of his hand, they were no larger than Monopoly money. I wanted to protest the amount, but for once I kept my mouth shut.

"You look like a cop," Kathy told Dmitri after locking the shop door behind her.

"You know cop paying five Jacksons?" Dmitri gave me a proud look at his use of slang.

"Sometimes," Kathy said dubiously. "Though taking is more their style."

"You know cop with Russian accent?"

"They talk, I don't listen."

"On Lenin's grave I swear."

"He's into hair," I said to help things along.

Dmitri shot me a withering look. It was my turn to play sidekick. Dmitri had whispered, "Kathy mine," while I removed my dripping foot from the pail. I had no objections. Kathy hadn't taken to me the first time around and Dmitri had "three important informations." He'd given me only two. My incredible acuity told me the third one was coming.

The barbershop was empty, with a pleasant smell of shampoo and aftershave. The floor was dusted with hair. I saw Dmitri glance down. Men's hair. Too short. I sat in one of the three barber's chairs, toweling my shoe dry. Dmitri stood in front of the glass door, blocking the view in or out, the five bills still clutched in one fist. Kathy eyed the money in the mirror while she dusted the counter with a rag filled with the dirt of the entire garment district.

"If you're not a cop, what do you want?" Kathy was almost six feet tall, bone thin, with a sharp angular face that had been handsome many cleaning jobs ago. She was somewhere in her fifties, with thin gray hair that slipped from the knot on the top of her head.

"Phyl friend of mine," Dmitri said, looking appropriately sad. "Good friend."

Kathy wiped the mirror, leaving a trail of dirt. She was watching me with diamond-hard eyes. "Who is she?"

I opened my mouth. Dmitri beat me to it again. "Another good friend."

"Phyllis didn't have friends, that's what I hear."

"Friendship of passion. I give her gold chain. She always wear it. You notice gold chain on her neck?"

"Why should I? In the ten years I clean here, I saw her maybe a dozen times."

Gold chain? What was he talking about? I tried to focus back on Sunday. Phyllis standing in her bra and panty hose. I hadn't noticed a gold chain.

"You see her dead," Dmitri said. Kathy picked up a can of hair spray. She wiped it with her rag. "What I want to know," Dmitri persisted, "you see chain?"

I *had* seen it! There had been a flash of light on her chest as Phyllis bent down to scratch her knee. I remember thinking it matched the gold at the back of her mouth.

"Eighteen carat," Dmitri said. "Italian, heavy, too."

Kathy wiped the top, pressing the nozzle by mistake.

Hair spray covered the mirror in a wide arc. She flung the can on the floor. "You're saying I stole that gold chain, aren't you? You're no better than the cops! Some guy with a record as thick as your waist fingers my brother as a thief and they believe him. No evidence, except that he was there when it happened. Just like me. I clean, that's my job. And the first thing that gets cleaned is the bathrooms. Yes, I'm the one who found her. That doesn't make me a thief. If I find something in the bathrooms and laying about where it has no business being, I bring it right down to security and sometimes I get a tip but mostly I get no thanks. I don't do stealing."

Dmitri lifted his shoulders, a mountain moving. "I pay hundred dollars to thief?"

She laughed at that, showing teeth that looked oddly dainty in her wide mouth. "You'd be dumb if you did, but if that chain was worth a lot of money, maybe dumber if you didn't."

"Dmitri supremely intelligent and chain worth money, but more in sentiment, you understand." Tears actually appeared in his eyes. What an actor!

"Was Phyllis wearing the chain when you found her?" I asked.

"Who says she wasn't? The police didn't ask me anything about a gold chain. Not that I listened too carefully. I gave them what they wanted to hear without pointing any fingers. Asked me down to the precinct to sign a statement. I went home and took a long bath after that. That place was even filthier than this rag. I don't use this, you know." She addressed me, a wily look in her eyes. "This is only for show. It puts people off, like body odor. You didn't like it none too much." She shook the rag in front of me and a cloud of dust wafted down to the floor, barely missing my lap. "I'm good at my job. Otherwise I'd be out on the street. The management here is very particular."

"Phyllis got no relatives," Dmitri said. "The police send her clothes to Mrs. Riddle. Chain missing. Beverly tell me this. She remember Phyllis wearing chain day she was killed. So, Mrs. Kathy—"

"Miss, thank you."

"If no heirs, I want chain back."

"The police took it. Wouldn't put it past them. Liquor store owner down the street from me had a kid hold him up. The cops caught the punk not ten yards from the store, but the money, six hundred dollars he took, gone. Cops said they found nothing. You believe that? I don't."

Dmitri crackled the money. Kathy sat.

"Mrs. Riddle thinks I don't like her because she doesn't tip enough. She tips as well as the rest of them."

"What does Roberta have to do with the gold chain?" I asked.

"They had a fight, you know. I was cleaning the stairs, they're next to the wall of her studio. I'll tell you what I told the cops. It's the truth too. At first I thought the noise was just Mario and his operas again. Then I picked out Phyllis, she was a screecher. Mrs. Riddle got in there, too. That's when I knew they were fighting. Mrs. Riddle never raises her voice, not that I know of. She was yelling back, but I couldn't make out any words. The singing was too loud."

Dmitri pocketed the money. Kathy sagged back into the barber chair, her skinny legs long enough to touch the floor.

"Look, Kathy," I said, "we're trying to help Charlie Angelo. His fingerprints were in that bathroom and the police almost arrested him. They've been waylaid by something else—"

"The stolen money. I know all about that. I got the cops on my back again over that one. And I didn't tell them the whole truth this time. That man's heart and his name are one and the same. Gold. He's in love with Mrs. Riddle, and he'll do anything to help her. I heard about Charlie being in trouble, and I don't like it. Charlie's no murderer. I'd help him, but it's going to have to be two hundred if I'm risking the cops. No, make it three hundred. I could get jailed for an accessory after the fact." She folded her arms and leaned back, her face set.

Dmitri's eyes shifted my way. Barely. He didn't want to lose face, but the money had to come from me. I nodded once. Roberta would pay. With the deftness of a magician, he reached deep into his pants pocket and came up with a fan of nine twenties.

"Tops," he said.

Kathy held out a callused hand. He released two twenties, held on to the rest, an expert at this game. She was, too. Kathy rolled the money into her socks and sat back, the gleam of the storyteller settling in her eyes.

"The month before the New York shows I get overtime for coming in on Saturday and Sunday. The designers work around the clock and they're nervous and make a mess. On Sunday I started on Mrs. Riddle's floor. I always start on the thirtieth. The Nina Ricci people in the penthouse have their own gal. I start with the bathrooms first, except on Sunday I couldn't clean the men's or the ladies'. Somebody had filled the locks with Crazy Glue, not that I minded, just as long as nobody thought I'd done it to shirk off work. I vacuumed the corridor, didn't bother with Mr. Mannucci because he's no designer and I'd cleaned up the place Friday night. Did some mopping on the stairs. That's when I heard them fighting. Then I went down to the twenty-ninth floor. That's where I made my mistake. I didn't do the bathrooms right away. If I had, I wouldn't have found her. Instead, I let myself into Mr. Nite's showroom and went into his office, where he keeps a nine-inch TV. I sat down and watched myself a Fred Astaire movie on AMC. *Top Hat*. I was in there for ninety minutes, but I didn't tell the cops. I'd be in jail for stealing a hundred and eighteen thousand dollars. Which I didn't!" She paused and extended her hand. Dmitri dropped two more twenties. At this rate I was going to have shaving soap for dinner.

"The gold chain?" I murmured.

"I found Phyllis. I skipped screaming, a waste of time. Although I did drop my bucket. Thank the Lord it was empty. I called Mrs. Riddle first. She was Phyllis's employer, it was proper. She was down in no time and when she looked at that poor dead woman, she didn't scream either. She made this funny sound, almost like a belch, it was so loud. Then she told me to call security. I started to—she must have heard my footsteps going to Mr. Nite's office—but then I thought of that sound she'd made, like she'd just gotten rid of something awful in her stomach, and I got curious. I tiptoed back. She was leaning over the body, I could see her in the bathroom mirror. Mrs. Riddle's hand, as fast as the tongue on a snake, unclasped that gold chain and slipped it in her bra."

"Roberta? I don't believe it." We were eating hot dogs in the car on the way to the Upper West Side and home. I sat in the backseat again, to give him room up front, and my chin was speckled with mustard and ketchup. Dmitri drove with one hand and ate with the other. His mustache, for once, was impeccable.

"What reason on earth would she have to steal Phyllis's gold chain?" I asked. "She doesn't need money that badly, she doesn't wear jewelry."

Dmitri stuffed the hot dog in his mouth and reached under the seat. A paperback tome hit my lap.

Jealous Night. Which must have been the name of the aftershave Kathy had sprayed on him after he paid her. The smell was cloying enough to evoke murderous rages.

"I get it," I said, licking my fingers clean. "The chain was a present from Saul. Roberta knew it."

"For certain, Phyllis tell her."

"So Roberta took it back."

"*Exactamente.*"

"*Esattamente.*" I threw the book back up front. "I don't buy it. Stealing a necklace from a dead body. That's maudlin and pretty stupid and I don't think Roberta is either."

"You don't believe Kathy? We waste hundred and eighty dollars."

"Funny enough, I believe she's telling the truth as she sees it. Watching *Top Hat* on Mr. Nite's TV won me over. That could get her into real trouble if the money turns out to be stolen after all." I wiped my chin. "If Roberta took that chain, it wasn't to steal it. Maybe there's a practical reason, evidence against the murderer, or—"

Dmitri's cellular phone chirped.

"—or something to do with the business. Now what can a chain stand for?"

"For you." Dmitri launched the receiver to the backseat.

It nearly hit my head.

"Hello?"

It was the CEO himself. In a truculent mood. "Why did you take the day off when you keep claiming the creative department can't operate without you?" He was overstating it a bit. I explained I was helping *his* client out on a matter, that it was October and I hadn't taken any personal days yet, I was entitled. I also almost told him to go to *quel paese*, as we say back home, "that country" never properly defined.

He told me to get back to the office. He was calling a meeting of the entire creative department in half an hour. We had a chance to pitch a car account. A first for HH&H. Car accounts are extremely lucrative. This one was Japanese. Even better.

"When Roberta Riddle's billing is a million dollars," the CEO said, "then you take the day off to help her."

The conversation ended. I almost threw the phone back at Dmitri. I was furious, but I liked the job, I liked the people I worked with. Every second Friday, I even liked the CEO. Especially his signature. I called Stan and told him I was going back to the office, where I was perfectly safe. No one gets past Reception without a pass. After hours included. Stan told me Willy wanted to talk to us both.

"How are we going to do that? Conference call?" It wasn't safe for his son to be seen with us.

"I told him it wasn't a good idea right now, but he insisted. Irene plays into it."

"Poor kid."

"I couldn't tell him no. Get Dmitri to drop you off at the Waldorf Astoria at eight o'clock. Think you can make it?" It was now six.

"Nine is better. Why the Waldorf?"

"It's close to home for Willy, and I know the head detective over there. He's got a room set aside for us, 813. Call up first."

"What's the code?" I asked, laughing.

Stan didn't join in. "Who knows, he might be telling us he wants to move in."

Mamma mia! I love the boy, but I still had to get used to Stan as a permanent fixture.

"Dmitri, you've got a few hours off." If the CEO's meeting was the usual pep talk about squeezing our masterly brains for innovative ideas, it would take thirty minutes at the most. Then I planned to breathe by hanging around the office awhile. Maybe even show how productive I could be. The thought of what Willy had to say was giving my stomach goosebumps.

"Meet me at eight-thirty in front of the office." What if he was going to ask me to move out of his dad's apartment? "I'll be meeting Stan at the Waldorf, so after that it'll be home for you."

"I go to Kennedy airport. I got new hair shipment."

"A shipment?" I was impressed. "You have that much hair?"

"Pavel's wife coming. She bring suitcase full." His face spurted happiness.

For the suitcase? For Pavel's wife? Who was Pavel? I didn't ask.

The pep talk took twenty minutes. If we didn't win, we were dead was the gist of it. Afterward the art directors and copy editors clustered in the conference room, babbling with excitement.

"How about not showing them the car, just the sensation it gives. Power! Luxury! Sex!"

"Yeah, you've always got to put sex in it, even if you're selling shoes."

"Especially if it's shoes."

"No, show them the wizardry of the motor. Now that's sexy!"

Really, these are nice people. Take my word for it. I snuck out and made it to my office with no one the wiser. I scrapped the note Linda had left me, apologizing for revealing Dmitri's phone number. I sat down, kicked off my shoes, and propped my feet up on the desk. The CEO darkened my door. I sputtered to a standing position. The CEO in my office cubicle? He shut the door behind him. I had no windows. He wouldn't stay long.

My CEO: Harold Harland, the first of the three HH&Hs, dressed in an English houndstooth wool suit, Turnbull & Asser shirt, Ferragamo tie, and Cole Hahn black wingtip shoes. A perfect example of advertising gullibility: the label makes the man. Har Har, as he is sometimes called, is a sleek, handsome man in his sixties who is so impressed by elegance that his underpants are probably monogrammed. His face has been designed in sleek lines, with no uneven edges. His hair is as white and smooth as mother of pearl. For that evening he was donning a red, visored cap. Not elegant at all. But then he'd had a golfing accident, someone had whispered.

I looked at the cap, looked back at the marketing manual he clutched to his chest like a preacher with his Bible. I went back to the cap. "I'm sorry about the accident."

"I had to have a few stitches. Golfing accident."

"You fell from your cart?"

"A golf ball met the back of my head on the seventeenth hole."

"They shook hands?"

He didn't find that funny. Neither did I, but I had the queasy feeling that I was in trouble. Why not make it worse?

"I hope you weren't winning," I said.

His jaw tightened.

I murmured further regrets. He told me the reason for the tête-à-tête. He was giving me a week to decide whether to come upstairs and work as an account executive.

"Or?"

"I'll have to let you go. The creative department is over-staffed, the account department is understaffed." That was because he had fired over half of them.

"What if we get the car account?"

"It's a long shot. You have a well-trained assistant. She will handle the job by herself."

Well-trained thanks to me and sure, she could handle the job, except that Linda was pregnant and planning to ask for a year's leave. But I wasn't going to rat on her.

"I'll think about it," I said, giving it the importance of a choice between Caesar or Cobb salad.

"A week," he reminded me, and then left, taking his manual with him.

I dug up October's *Elle* and read my Pisces horoscope. "Mercury's retrograde motion will leave you baffled and apprehensive."

Baffled, apprehensive, and enraged.

Fifty minutes later, after having set up and written budgets for two print ads and saved HH&H three thousand dollars with my knife-sharp and to-the-point negotiations, I was thirsty, hungry, and still mad. I buttoned my coat, strapped my purse across my chest bandolier style, went downstairs, and headed for a Diet Coke and a large chunk of Brie.

I forgot all about security.

20

The sky was dimming down to night. The street lamps were lit. Cars swooshed by. The traffic sign warned DON'T WALK, but I rushed across Fifth Avenue, a true New Yorker in my impatience. Burke & Burke, my usual supplier, was closed. I rattled the door out of frustration, then spotted Au Bon Pain across the street. This time the sign said WALK.

I was about to step up on the curb when the car caught me. A grimy white Oldsmobile with its headlights off. I heard a thump, felt myself spin and tilt forward with the movement of the car. My knees buckled and scraped against asphalt. Something pulled hard against my chest. Cold metal hit my cheek. Fear and surprise twisted their way around my windpipe, choking off sound. I was falling. Down. Under the heat of the tires.

I was wrong. The sideview mirror had hooked my purse. I was being dragged, chest held up by the sturdy strap of a Coach bag. The car slowed down. I did not have the sense to look inside the open window, to see the driver. I was trying to survive the moment. A hand reached out, large, male. I clutched the window frame and tried to pull myself up. The hand jerked down. I heard the snap of the mirror.

I was free. In the second before falling, I grabbed that hand and scratched for dear life.

A shoulder hit the garbage can, a hip caught the curb, and my leg twisted under my weight. The Oldsmobile sped away, license plates too muddy to read. I lay on the asphalt with my scratching hand balled into a fist and screamed.

I got most of this information from Dmitri, who, early for our eight-thirty appointment, had been circling the block looking for a parking space. When the Olds left its parking space to try to make Bolognese sauce out of me, Dmitri was right behind, aiming for the empty spot. He wanted to chase after the car, but I kept screaming. For the excruciating pain in my left leg, for the humiliation, for my sheer stupidity. Dmitri, with his passionate heart, felt that he could not leave me.

At St. Vincent's—the nearest hospital—they X-rayed, cleaned me up a bit, gave me two Tylenol with codeine. Every time they got near my fist, I yelled, "Don't touch the evidence!"

They left me lying on the gurney. I heard a nurse call the staff psychiatrist.

I wasn't crazy. I was waiting for Dmitri to bring Stan from the Waldorf Astoria. My fingernails held evidence, the skin and blood of the hit-and-run driver. Match the DNAs and we had our man.

Stan, face scrunched with worry and fear, arrived in time to hear the X-ray results. Intact skull, bad bruises on my hip and shoulders, and a closed fracture of the fibula—the smaller of the two bones that go from the knee to the ankle.

"Let's make sense here," I said, grumpy being a

mild way of describing my mood. "How can a fracture be closed?"

"Hon," Stan muttered, meek in his concern. Dmitri sniffed into a handkerchief. The doctor told me I was one lucky lady.

"You weren't even wearing heavy clothes. You should have had all your bones broken! Three to four weeks with a short leg cast and you'll be as good as new. First four days with crutches, then a cane. Now let's see the damage in your fist." He extended an arm. I growled and told Stan about my dirty nails.

"Quick thinking!" Stan rocked on the balls of his feet, moving his arms, getting them tangled. He wanted to punch my shoulder, pat my arm, ruffle my hair in approval. He was afraid I'd break. I didn't tell him that my scratching had been a purely instinctive gesture of anger. It was only later, on the way to the hospital, that I realized I had evidence under those short nails of mine.

"You're cute when you worry," I said. A warm glow was spreading in my chest. I thought it was love. Codeine is more likely. "Remind me to break another leg if we get into a fight. How about covering my fist so I don't lose anything?"

"Right. Five more minutes. Hold on, honey." Stan ran, light-footed, to call for a medical examiner's manicurist. I guess he didn't trust St. Vincent's to do a good job, or it wasn't proper procedure. I lay back on the gurney and tried to let the codeine wash over all of me.

Dmitri hovered, fist and hand punching each other in penitence. "Why I not chase him? Why you not wait for me? Why you hurt? I saw this woman dragging next to car. I think perhaps something funny, I think to myself I save her, but seat belt get stuck. I not recognize you till you hit sidewalk. Your mouth wide open."

"Thanks."

"Are you hungry? I go buy hot dog."

"No, I've got work for you." I sat up again, beginning to feel woozy.

The doctor fit a stockinette on my leg and rolled my calf in cotton wadding as if he planned to ship it somewhere. Not a bad-looking leg. One of my best attributes, in fact. Thin.

"Dmitri, *amor mio*, it's my fault, not yours, so stop worrying." I pulled him toward me and started whispering. I could see the doctor eyeing me warily and the nurse grinning. Ours must have looked like a lovers' embrace.

"We're in St. Vincent's. That's where Phyllis came after the accident. I know it's twenty-eight years ago, but maybe they keep records this long. Can we get hold of them? If you need to pay some money, do. Not more than fifty this time. See if there are any old-timers around who might remember how she got here."

"You still want me on case?"

"You're the best." And he was. At that moment I loved him dearly because he cared. Somewhere in our wanderings and questionings we'd become oddball friends. Sancho Panza and Don Quixote sharing a quest. For no other reason maybe than the sheer joy of discovery. "Say you're a private investigator or whatever you think will work, but don't pull out that gold police badge! I don't want you arrested."

He straightened up, a pout hanging on his mustache. "You boss me."

"I'm war wounded. It gives me rights."

"What color do you want?" the nurse said, snapping on rubber gloves. The gesture made me think of crime scenes.

"Color what?"

"The cast. We use a synthetic cast. You can't write on it, which gets the kids riled up, but you can cover it up with decals if you like." She lifted a roll of gold stars.

"Best kid in the class is all I got left. So what color are we havin'?"

"Pink," Dmitri bellowed. "For Cadillac office."

"Green. For Greenhouse. And no stars." That's when I decided to throw up.

What followed is slightly muddled in my head. I got moved to a clean gurney. Some police expert did clean my nails, and I vaguely remember worrying that all she'd get was a mustard and ketchup combination. Stan held my free hand and told me Willy sent his best. I felt as foggy and wanting as a newborn. Now that the initial elation of survival was gone, I was overwhelmed by a sense of unfairness. A muddled murder case, an angry ex-wife, a new home I couldn't enjoy, a vanishing job, and two stupid hit men. What had I done to merit all this *merda*?

When I finally bothered to look down, my foot was in a walking boot and my leg was shining pink up to my knee. The nurse shrugged at my look of dismay.

"We ran out of green."

At least no stars.

The next four days were spent not in New Jersey with my friend Gregory or in upstate New York with Stan's relatives as threatened, but in an inexpensive hotel in the East Thirties—a section called Murray Hill. Stan got me a suite with a closet kitchen, nubby beige upholstery, orange-flowered wallpaper, black drapes with identical orange flowers, blankets that looked and felt like peach fuzz and set my teeth on edge. For company I had a cellular phone, TV, Dmitri's romance paperbacks, a loud-voiced astrologist next door, and two retired cops, ex-colleagues of Stan's, who guarded door and windows with their eyes locked on the sports channel.

Chasing a ball of any size is behavior fit only for quadrupeds. I shut the door to the sounds of male hormones raging on a muddy football field, lay back on my bed with my broken leg stretched out, popped painkillers, and buried my nose in quivering breasts and throbbing swords.

Stan ordered no visitors for fear the hit men were watching my friends and would follow. Dmitri sulked back to Brighton Beach in his borrowed Cadillac, still blaming himself for not catching the men. Willy had not gotten a chance to get anything off his chest at the Waldorf, but now he and Irene were safe in the house of friends, with another pair of ex-cops guarding them. Just in case.

Stan called often to encourage me. At my bidding he'd told Roberta I'd be away in the Berkshires for a few days to recuperate from a broken leg. The office got the same story. I wondered if I was ever going to go back to any of them. Stan kept apologizing, kept telling me he loved me. I listened but didn't participate. A part of me was angry enough to blame him.

I didn't use the phone. I wanted nothing to do with life outside my room. My leg hurt, my bones ached, half of me was the color of rotten eggs and mold. While the astrologer promised major changes for Sagittarius and warned Aries that this was often a tough time of year, I ate pretzels and read about thwarted love in Regency England. The dependably happy endings cheered me up.

I missed Phyllis's funeral.

Saturday night Stan brought presents. Himself, first of all. He swore he hadn't been followed. Then Raf's paella with extra shrimp, a chilled bottle of Pinot Grigio, Thursday's and Friday's *New York Times*, a huge arrangement of flowers from Roberta, a box of Perugina *Baci* chocolates from Gregory and Linda, and a new romance novel from Dmitri.

"We think we've found the car." That was the best present of all.

"Reported stolen not five blocks from D.T.'s, the bar underneath Victor Delgado's gym. We found it abandoned over on the West Side Highway. Unfortunately, the car had just been washed so we can't match the grime we picked off from your coat."

"Fingerprints?"

"Wiped clean."

My elation was shriveling rapidly. Stan put on an optimistic face.

"We're checking all the car-wash places, starting with Manhattan. We're scouring the neighborhood where the car was stolen. Maybe someone saw something. Dmitri is ready to testify that's the car, but he's not a reliable witness."

"Too passionate."

"By far. He's taken the attack as a personal affront. It's a game of patience, honey. You have to wait it out. I'm sorry." He stroked my cheek.

"What about the skin under my nails?"

Stan grimaced. "We've got to get a match, which means getting those two to come in and give up some skin and blood. Their lawyers won't hear of it."

"Force them! I want to get out of here!"

"The chief is balking. Those two are going to stumble sooner or later. They're not bright, they've just been lucky. That's how we catch most criminals. Stupidity."

"They went for me four times and missed. You'd think that was really dumb, but looking back, I don't think they ever meant to really hurt me. At least not this last time. Dmitri said the car was going slowly and slowed down even more when my purse got caught. Victor or the other guy, the supposed hired killer, what's his name?"

"Sonny Petruzzi."

"Great! An Italian. Anyway, the driver—there was only one man in the car, Dmitri confirmed that—he snapped off his rearview mirror to unhook me. That's not the action of a killer." I scooped saffron rice onto a mussel shell.

"I bet Sonny was driving. Forced into it by Victor. Sonny's the weak link. We've been trying to work on him, but Victor's got his own lawyer onto it. We've got to tread carefully. I can't risk any coercion charges."

It didn't sound promising. "What's happening with our Riddle murder? Did you find the missing hundred and eighteen thousand dollars?"

"Sim."

I played deaf and scooped again. The food lifted my spirits somewhat. "Just asking."

Stan looked at my leg propped up on a chair. We were eating in the living room on a small round table. My bodyguards had discreetly retreated to the hallway.

"Does it still hurt?"

"*Da morire.*"

"To die?"

"Yup." I sucked on a shrimp shell. He took pity on me and confirmed what Dmitri and I had already suspected. Mr. Nite had made up the theft story to throw suspicion away from Charlie. When the managing agents confirmed that he'd paid his $7,000 rent in cash on Monday afternoon, two days before he'd said he'd discovered the theft, Mr. Nite had confessed that he had only wanted to help Roberta.

"What about you?" Stan asked casually. "What did you and Dmitri find out?"

"That Mr. Nite was fibbing." Way before you did.

He looked surprised.

"Deductive reasoning."

He checked a laugh. I ignored the slight. He means well and he's not often wrong. "Roberta's hundred-dollar check says that's all I can tell you, *bello mio.*"

"Confidentiality only works for lawyers."

"And for psychiatrists, priests, and yours truly. Where do you stand now?"

"I've got two cases on my desk, my family in hiding, and an old boyfriend of Phyllis's who keeps skipping out minutes before we get there."

"An old boyfriend?" It was my turn to be surprised. "When did he turn up?"

"You dig deep enough, you find people."

"Is it Jerry?"

"Someone new."

"Does that mean the heat is off Riddle Solutions and its employees?"

"I wouldn't go that far, but that's all you're getting from me. If you were dying of pain, you wouldn't be gorging yourself."

"Raf's paella resuscitates the dead! Tell him I love him desperately."

"What about Dmitri?"

"I love him, too."

"Gregory?"

"As good as bread. My best friend. I know, I love a lot of men, but you, I adore you."

The conversation degenerated into further silliness as we cleaned out the mussels, the chicken, the shrimp, licked up every kernel of rice, and polished off the wine bottle. I hopped back to the bedroom on crutches while Stan cleaned up. We did a little smooching and pawing, with my pink cast and extended contusions getting in the way. Stan wanted to spend the night with a fresh couple of ex-cops keeping vigil in the living room. I sent him home, knowing that I wouldn't sleep a wink with him beside me, imagining the killer getting both of us. I simply felt safer with Stan far away. I found that sad.

21

"So what did you find out?" It was Sunday noon. The New York Fashion Week for Spring was starting that very minute. Donna Karan, Marc Jacobs, and Miu Miu. Roberta was going to show in two days. I'd had it with playing the victim.

"No hair," Dmitri said over the phone. "Pavel's wife forget suitcase."

"At St. Vincent's?"

"They have records. Microfilm in basement. But only patient or immediate family can see. I say I am cousin from Russia, I was in car night of accident, I got bad kidney now. I got to look up records. She tell me to come back Monday. I say no, Friday. She say Monday. I show money, but no good."

"It's a game of patience."

"You okay, Simona? I worry and miss you." He had a heart the size of his country. I told him my problems. First about having just moved in with Stan and the crimp Willy's mother had put in the arrangement, then about my CEO threatening to fire me—something I hadn't mentioned to Stan because he had enough to think about.

Dmitri offered to work over my boss. When I refused his help he advised, "Concentrate on case."

I read him the list of suspects I'd prepared to keep from screaming.

"Flossie Sarnowski—disliked Phyllis, very protective of son. Denied any design stealing going on, which could mean she knew Jerry was the thief. Might have killed Phyllis if it would help her son."

"My mother first to cut hair for me," Dmitri announced. I read on.

"Jerry Sarnowski—big gambler, needs money. Admits having means and opportunity. Denies any motive. But Phyllis, according to Mario, knew he was stealing. He also admits having slept with victim. Dislikes Charlie. What if he knew of fingerprints on bathroom door and thought he could kill two birds with one stone. Phyllis and Charlie? Too far-fetched?

"Mario Lionello. A bitter man, Roberta describes him. I see him as sad, weak. Abandoned by wife and son. Because he is in love with Roberta? Probable. Relationship to Phyllis none, according to him. Could have killed Phyllis to help Roberta."

"Crime of passion."

"That's what you would like." I went back to my notes. "Lourdes Montalvo. She admits to not liking Phyllis despite fact that Phyllis helped her get the job with Riddle Solutions. But no one liked Phyllis except Jerry. Has no motive that I can think of. Is Lourdes telling the truth about baby conversation between Phyllis and Roberta?"

"Lourdes innocent!"

"You mean she's pretty."

"That, too."

"Ed Mannucci. Was in the building from four to

four-thirty. According to Stan his alibi around the time of the murder isn't airtight. Knew Phyllis. May have slept with her. Dislikes Roberta. Wants her company. Killed Phyllis to deliver the final blow to Roberta's company so he can then buy? How did he get hold of the Buddha, which was behind locked doors? Again far-fetched?"

"What about wife, Sally?"

"Out of the picture, Stan said. She was in Port Washington visiting her mother with two other witnesses. They were playing canasta."

"What else?"

"Nothing more from Stan. Roberta's our last suspect. She has two motives. Phyllis took her husband, and Phyllis convinced Mr. Nite not to invest."

"But she pays you to find truth!"

"I know, it doesn't make sense unless she's innocent."

"Innocent, but knows who is killer."

"Maybe. She knows, but she can't bring herself to or doesn't want to point the finger. She wants me to do it for her."

"Battered wife mentality," Dmitri offered. "I read in serious book. What we do about it?"

"We have to get me out of here." I went on to tell Dmitri all about the Delgado case. Mrs. Cordova's telephone records showed there had been calls made from Victor Delgado's gym to Sonny Petruzzi's apartment in Long Island City. Stan and Raf had checked with the regulars at the gym and found one guy who knew Sonny. He didn't remember making a call to Sonny from the gym, but he couldn't swear he hadn't. A long time had passed. And no, he didn't know if Victor and Sonny knew each other. Sonny didn't work out. Victor Delgado and Sonny Petruzzi were still refusing to give the police blood and skin samples.

"I have more informations," Dmitri said. "I talk to

doctor at hospital. I tell him I am journalist from *Pravda* doing story on American nurses in emergency rooms. I ask for old-timer. I get name of Irish woman in Village Nursing Home. I wait for you to go. I look too fearsome for someone so old."

"*Fantastico*, Dmitri! You're the cheese on macaroni. Call me tomorrow the minute you've checked the records. And now, let me tell you about an idea of mine."

At five o'clock that Sunday afternoon, Dmitri picked me up in the pink Cadillac and drove me to a bar on Tenth Avenue and Fifty-fourth Street, luckily a bar within Stan's precinct. D.T.'s was Victor Delgado's and Sonny Petruzzi's hangout, where they were committing their lies to paper with the help of a reporter who had been fired from the *Daily News*. One of Dmitri's men, Mike— known in his home country as Ivan—had sat at D.T.'s most of the afternoon drinking beer, making sure that Victor and Sonny didn't budge. He'd also checked out which man had the scratched hand, information that he had called in to my hotel. Another Dmitri henchman, Phil—once known as Igor—came with us in the Cadillac.

I hobbled into the bar on my crutches. A small, narrow space with room for three wooden booths on one side and an overly ornate pine bar on the other. The usual mirror lined with bottles covered one wall. Grime covered the rest.

Victor and Sonny sat in the middle booth, bent over a laptop. The other booths were empty. The ex-reporter wasn't in sight.

I recognized Victor from the photo Stan had shown me. The bowling ball of a head was circled by a few remaining hairs that looked like a rubber band keeping his brains together. He had pinpricks for eyes and the smudged look heavy drinkers get. His navy sweats advertised VIC'S MUSCLE, the name of his gym.

Sonny Petruzzi was a different category of man. All I needed was a glance to wonder if it had been his looks that had gotten Anna Delgado to contemplate getting rid of her husband. In profile he reminded me of Tony Curtis in the days when he had been my mother's idol. Wavy black hair, five nine at the most, full lips and cheeks, big, languid brown eyes. He had the same strange mixture of baby-faced innocence and threatening good looks. He had to be one hell of a bad actor to end up at D.T.'s with Victor Delgado running his life.

With Phil at my side, I noisily settled down in the booth behind Victor. Mike stayed at the bar, his armpits looking ready to crunch coconuts. Dmitri leaned his bulk against our booth and held my crutches. They were matchsticks in his hands. I ordered a Bloody Mary to match my mood.

Victor clicked at the laptop keys. The blue screen was filled with type. I stole a quick look and read, "I fell in love with Anna's tits the day I first saw them." With breath suspended, Dmitri read on. I shifted my eyes back to Sonny and mouthed, "Remember me?"

He did. His nice mouth twitched, his tongue licked his teeth. His left hand, yellow with iodine, dropped under the counter.

I smiled at him. Mike had studied their body parts for several hours. He swore they carried no guns. I felt perfectly safe.

"That's him," I whispered loudly to Dmitri. "That's the guy who ran me over!"

Victor whipped his head around. Sonny blanched.

My plan was to unsettle the weak link, the driver I had scratched, Sonny Petruzzi. Stare him down, make him think I was ready to make a positive ID, then loudly declare I was ready to go to the precinct and make my statement. He would tremble at the thought and rush to plea-bargain, pointing the finger at Victor. Not as lame a plan as it may sound. It might have worked given the IQ's of the gentlemen involved.

Dmitri had a more forceful idea. When Victor turned around, Phil held up a camera and snapped. The flash popped.

Victor half stood up, arms flailing. "What the fu—"

"You are excrement of rat!" Dmitri shouted. He threw my crutches across the room for emphasis. "The urine of chickens, the turd of cows!"

Victor started laughing. Sonny looked unsure. As Dmitri's insults escalated into more in-vogue epithets involving mothers' professions and male body parts, his voice lowered into coal-dark depths, his black-clothed hulk leaned menacingly over his victims.

Victor's laugh stopped in his throat. "What the fu—" Dmitri dropped one of his oversized palms on the laptop. The power button clicked. The screen went blank.

"You didn't save!" Victor jumped up with a howl and swung out. Dmitri ducked and let his elbow push the laptop to the floor. Sonny snarled and popped a fist in Dmitri's face.

Dmitri fell on top of him, kicking the laptop across the floor. Sonny struck again. Dmitri caught his right hand in midair. Slowly, deliberately, as he sat on a squirming Victor, Dmitri curled his fingers and scratched Sonny's good hand. Mission accomplished, he stood up, a malicious grin plastered to his mustache, and let himself be pummeled by both of them.

In my effective way I threw an open ketchup bottle at Victor's head and screamed, *"Basta!"* Phil sipped his Coke. Mike called the police.

Four hours later, we were still sitting on a wooden bench at Mid-Town South. Dmitri's face was growing mushrooms, the blue and red variety. A bandage covered one ear. One eye had disappeared. His nose was cut. His lip was swollen from where the ketchup bottle had hit him. He had not brought charges against me. The ketchup had stayed in the bottle.

I worked my way through a Mars bar Raf had dropped on my lap on his way back to the interrogation room. He was softening Sonny with cigarettes, apple Snapple, and promises of great understanding. Victor was barking in another room. Mike and Phil had given statements and been released. Stan was honoring us with a stern lecture. I had shut down my ears as soon as his eyes started twinkling.

"Dmitri, I'm going to have to charge you for verbal assault and destruction of property," he concluded. He had a diamond glint in them now.

Dmitri shrugged. "Accidental. Pure accidental. I never hit them. Only words. And then I fall. I cannot help it. And yes, I get mad. After so much beating up. But I am dangerous machine. If I hit, I kill. So I use safe, woman's method. I scratch. What about skin and blood from my nails? Everyone in bar see I take from Sonny Petruzzi. Thank God I not cut nails for two weeks. When skin from Sonny match with Simona's scratch, we are on top of mountain." He rested his head against the wall and closed his good eye. A warrior at peace with himself.

Stan gave me a doubting look. "I don't know what they'll be able to do with that in court." He looked around to see who was listening. We were in a small, windowless room with a metal table, one chair, the bench, and countless gray metal filing cabinets. The walls were painted baby blue. There was no one to listen, but Stan has always been the cautious type. He leaned forward and dropped his voice.

"Thanks, Dmitri, for supplying a reason to bring them in."

Dmitri snored. Stan offered to have a cop take me

back to the hotel. I refused. "Sonny will break any minute. I know it."

Stan kissed my forehead and left the room. It was his turn to interrogate. I grabbed my crutches and went looking for Raf. I found him crunching his knuckles over a pizza box in the squad room.

"Simonita, you look beat." He offered a chair and a slice of pepperoni pizza. I took both.

"I need a favor," I said.

"Nothing on the garment-center case. You know I can't."

"I just want everyone's address. Victim, suspects." I didn't want to let on that I was only interested in Roberta. "Addresses all the way back to their births, if you've got them. Come on, Raf, you're not giving away secrets. I could ask for those addresses at Riddle Solutions, but I don't want to raise any questions. I could also dig up those addresses, but that would take forever."

"Why do you want 'em?"

"To test a theory about the past and people who don't fit well together. Like Sonny and Victor. They're an unlikely pair."

"They're both dumb. My hunch is that Sonny offered Victor the info about Anna Delgado wanting to rub him out for a price. Then Victor gets the idea to take it a step farther so he can get rid of his wife without having to kill her. Victor had some money, and Sonny's hungry. He hasn't had an acting job in two years. Simonita, I gotta go. This pizza's for him. After Stan gets through with him, he'll be real hungry."

"Is Stan that cruel?"

"No, Stan wouldn't hurt a roach, you know that. He just gets to be like a piece of ice. You've seen that, when he gets mad."

"Luckily, I haven't."

"Good. He does the reality bit, you know, how many

years the jury will give the guy, what happens to men and their spirits while they're in jail, not to say anything about their rear ends. All matter-of-fact, no emotion showing. Stern father bit. Most of the people we see in here don't know from father, or if they had one, they want to forget him. Stan leaves them feeling that they don't have a friend in the world. Then I come along and feed them the fantasies. When you got something on your chest, the fantasy looks real good and you buy it. Stan's the real salesman. He gets them to buy what I have to offer."

"It sounds cruel."

"Maybe it is to you, but what most of 'em have done out there would make you puke. Now I gotta go."

I didn't ask for the addresses again. Don't belabor a point, Raf had taught me. Stan had taught me something too. Raf, as a cop, had one weakness. He wanted to be liked.

I swung myself back to the little room where Dmitri was sleeping. An hour later Sonny hadn't broken down. I needed a bed. Dmitri still snored.

Stan saw me into the backseat of an unmarked police car. My pink leg looked like a wad of bubble gum retreived from under a desk. My broken fibula throbbed and I had a blinding headache. I was going back to the hotel. I still had to hide. Stan didn't know how much longer he could get away with holding Victor and Sonny. Once out, they might be stupid enough to want revenge.

I focused on Sonny just as the car doors slammed shut. Sonny, the actor. I had, in Rome, dubbed films for a living. Actors had been part of my life. Most of them are volatile, vulnerable, egotistical children. When they're working, the director is God or Mother. But Sonny was jobless.

The police car took off. I waved at Stan and shouted, "Get ahold of his acting teacher!"

22

―――――― ◦━✦━◦ ――――――

Sonny broke down at four o'clock on Monday morning.
Stan brought the news himself at seven-thirty along
with what he insisted on calling a *latte,* which in Italian
means milk and which turned out to be coffee and
milk, *caffè latte.*

"Americans have this mania for shortening everything!" I hobbled to the bathroom, brushed my teeth,
and splashed water on my face. Look good! I commanded my reflection.

"That's in the interest of efficiency. Do you want to
complain or hear about Sonny?"

I got back into bed and pulled Stan down. His eyes
were creased with fatigue, his shirt smelled of second-
hand smoke and pizza sauce, and his breath was stale.
My reflection had refused to obey, which made Stan
and me even. I gave him a long kiss. "When do I get out
of here? I have to go and defend my job. Never mind,
I'll tell you later." I pushed Stan back into the chair and
picked up my *caffè latte.* "Tell me everything."

"The acting teacher turned it around for us. She told

228

me he was stuck, an actor who'd lost his lines. She went back into that room and got him to do an improvisational exercise. 'Use your anxiety,' she told him. I thought I was in for a long night of nothing, but actors are crazy. He finally let it all out. He met Anna Delgado in a bar a couple of times. They got friendly. She got sloshed one night and asked him if he'd kill her husband for her. She even offered money, that's the part the waitress overheard, but Sonny knew it was just wishful thinking. She even admitted it was a joke later, unfortunately when the waitress couldn't hear her. Anna hated Victor's guts but she'd never harm a hair on his head.

"Sweet Sonny thought he might make a few bucks out of Anna's ambivalent sentiments and called Victor up at the gym from a pay phone. Victor met him down on Mott Street in Chinatown, where he was pretty sure no one would spot them, paid him a twenty to hear what Anna had said about him, then offered five hundred dollars if Sonny would teach Anna a lesson. The lesson was to scare her into thinking he'd really killed Victor. Sonny, none too bright, went along, and when the lesson got serious Victor threatened to have him knocked off. Sonny was too scared to pull out."

"You got all this from an improv exercise?"

"The first part. The acting teacher, Rita, she played Anna. That helped."

"Is this going to hold up in court?" I hopped back to the bathroom and turned on the shower. The thought of freedom was making me itchy.

"Not the acting part." Stan sat on the spot I'd vacated. "Sonny felt like a heel after acting out the scene with Rita as Anna—Rita started crying, she's really good. He adores her. Now we have a deal, a confession, and two arrests."

"And I'm gone from here." I undressed. From the bedroom I heard something about tomorrow and bail.

Bail! I shuddered and wrapped a tall garbage bag around my cast, tied it up with string, set a stool in the shower stall, and stepped in. Freedom and my first shower in four days! Bliss—or as the Romans say, *me va l'acqua pe' l'orto*. Water was running down my orchard.

By the time I got out, a good fifteen minutes later, Stan was fast asleep on the bed. On his chest, underneath his folded hands, a folded sheet of paper. I covered Stan with the bedspread, kissed him good-bye, scribbled a note as to where I'd be, and slipped the sheet out. Raf, the good cop, had come through. I had my addresses.

Roberta had lived at the same address on Fifth Avenue since 1966 except for an eighteen-month period when she had lived with her mother. And her mother had lived in Brooklyn Heights, on Pierpont, one block from the Promenade where Charlie had recovered his baby memories. My Roberta-Charlie-mother-son theory was tightening.

Back home, I called Charlie's mother. No answer. I tried Dmitri's apartment in Brighton Beach. I got the answering machine, the message delivered in English and Russian. I tried his cellular phone. It didn't even ring. I called the apartment back and left a message. The bad guys were in jail. I was free. He would understand the implications. His bodyguard services were no longer needed.

I didn't stop to think about how I'd miss him.

I got dressed in my power suit, an Armani knockoff I'd nursed along for five years, and headed for HH&H.

I gathered my immediate boss, Bertrand Monroe, who was the head of the creative department. He had been shooting an ad in London and didn't know the new developments. I gathered Linda. I gathered all the print ads I had collaborated on, the letters of thanks from stylists and photographers for pulling white rabbits out of hats. Once I had my defense assembled, I ushered everyone and everything to the seventeenth floor and Harold Harland, the baseball-capped lord of the manor.

I gave the most heartfelt presentation the agency has ever produced. At the end, after the letters and the ads, I shamelessly listed my good points: unrelenting enthusiasm, quick on the uptake (if preceded by enough sleep), tireless energy, can shift direction with the wind (a necessity in advertising), follows orders well (if orders make sense), understands and is supportive of the creative mind (they're all nuts—the creative director gave a nod), a good manager (Linda hid her face behind a Kleenex), and an excellent delegator (Linda nodded far too vigorously).

"What more can I say? I hate manuals, rules, statistics. I love what's crazy and awe-inspiring. If I leave I'm going to miss the creative department, and what's more important to you"—I flinched at being so brazen—"the creative department is going to miss me!"

"Besides," Linda said, putting her Kleenex away carefully. "I'm pregnant."

We left the two stunned bosses in the top corner room with its chrome and onyx desk and the jade plant the size of Dmitri and went back to our cubicles to work. I called Roberta to announce that I was back on the case. I got Charlie instead.

"Did you see *WWD*? The little belt. It's all about the little belt. Retro's genius." Charlie's voice was high and edgy above a flow of opera. "Roberta's right on. That's what her whole collection is about. Nostalgia. Neoconservative chic, Norwich calls it." He laughed. "I told you, instant fame."

"Where is she?" I had hunches, half-formed ideas that might explain Roberta stealing Phyllis's gold necklace. Those hunches did not clear her of suspicion, but she had hired me and I, like Charlie, hold on to the old-fashioned notion of loyalty. "I have to talk to Roberta about Phyllis's death!"

"You don't understand, do you? In twenty-eight hours we're sending our life down that catwalk. And those bastards, the retailing directors, the critics, they're going to take a quick, smug look and decide whether we live or die. Phyllis? Who's Phyllis?" He started to hang up.

"Your lover, Mark," I screamed.

"What?"

"Can you produce the letter he wrote to you?" In the background, Flossie was yelling at Mario. "The one you didn't want the police to see."

"No."

Flossie declared herself deaf. A blast of *I Pagliacci* hit my ear.

"There was no letter from Mark that day," I said. "Phyllis wrote to you."

"No! Why should she?"

"You paid her thirty thousand dollars. You tell me."

"Darlings!" That was Roberta, her voice like water on fire. The radio faded into the background. Mario apologized. Lourdes giggled. I pictured Flossie squaring her shoulders and getting back to the business of sewing. A happy family.

"Let me talk to Roberta."

"No! I don't have the letter, but I know it was Mark. He told me he still loved me, but he was scared. That's it. He still loved me."

"Was it your idea to have Roberta pick up your mail the day after the murder?"

"What difference does it make? I mean, we discussed it together first. Mark had told me he was going to write, to explain things. I didn't think my love life was cop business, so I gave Roberta the keys. And then you tagged along."

"And you destroyed Mark's letter?"

His voice got even closer, a dry whisper. "She never let me see it."

"Then how do you know what the letter said?"

"Roberta told me, then she burned it. She had to. The cops came to her place, too."

"And the letter from Happy Futures, did she let you see that?"

"Yeah, she handed that over. Unopened."

Of course she had. Roberta knew the agency couldn't tell him anything. New York was a closed-record state. Phyllis's letter was a different matter. She had probably written out the truth.

"Are you adopted, Charlie?"

He hung up. Before I could redial, Bertrand Monroe appeared in my doorway. His handsome face was glum.

I dropped the receiver, eyes on my creative director. "What's my destiny?"

"You made a great presentation. I told him you were indispensable." Pause.

"Yeeees?"

Bertrand broke into a grin. "You stay, and you have the week off. That pink cast seemed to have moved him."

I blew him a kiss. "*Grazie* from my heart." I buzzed Linda. She congratulated me. I buzzed Gregory. He offered a party. That instant. With wine and chocolates.

Stan I saved for later.

After celebrating my escape from the realm of the Living Dead, I went back to my office and tried Riddle Solutions again. This time I got Flossie.

"You okay? How's the leg? Who's trying to kill you?"

"How did you find out about that?"

"You get run over by a car that doesn't stop and we

don't know? In the building here they're saying Phyllis's killer is after you for asking questions."

"This has nothing to do with Phyllis. Somebody is trying to get back at my lover."

"The homicide cop? Smart choice you made. Instead of protecting you, he gets you killed. I gotta go."

"I want Charlie."

"Charlie just left."

"Roberta, then."

A reproving sigh, then the sound of rustling. "Simona wants to talk to you."

Roberta's voice floated over. "*Domani*. Tell her *domani*, after the show. Did she get my invitation?"

"I got it."

Flossie came back to the phone. "She's *meshugga*, got her battle hat on. She's been rehearsing the show all weekend. At the tent. It's like the Bellevue psycho ward in here. I can't hear myself sew. Now she wants to do another edit. That green suit you like so much? It's hitting the wall as I talk. If you're a size six, it's yours, but believe me, better you shouldn't come. You could end up against the wall, too." Another sigh. A short one. "Maybe you're not a size six."

"Yes, I am." If I ate steamed broccoli for a month. Maybe. "Phyllis always wore a gold chain around her neck. I saw it on her the night she died. Was anything hanging from that chain?"

Flossie paused. Much too long a pause. "What's to hang from a chain? A star of David, that's what."

"What about a key?"

She sniffed, cleared her throat. "Never saw a key." She wasn't very good at lying.

"Flossie, I can find out just by asking the others. Someone will tell me the truth."

"The woman's dead. Let her rest in peace."

"What about her murderer?"

"So she carried a key close to her heart. Not a big heart, but still, does a key get you justice?"

If not justice, a little more light on the players. Roberta had stolen the key from Phyllis's neck because it unlocked a drawer, a safe-deposit box, whatever. And in that whatever, Phyllis kept information that she had used against Roberta for all these years. Information about Charlie. A copy of a birth certificate, perhaps, or proof that Roberta had checked into a maternity ward. A photograph of Roberta pregnant.

Roberta wanted to destroy the evidence. With Phyllis dead in front of her, she had seized her chance.

Did that mean she was not a murder suspect? Probably. Unless, after killing Phyllis, she had heard a noise, panicked, and run away without the key. Only to get the chance later. It was a possibility I didn't like.

I thanked Flossie, hung up, and called Mrs. Angelo again. I would have preferred to chat with her *a quattr'occhi*—at four eyes. But Dmitri was unreachable, cast plus crutches made getting in and out of subways a risky business, and the cab ride would have cost fifteen dollars. Besides, my presentation to the CEO had left me exhausted. Not to mention that after three days of painkillers, the glass of wine I'd just imbibed at my survival party had me wondering who had filched the floor. A conversation over the phone would have to do.

Mrs. Angelo was finally home.

I introduced myself, she remembered my messages. "I'm sorry I didn't call you back, but with this death in Charlie's company, and the police coming in and out, it's got the whole neighborhood nervous."

I tried to reassure her. I explained that Roberta and Charlie were my clients. That Roberta was nervous, too. I was trying to help.

"Charlie's done nothing wrong. Why are they picking on him?"

"Nothing's over until the police find the murderer, Mrs. Angelo. Forgive me, but I need to ask a very private question."

"Charlie's a good boy. Always has been." She had a warm voice. "He can't help himself, you know? Tell that to the police. It's not something you can choose, who you love. It's just something that happens."

"My question has nothing to do with Charlie's sexuality."

"Then what? What is it?" I could cut week-old bread on the edge of her voice. "What do you want?"

"I was wondering if Charlie was adopted."

"Who said that? Who told you that? You been talking to Dominic? Don't believe a word of it. My brother-in-law says that 'cause he can't face havin' a gay nephew. Let me tell you something, I'm proud of my son. He's a good man, and you can't say that about too many people these days. You tell the police Charlie's the fruit of my loins. Eight pounds, seven ounces' worth!" she yelled. "And if they don't believe me, I got a birth certificate to prove it and the midwife who can still show you the marks where I bit her."

"I'm sorry to upset you, Mrs. Angelo." I had been so sure, and in my eagerness to prove myself right I hadn't cared whom I trampled.

"My Charlie is blood." Mrs. Angelo's voice leveled off. "Why did you think he's adopted?"

I told her about the Happy Futures letter I'd found in his mailbox, about my visit to the adoption agency.

"Charlie, what does Charlie say?" She had started to cry.

"He hung up on me."

"He's looking for his real mom. He knows. How does he know? Oh, God, he'll never forgive me."

"There's nothing to forgive. Charlie talked about you a week ago, the day I picked up his mail. He knew then. Here, in my office, he told me what a great mother he had. I'm not making it up, Mrs. Angelo."

"He said that? A great mother?"

"The best."

She blew her nose. "My husband made me swear I wouldn't tell. He said Charlie wouldn't love us if he knew. We moved down to Argentina, 1969 it was. Two years we were down there, my husband working for a trucking company. Time enough to produce a baby. When we got back to New York with Charlie, no one asked nothing except how much he weighed and did I have a hard time with the birth. A year later my husband quit us."

"You got Charlie in Argentina?"

"A private adoption through the church. How am I gonna tell Charlie after twenty-six years?"

"Just the way you told me. Maybe something good will come of my meddling," I said, trying to feel less like a heel. I apologized again, even told her my suspicions about Roberta being Charlie's mother.

"That's right, the inheritance," Mrs. Angelo said. "Charlie's been trying to figure it out since the old lady died. Maybe that's why he started thinking he's adopted. I keep telling him it's because he's good at his job, but he don't believe me."

"Roberta's mother lived in Brooklyn Heights," I said. "A block away from the Promenade that Charlie loves and which seems to bring back childhood memories for him. That's another reason I thought Roberta and Charlie were connected."

"Every Sunday, after the divorce, the Promenade's where my husband took Charlie. For ice cream and a stroll. For about two years. Then my husband moved back to Argentina, and we haven't heard a peep out of him since. Poor Charlie. How'm I gonna tell him?"

23

────────── ◦═╋═◦ ──────────

Dmitri called before I had a chance to piece my thoughts together.

"Phyllis file white paper. No words."

"You're at St. Vincent's?"

"In my office." The car. "Woman agree to look for information about my kidney in file. I wait twenty-four minutes. When she come back she show me empty paper."

"Has she shown the file to anyone else recently?"

"She does not remember. I call in other employee, make big fuss. My kidney will kill me. Other employee woman big like me. She says to me, 'Lower voice,' and she says, 'No, no one ask for file in past year.' I believe her because paper yellow on edges. It has been in file long time."

I didn't know where that got us. Why would Phyllis go and clean out her file? Assuming it was Phyllis. Anyone could forge a permission slip. Phyllis's handwriting looked easy to copy. A few curlicues would convince the reader. What was in that file worth stealing or hiding?

I thanked Dmitri and told him I wouldn't be needing him anymore.

"I stay on."

"I can't afford to pay you anymore."

"You give me hair."

"I like my hair."

"How do you solve case without me?"

I could picture his mustache sagging with disappointment. "It's going to be hard, Dmitri, but I just don't have that kind of money."

"Ask Roberta."

"She doesn't want me investigating anymore." Besides, she had stolen a key from Phyllis's body and I didn't know why. Which made me nervous. I thanked Dmitri again, asked him to add up what I owed, and I would send him a check. "I'll miss you," I added, meaning it.

"Tell your woman friends about Dmitri. I pay good money."

I said I would and, for a moment of sheer nastiness, pictured myself sneaking up on Stan's ex and chopping off her blond locks. The moment passed guilt-free and Dmitri and I vowed to call each other at the end of the week. Maybe for a coffee and a vodka in Brighton Beach. We hung up.

I called Sally Mannucci at the Très Français showroom. We made a date to meet in an hour at Barney's on Madison and Sixty-first.

"I've been in retail. They don't have to get snotty with me. You'd think I was trying to sell them crap!" Sally shook a shoulder-length mass of bottle-bright red hair. "Our line of evening dresses is in Lord & Taylor, Saks, Bergdorf's, Neiman Marcus. Barney's? God forbid! The buyer took one look at the colors of the samples and just shook her head. A shaved head, I want you to know. She thinks that's fashion. A shaved head and brown knit from neck to toe. She looked like my mother's crochet hook, is what she looked like." Sally was dressed in a tight purple and green knit suit, diamond studs in her ears, and a Gucci flowered scarf that almost covered the neck wrinkles her plastic surgeon had missed. She was about five foot five, late forties fighting for late thirties, with a pointy, bottle-tanned face and expertly applied makeup. She must have weighed all of one hundred pounds. We were sitting upstairs at Mangia on Fifty-seventh Street instead of mad.61, Barney's hot food stop, as originally planned. She was that angry.

"I told the buyer fashion is color this year! Milan, Paris, New York. Color! But for Barney's, nothing doing. They're so blind in there, I can't stand it!" She sniffed at her grilled vegetable plate. Inhaling aromas, I suspect, was Sally's idea of nourishment.

"The baby," I prompted, and did as the restaurant's name commanded. I ate, biting into penne glistening in a light tomato and shrimp sauce. They were cooked to perfection.

"The baby! That's right. You wanted to know about that poor girl. I don't know why I came up with this baby idea. It just popped out, and I couldn't remember where it came from. Mom didn't know. So I called my usual pool of girlfriends. My friend Marie, I've known her since nursery school, she thinks she remembers that the poor girl was pregnant when Phyllis killed her with the car."

"The papers would have mentioned that. Human interest, whip up sympathy for the victim."

"Not if no one told them. I mean, she was eighteen or something. And not married. This was back in the sixties. It was nothing to brag about back then.

Anyway, it doesn't matter, because my friend Janice, remember I told you about her, she graduated from high school with Eddie, my husband. Janice is more dependable than Marie, she's got a Master's in English and she teaches now in Palm Springs. Janice remembers that the girl had already had the baby and had put it up for adoption just before the accident. Is that any help?"

"I really don't know, but thanks for asking around."

Sally clawed purple nails in the air for a waiter. "Refill. Decaf. Whoever it is should get off. I let Phyllis know what I thought of her while I was working for Roberta. 'If you even look at my Eddie, I'll file my nails on your eyeballs,' that's what I told her."

I eyed her grilled vegetables. "Phyllis went after your husband?"

A nail speared a black olive. "Saul had just died. I just wanted to make sure. That warning works like a charm." The olive got flicked back on the plate. "You wanna hear something funny? You know who told Janice about the baby? Phyllis. Can you believe? Then I checked with Marie. She remembers now. It was Phyllis who told her, too. Wouldn't it be something if the baby grew up and bumped Phyllis off?" She laughed. "Now tell me what happened to you and your poor leg. I love that pink. Pink's in this year."

"Someone's after me."

Her eyes popped. "Wait till Mom hears this. How after you? To kill you?"

"Maybe. You see, I live with a homicide cop and these two—"

"Oh, my God, a cop! My friend Irma is dating one of those, and he's got these handcuffs—" She went on about Irma's sexual kinks. She went on about wanting Eddie since the minute he walked into study hall. She went on about the soaps having too much sex. She went on about fixing me up with her cute aerobics instructor, the last with a pointed look at my waistline.

I finished my penne, I finished her grilled vegetables, I finished a poached pear and two cups of decaf coffee. She went on.

"DimSim," Dmitri announced. He was waiting for me outside my office building, Cadillac in tow. He flourished a business card. This one a subdued silver on white. Cyrillic on one side, English on the other. He read the card to me. "DIMSIM, DMITRI-SIMONA DETECTIVE AGENCY. FIRST CONSULTATION FREE. My phone number. No address. We work from Cadillac. If you want, I make Italian card, too." The sight of him in the entrance, looking like a Samson about to bring down the temple, warmed my heart. "For Roberta case, no money. Friendship better."

"Friendship you've got. I'm still going to pay you."

"No, we are team. You are heart of bread, me the crust. We go far." He walked to the curb and opened the backseat of the Cadillac.

"No, front seat," I said. He grinned and threw his files and magazines in the back. I got in, slowly, with his help. My crutches joined the mess in the backseat. "DimSim sounds like we're offering dumplings. Why not the reverse?"

He got into the driver's seat. "Who comes last more important."

We both laughed, happy to be together again, and headed for the Brooklyn Queens Expressway, on our way to Long Island. It felt wonderful to be out, on the move again with my new friend, tires splashing through puddles from last night's rain, Manhattan a study in distant grays. The sky ahead of us reminded me of one of Roberta's fabric swatches—"Blue Innocence."

"I'm glad I met you, Dmitri Yakov Karamasov. Or whatever your last name is." I meant it. I liked his humor, his generosity, and his heart.

Dmitri confessed that he was lonely. He missed Russia but had left because he was in love with Pavel's wife. Yes, the woman who had forgotten the suitcase full of hair because she was too anxious. She loved him back.

"With excuse of hair, she come every year. With excuse of buying hair, every year I go back to Moscow. When we together, after six months when I do not see the color of her eyes, after six months when blood has dried in my heart, we look at each other and talk. No more. My blood goes again—it goes too much. We do not dare kiss. Because after kiss . . . how can I betray my brother?"

"That's very noble of you."

He agreed. "I read romance novel not because of good English. English is better in Shakespeare. I read because in story, my life ends good."

"Oh, I hope so, Dmitri." I planted a kiss on his cheek. "Well. Your life will end well. Shakespeare's English."

"I hope your mouth is true." He smiled. "Now tell me why we go to Manorhaven."

"That's where Lourdes's mother lives. The girl Phyllis killed also came from Manorhaven." I relayed what Sally had told me and my conversation with Mrs. Angelo.

"We back to first square."

"I like to think we just took a wrong turn and are now back on the road." Mrs. Orengo was expecting me at four-thirty.

"You think Lourdes dead girl's baby?"

"At this point I'm scared to commit to any thought. I was so sure about Charlie, I could taste it. Lourdes could be the missing baby. She's the right age, she's Hispanic like the dead girl, but then so is half of New York."

"But Phyllis bring her to Riddle Solutions. We go to Manorhaven and find out why."

"Right on, Dmitri."

Manorhaven, Incorporated Village, is on a curved finger of Long Island that reaches out into the Sound. The town, mostly blue collar, is surrounded by what was once Gatsby country—sprawling, gated estates with water views and velvet lawns the size of Central Park. In recent times the old estates had been broken up and the new homes had eight bedrooms instead of sixteen.

Lourdes's mother, Mrs. Orengo, lived on Coxwood Road. Her front lawn was pizza-box size compared to what we had seen along the waterfront, but the narrow frame house covered in cedar shingles and trimmed in white was the prettiest on the block.

" 'ector!" A flow of Spanish accompanied the chimes I'd just rung. I was alone. Dmitri had suggested that the delicate subject matter of adoption required an intimate approach. That was after he had spotted Razzano's Bakery two blocks away, a food haven that could rival Balducci's. He was stuffing himself, and I was sweating. I didn't want to make another woman cry.

Mrs. Orengo opened the door. "Excuse me," she said, running after a two-year old boy, Lourdes's son. " 'ector, you kill Pookie!" Hector was beetling after a gray and white cockatiel. The bird hid under the sofa.

"*Mi vida!*" She lifted Hector up, a round-faced boy with black straight hair and cheeks red enough to make Charles Dickens proud. She spun him in the air. "*Mi amor!*" The boy laughed. She picked up a toy fire truck, wound it, and unloaded both boy and truck in the corridor. The truck wailed and sped toward the kitchen. Hector went after it, diapered bottom swaying.

Mrs. Orengo gave me a smile that made me want to settle in permanently. She didn't look anything like Lourdes. Her face was square, not round, with sharp cheekbones and a long, hooked nose. Where Lourdes was soft and pretty, she was strong and handsome, with salt-and-pepper hair tied in an elegant bun at the nape of her neck. She wore a hot-pink jogging outfit that could have come straight from Mannucci Sportswear. Her figure showed that she didn't use it only to lounge in. She was much older than I had expected. Well past sixty.

We sat down in the small living room on the black leather sofa. The birdcage rested on the coffee table, next to a pile of just-laundered cloth diapers. I could smell the softener. The windowsills were filled with toys. On the striped wallpaper, enlarged photos of Manhasset Bay.

"I take photography class," Mrs. Orengo said after offering coffee or a soft drink, both of which I declined. "Before Lourdes have 'ector. Now he is full-time employment." She had a strong accent. "You said you need 'elp with this 'orrible murder?" She seemed eager, curious, open.

I started out with Gloria Hernandez and the accident. Raf's address list had told me that Lourdes had grown up in this house. Maybe Mrs. Orengo had lived here back in 1967?

"No, we live in Port Washington. Seven minutes from this 'ouse, fifteen minutes from the accident. *Povrecita* Gloria!" She stopped smiling. "I know her parents good. They dead now. One cancer, the other heart." The bird flew to her shoulder.

I mentioned the rumors about Gloria being pregnant.

"Who say Gloria 'ave baby?" Hector waddled back in, eyed the bird, and started climbing on his grandmother's lap.

"Phyllis Striker, the dead woman."

"Gloria no 'ave baby. What does Miss Striker know of Gloria? I know Gloria. I see her almos' every week. She no 'ave belly." She wound another toy, a sports car this time, and sent Hector barreling after it. The bird got slipped back into the cage. She looked at me, her face furrowed. "No baby. Jus' the tragedy."

"Phyllis Striker. She was known as Phyllis Cirni at the time of the accident."

Mrs. Orengo dropped back against the sofa. "Phyllis Striker, the woman who 'elp my daughter get the job, is Phyllis Cirni, the woman who kill Gloria?" She looked horrified.

"One and the same."

"I no recognize 'er from the pictures in the paper. I no recognize 'er." She sounded angry with herself.

"It was a long time ago."

"But I know 'er! I see 'er in the face. After she come out of the jail. In Pittsburgh. You see, Lourdes was a miracle. I was forty when I get pregnant. An old woman. And I go to my sister in Pittsburgh because I am scared I will lose my baby. My sister is the nurse in the 'ospital, she knows the doctors. So Lourdes is born in Pittsburgh, December eight, Conception day, 1970."

"1970? That would make her only twenty-six years old. Her job application says twenty-nine years old."

"Miss Striker tell her to write twenty-nine years old. Older. More experience. Easier to get job at Riddle Solutions, she say. It's a good job. Lourdes and 'er 'usband need the money." She assumed my understanding, my not telling.

"I don't think Roberta would care one way or the other," I assured her. "Why did Phyllis want Lourdes to lie?" I asked.

"I don' know." Hector was back, rattling the cage door.

"You said you knew Phyllis?"

Mrs. Orengo picked up her grandson and laid him on her lap as if he were a cat. In his cage the bird trilled. "Now, no. Lourdes jus' tell me about the model, Miss Striker, she works sometimes for Mr. Jacobs at 480. Lourdes work par'-time for Mr. Jacobs. Miss Striker promise her full-time job and get her job with Roberta Riddle." She lifted Hector by his feet. The boy yelled with delight. I would have thrown up lunch.

"I know Phyllis Cirni from Pittsburgh," Mrs. Orengo said, starting to tickle Hector. "Imagine, me and Gloria's killer in the same room in the maternity ward."

Hector was laughing so loud, I had to ask Mrs. Orengo to repeat what she'd said.

"Phyllis Cirni and me, we bring a baby into the world. She a boy, me my beautiful Lourdes. Life is tragic, but life is also funny, no?"

Hector thought so.

24

———— ❦ ————

"Willy, you're home!" Fifteen years old, five foot eight, with a natural, lanky grace that new muscle was beginning to harness, drooping blond hair, deep blue eyes hidden by corn-silk lashes, and freckles over a straight nose. A boy/man with his mother's lovely features. And now he was standing in Stan's kitchen again, with his father. With me.

"Bello mio!" I gave Willy a tight hug, which I knew he hated at his age, but I couldn't help myself. The crutches thumped to the floor. "I'm just so happy to see you!"

"Hey, watch it, you'll fall." Willy steered me to a chair. Stan watched, cheeks blazing with pride.

"The leg okay?"

"Fine, fine." I raised my hands, wanting to grab him again. Willy placed crutches in them instead. "You look great."

"Thanks. You, too."

"Liar." I squirmed. "How? Your mother . . . It's okay now?"

Willy popped open a Coke, looked at his dad, who was making noise with the plastic grocery bags. Why weren't we all screaming with happiness here? What was holding them back?

"Nothing's wrong? Your mom's okay?"

Willy flicked a lock back, took a long sip of Coke. "She's fine."

We were going nowhere fast. I offered food. Stan wanted to order in. Pizza or Chinese.

"Not even in your dreams. I'm cooking to celebrate." After the stunning announcement about Phyllis's baby— stunning only in showing me how wrong I had been— Dmitri and I had stayed in Manorhaven to splurge at Razzano's. A display of food clarifies my mind, and I had a lot of furious thinking to do. Dmitri had understood and been silent as we'd eyed rows of manicotti, lasagne, chicken balls, veal parmigiana, spinach rolls, eggplant rollups; watched the pizza man flour the counter and fist the dough; picked our way through bread sticks, bagels, and loaves. Tall boxes of *panettone* had already arrived for Christmas. A corner had been stacked with Halloween pumpkins and varnished gourds. With my head beginning to clear, I'd bought bacon, garlic, parsley, dried porcini mushrooms, a large can of Italian tomatoes, two pounds of wild mushrooms, and a pound of fresh pasta sheets. Dmitri had settled for three pounds of meatloaf with tomato sauce. If nothing else, we were going to be a well-fed team.

In my new kitchen I sat on a stool and peeled garlic cloves. Stan cleaned mushrooms. Willy hung out, making chitchat. Stan's eyes never got enough of the sight of his handsome son. Willy leaned against the window, drinking Coke, unaware of the love he generated. We talked about school, the hockey team, whether Steve Martin was funnier than Billy Crystal, and which cop show we preferred.

It felt good to be together, to make the chitchat of ordinary families, but Irene was with us, an univited guest. When the sauce was sputtering quietly in the pan and the pasta water was on, I took the plunge. "Does your mom know you're here?" I asked.

Willy let out a long, slow breath and sat down next to his dad. Stan looked frozen. I crinkled an onion skin.

"I had a long talk with her," Willy said. "That's what I wanted to talk about the other night, you know, when that car ran Simona over. I'd just told Mom, and I guess I was all excited and, I guess, scared, too, and I wanted to get it off my chest to all of you." He turned to me. "I saw you at the *Intrepid*."

"I tried to hide. I didn't want to embarrass you, but I did want to defend myself."

"Mom didn't like it much." His expression said that he hadn't liked it either. Loyalty demanded that he keep us separate. "She asked me if I would always love her. I said sure, why shouldn't I? Look, I don't want to talk about her. I've thought a lot about this. I've been worried about hurting Dad, Mom, and now you. I've been doing that since the divorce. That's a lot of responsibility, and I hate it. It's not fair."

Stan opened his mouth.

Willy raised his hands. "I'm not trying to lay on a guilt trip. I'm not. Really. All I'm saying . . . all I said to Mom was that I'm fifteen. It's my life, and I get to decide who I get to see. I want to be with my dad, my dad wants to be with me. And he also wants to be with you, and that's fine. In fact, it takes a load off my chest because I don't have to worry about spending all my free time with him. And I also told Mom that she's got to trust my judgment. I'm not going to do anything dumb. She understands. She really does. And she's a great mom and I'm always going to love her even if she has a fit if I want to drink a beer." He gave us a lopsided grin. "Besides, that stuff she's worried about, you know . . . "

"What stuff?" I asked.

Willy shuffled brand-new sneakers. "You know, the bed stuff. That's no big deal with you guys. Not at your age."

Stan and I made gentle love after Willy left that night. Not to prove Willy wrong. Another celebration. Afterward, I rested my head on Stan's stomach. The pink walls of the room radiated welcome. The soft bed embraced me. My leg had stopped hurting. My new bureau gleamed. We both felt relief, happiness, a sense that all would be right with the world.

"We're going to be fine, aren't we?" I said.

"No bail for Sonny and Victor." His fingertips circled my neck.

"Thank the heavens."

"I want you to stay away from the Riddle murder from now on."

"Why?"

"You could get hurt."

"I'm no threat to anyone. I haven't gotten one thing right since I started." I told him how I thought Roberta had been blackmailed by Phyllis, that Roberta had closed up shop for a year but that it was Phyllis who had given birth to a son, a son who couldn't be Charlie. I told him about how Phyllis had spread the word that the girl she had killed had a baby she'd given up for adoption. How Lourdes could have been Gloria's daughter but wasn't. Then I lay back on my pillow and let Stan rest his head on my chest.

I moved on to another theory, which had come while I sorted through shiitake and portobello mushrooms.

"It all revolves around that accident back in 1967. It makes no sense the way it was reported. How did

Phyllis drive herself into Manhattan bleeding as much as she did? Someone helped her. And if we find out—"

"Stop thinking about this case. Get Roberta's check. Tear it up."

"Are you kidding?" A queasy feeling settled in my stomach. "I cashed it."

"Tear it up mentally."

I sat up and turned on the lamp. "What are you going to do with Roberta? What? She didn't kill Phyllis! What about Phyllis's old boyfriend, the one who kept dodging you?"

"He has an airtight alibi. Playing poker in New Jersey with two cops."

"Then why did he keep slipping away?"

"Because he owes one of his ex-wives twenty thousand dollars in alimony."

"You can't arrest Roberta!"

"Kathy Breen's brother was released this morning, free of any charges. Kathy came forward and told us about the gold chain. Something you forgot to tell me in your exposition just now."

"I don't rat."

"Fair enough. We found out about the key. A key to a safe-deposit box in Phyllis's name in Elizabeth, New Jersey. Two weeks ago Roberta took home a bank form that would give her access to Phyllis's box. All she had to do was fill it out and forge the original signee's signature. Phyllis didn't have to present the form in person. Roberta now had access to the box. All she needed was the key."

"I told you, she was being blackmailed! Phyllis was lying there dead and Roberta saw an opportunity to help herself."

"Roberta saw an opportunity to transfer money. Five weeks ago a bank employee saw Phyllis open her box. It was one of the large ones, filled with stacks of hundred-dollar bills. When we got to the bank all we found was her birth certificate."

"Why did this bank employee wait a week to tell you?"

"He didn't tell us. We tracked it down. A new employee was on duty Monday morning. She'd never seen Phyllis in person. Roberta wore some ridiculous hat with concealing veils and the employee didn't make the connection."

"Do me a favor, please. Her show's tomorrow at noon. Guard her, follow her, confiscate her passport, but don't arrest her until afterward. Give Roberta her twenty minutes of glory."

Give me the time to prove you wrong.

25

―――――― ❦ ――――――

It was hot in the Josephine Pavilion. A blinding-white tent. Overcrowded. Photographers crouched along a muslin-covered catwalk like hungry frogs on a river's edge. Surrounding them, climbing rows of retailers and journalists sipped Evian water, waving programs to move hot air from one cheek to another. High in the back at least two hundred lesser mortals stood, gaping and gossiping. The required spattering of celebrities had shown up. Lauren Bacall, who was a friend of Roberta's from way back. Lauren Hutton swinging a red motorcycle helmet. Candice Bergen looking radiant. Facing the end of the catwalk, under a bank of searing spotlights, television cameras veered left and right, trying to catch the stars and the aristocracy of fashion. Across the catwalk, in the coveted first row were fashion editors Anna Wintour of *Vogue* with her signature sunglasses, *Harper's Bazaar*'s Liz Tilberis, Polly Mellon of *Allure*, John Fairchild of *WWD*. Ivana Trump was on my side, in the front row being cooled by the battery-powered fan of Bloomingdale's fashion director Kal Ruttenstein in silver sneakers. Ivana wore Gianni Versace. Her hair was a leaning Tower of Pisa.

Roberta Riddle had attracted the big time. Whether they were here to see fashion or gawk at a possible murderer, I couldn't tell. I picked up the latest issue of *Elle*—one of many sponsor favors—and fanned myself. Mr. Nite, sitting next to me, used his hat.

The show was supposed to have started at noon. It was now twenty past. There was no music, just the cicada buzz of dimming expectation and growing impatience. The heat and the wait were getting to be unbearable. The bulletproof vest I was wearing didn't help.

An unnecessary precaution, I'd told Dmitri. Most of the players in our little drama were backstage. Those who weren't couldn't get in. Trying to crash an "in" fashion show is next to impossible. Besides, the killer wasn't stupid enough to shoot me in front of eight hundred witnesses. Dmitri reminded me of political assassinations. A crowd was the best cover of all. I was to put on the vest or he would not let me go. His hand had dropped on my shoulder as a gentle persuader.

"Vests are all the fury in fashion," he added as an extra incentive. He'd heaped the vest on my shoulders. My knees had buckled. So had my will.

The vest was his, bought in Russia where they were selling out fast thanks to the crime wave freedom had brought. Dmitri's vest. Cut to his size. The color of sackcloth.

"Under, you will look thin," Dmitri said. "Kate Moss." I prefer sexy Claudia Schiffer as a role model, but instead of arguing, I had sheathed myself in a navy turtleneck sweater and black tights. The bulletproof vest I wore on the outside, for a Ninja Turtle effect, with my red AIDS Awareness ribbon pinned over my heart.

To the killer I seemed to be saying, "Aim for the head."

That Tuesday morning Dmitri and I had paid a visit to the Village Nursing Home, where an old emergency nurse had remembered only too well. We had then gone to Roberta's home on Fifth Avenue. While Dmitri walked the Chinese rugs of her living room like a bear treading on bees, I sat in a darkened bedroom.

"Your timing stinks, darling," she said. She was lying down on a brocade chaise longue, covered in a silk robe and turban. "Your boyfriend's is worse. He came at seven this morning. I'd just come home from the studio. Thank you for convincing him not to arrest me immediately. I've put my life into this show."

"I want you to answer two questions. The rest can wait. Was the money you took from Phyllis's safe-deposit box the blackmail money you had been paying her for twenty-eight years?"

"Phyllis never wanted money from me. She took my husband, then she took my integrity. Now she wanted the very soul of me. My work."

"Why did Charlie inherit forty percent of the business? I know he's adopted and that he was looking for his birth parents at Happy Futures."

She didn't answer.

"I spoke to Charlie's mother. I know he isn't your son, but he is connected to you in some special way. Please tell me the truth. I won't judge you for it."

"I know. That's why I asked you to help." The silk of her bathrobe rustled.

"Did Phyllis find out that Charlie was looking for his birth parents?"

"Yes." She swallowed. "She promised to help him for thirty thousand dollars. Then she gave him a picture of me holding a baby from a bris we had all attended. She was trying to convince Charlie that I was his mother. It was her way of amusing herself. After she gave him the picture, she wrote him a letter to that effect, the one you picked up. I destroyed it and gave Charlie some comfort about his lover instead."

"Why did he inherit?"

"He was young, adopted, gay. I hired him to make up for Saul's sins. And my own. After Saul had his first stroke, the doctor told him the next one was going to kill him. He was trying to stop Saul's smoking, his heavy eating, drinking. The warning only induced a confession."

She clicked on the lamp then, her face bare of makeup, yellowed by the light and too many years of being unhappy.

"What did he confess to?"

She wet her lips. "In 1970, while I was piecing my life together in Maine, Saul and Phyllis had a son. When the baby was six months old, Phyllis left the state and put him up for a private adoption without telling Saul. Eighteen years later, Saul got a letter from the boy's adoptive mother. The boy had AIDS. The family had no money left. Phyllis refused to help, but she'd given the woman Saul's name. Saul sent money. Then he flew out to Indiana to see his son. The boy died six months later."

She spoke to the garlanded ceiling. "Then when Saul died, I wanted to find someone I could help. I'd just lost my assistant designer to AIDS. I had a heavy conscience of my own. I looked and found Charles, full of talent and life. Elsa had no heirs of her own. Her health was failing. I suggested she leave him her share in the business. My own will, except for money left to Flossie, Mario, and Gay Men's Health Crisis, gives Charlie everything. He doesn't know this, of course." She looked at me with a faint smile. "I don't want to tempt him into bopping me over the head."

"Why did you steal the safe-deposit key?"

She looked at her watch. "You said only two questions. I'm on in two hours."

"You're finally talking."

"You can attribute my burst of honesty to preshow jitters. I didn't use the key to steal money. That was an added bonus. It was probably my husband's money, my money, that is, since Saul never earned more than change for cigarettes. I gave it back to your boyfriend this morning."

"You stole the key because Phyllis had incriminating evidence against you."

She clicked off the lamp, but not quickly enough for me to miss the wrenching despair in her eyes. "That's one too many questions."

"It wasn't a question." I stood up. I asked for three more passes to her show, then I made the rash promise that all would be solved by the end of the day.

I was pretty sure I knew who had killed Phyllis, but I had no proof. As soon as Dmitri assured me that his pals were standing by, I made a phone call. Filled with the fervor of clearing Roberta's name and proving my loved one dead wrong, I set a trap.

Now Dmitri, Mike, and Phil were standing guard high up in the rear of the tent. My partner had assured me that his aim was good. Exactly what I was afraid of.

The first ominous notes of *The Rite of Spring* silenced the audience. Heads turned to the backdrop, a heavy, unadorned white curtain. We were waiting for the first model to strut out. Instead the curtains parted, slowly, pompously. Mr. Nite clutched my hand.

Another backdrop. Black this time. Onstage a double row of sewing machines, cutting tables edged the sides. Tailors and seamstresses of varied ethnicities worked on flowing silver and gold fabric. Charlie, Mario, and Flossie flitted between garment workers.

Across the backdrop a large gold banner proclaimed: ALL I CAN KNOW IS WHAT I SEE, AND ALL I SEE IS WHAT YOU'RE WEARING.

Roberta appeared from behind the black curtain in

a white and black silk suit and a predatory black spider hat. She was smiling.

"Roberta is a genius," Mr. Nite whispered, tightening his grip.

The first model came out. The curtain stayed raised. She was wearing linen lime-green spiked sandals, no stockings. Huge purple-lace butterfly earrings. Her green-lace underwear would have done my collection proud. A green ball came flying through the air from behind me. I ducked, thinking of bombs. A few gasps. I peeked. The ball was a satchel. The model had caught it, shaken it open. A short, knit dress fell out. Standing in front of fifty popping bulbs, the model unfurled the dress over her head. She shook herself like a dog just out of the water. The dress slipped down, unwrinkled. Short, sassy, gossamer light, fitting tightly over her bodice and flaring at the hips. The model smiled. She turned one way, flicked to the other, swayed to the tip of the catwalk, swinging her satchel, paused, whisked herself around, and passed the next model, who was dropping another Riddle Nothings over her head, curry yellow this time.

The audience clapped. We didn't know where to keep our eyes. On the models, on the flying satchels, or backstage at the gut of the show. The music heightened its drama. We clapped louder with each satchel soaring through the air.

Riddle Nothings were followed by Roberta's signature suits in linen, raw silk, taffeta. Above-the-knee hemlines. An insistence on fitted waists, belts, and small shoulders. Butterfly buttons, small, big, made of metal, cloth, sequins. The models streamed down the runway already dressed this time, their walk more composed, their faces unsmiling until they reached the tip. They stopped in front of the TV cameras, pulled at their jackets. The fronts fell open. Underneath, wings unfolded over their breasts. Sheer silver, gold, copper wings as fragile-looking as real butterfly wings. The models flashed wicked smiles to the raucous sound of Stravinsky's sacrificial music and thunderous applause.

Then the traditional finale of all collections, the bridal gown. And another Roberta irony. The bride wore ocean waves of tulle topped by a high-cut, tight bodice of twisted silk rope. A beautiful, conservative design. Except the bride was short, stocky, and at least eighty years old. The curtain fell.

Everyone stood—except me, my cast, and my forty-pound vest. Everyone roared. The strobe lights exploded. Roberta came out to take her bow. She went back and pushed her staff out into the headlights of fame. She held Charlie's hand and gestured for the garment workers to rise. They stood and bowed in unison. Charlie shut his eyes and sighed. Flossie preened above her glasses. Lourdes looked like she might cry. Mario sucked his thimble finger. The rest of her staff clapped. Her models clapped. We clapped.

Roberta Riddle was a hit once more.

We poured backstage. I hopped, that is; everyone else pushed and shoved. I had graduated from crutches to cane, and I used my instrument to try to clear a path to the queen. The vest and my cast gave me no breaks. A spry Mr. Nite managed to reach Roberta first. Speechless, he kissed both her hands. She hugged him. The crowd of congratulators separated them. Bees sucking up to the honey of success. Cheeks brushing cheeks. Lips kissing air. Champagne corks popping, bubbles spilling. Bodies pressing. I joined the fray, with Dmitri and Muscles, Inc., not far behind.

"You have shown us the soul of fashion," someone declared above the noise.

"Major!" a woman behind me shouted.

Roberta flapped hands in the air. "No more riddles. They have flown away."

Like hell they have. I lunged for a champagne glass. I was hot, thirsty, scared. My gift bottle of designer water was finished and was now tickling my ribs in the form of sweat. In the next few hours my trap would spring. *Mamma!*

I had a mind to call Stan and tell him he could have Roberta on a spit. I was out of the case. I didn't want to get hurt, die, whatever. Why was I so persistently dumb?

Just as my hand touched a cool stem, an arm pushed me back. The champagne moved on without me. I was left facing Jerry.

My stomach clenched. "How did you get in here?"

"I worked for the woman until last Thursday, remember?" Jerry sneered. "I got a pass. I gotta talk to you."

"Go ahead."

"Not here. If Roberta sees me, she'll chuck me out." He lowered his eyes. "Some outfit you're wearing. Those guys still after you, huh?" His eyes gleamed as though he was ready to take a swipe at me right then and there.

"I had nothing to do with your getting fired, and I'm not leaving."

"You're too scared to come with me?"

My eyes searched for Dmitri. Phil. Mike.

"All right, I'll talk to you right here in the middle of these bozos. I want you to tell Roberta something. Your cop friend, too, while you're at it. Jerry don't handle dog shit. I stomp on roaches. I stay away from rats. You tell her that. I might have snitched a few ideas now and then to make ends meet, but that's only because she worked us to the bone and never paid us enough. But revolting tricks aren't my style."

"If not you, then who?" Were the boys watching me? Was Dmitri's gun cocked? I shivered at the thought. "Who, Jerry?"

"Phyllis. May she rest in peace."

It made sense. It fit into the plan. "How do you know?"

"That dead rat you found? She brought it in a plastic bag. I saw her."

I spotted Dmitri, ten feet behind Jerry. I couldn't see his hands. A crush of people filled the space between us. I slowly shook my head. My message not to make a move. "Why didn't you tell Roberta?"

Jerry grabbed a champagne bottle from a passing model and handed it over. I took a long swig.

"Phyllis caught me snitching a design once," Jerry said. "She didn't let me know until the knockoff got made. Then she brought in the dress and made this big deal in the studio. Her subtle way of letting me know she was on to me. You gotta tell Roberta, I didn't plant that rat!"

"I'll tell her. I can't promise the rest."

"I may be a thief, but I'm not scum. That's all I want her to know." He started to walk away, taking the half-empty champagne bottle with him. Halfway down the catwalk, he stopped. "You can tell Charlie something, too. He's good. I just don't like him." Jerry left the catwalk with a jump and wove his way through the emptying chairs.

The gang closed in on me. In full fashion gear. Which meant dressed entirely in black, topped by Armani sunglasses. The little round ones that make you look as if your eyes have been punched out.

"All is sunshine?" Dmitri asked.

"Not a cloud in the sky. You didn't have your gun out, I hope." I had visions of a gunshot soaring through the air like one of Roberta's satchels. I could hear and smell the ensuing stampede. And all because I had come up with one of my brilliant ideas. Actually, it had been Dmitri's. Hadn't it? I wasn't sure. French bubbles were bursting my gray cells. "Did you have your gun out?"

Dmitri frowned. "Trust me."

Mike flexed his smile. "I was right behind you."

"I was covering your flank," Phil said, his head nodding next to Mike's. "And I don't need a gun." He crunched bone. His own.

"Great. I just wanted to make sure you were all on your toes. The afternoon is young. Now let's form a discreet huddle and barrel our way to one of those Port-o-Sans at the very back of the tent. I have to tinkle."

"Yeah, me, too."

"That water really gets to me."

"I drink only champagne." That was Dmitri. He was wincing, the urge obviously great. "Champagne is worst."

There were four Port-o-Sans. Ladies first didn't apply to my stalwart guards when it came to relieving themselves. Nor did my safety. In unison, they pushed themsleves into the three available toilets. With an unerring instinct, I'd picked one in use. "Dmitri, you're fired!" I yelled out just as the door to my Porto-o-San opened. A Chanel-clad and perfumed woman started to come out. She took one look at me and changed her mind, slamming the door shut and clicking the lock.

Before I could figure out why, a slap knocked my cane out of my hand. Metal tapped the nape of my neck. An arm crossed my chest and hugged. "If you scream, you're dead." My bladder froze.

"What is it about toilets that gets you into murderous rages?" I asked.

"Shut up!" Another tap. Hard enough to jerk my head forward. In that blinkered crowd there wasn't much chance of being noticed. Besides, my hair was an unruly long mass covering my neck. Even if the gun did show, the makers and seekers of chic would only consider it an outmoded grunge accessory.

In other words, I was in something of a jam.

"Walk."

The voice was the one I had expected. What I hadn't expected was to have my three bodyguards caught in the toilet giving their masculinity a slap of fresh air.

"Walk out through that slit in front of you," Phyllis's killer commanded. The tear in the tent flap was only five feet away, behind the toilets.

"My cast," I protested. I felt myself rise a few inches above the ground. What was it about Bryant Park that didn't agree with me? And how long do men take to pee?

As the slit in the tent got nearer, I did what any self-respecting, unarmed woman encumbered with a pink cast would do in a similar situation. I faked a faint. Head drooped down and away from the muzzle of the gun. Knees buckled. My weight plus forty pounds of bulletproof vest fell against the hugging arm.

My assailant's head bent over my shoulder. The hugging arm tried for a better grip. In that fraction of a second of release, I lashed out and hit at what is most dear to an aging man.

He yelped, floundered backward, his arms grasping air in an attempt to catch his toupee. I twisted around and kicked at his shin with my cast. I screamed. For attention. From pain. He fell on his rear end. I was saved from crashing to the floor by Flossie's hefty arms.

My three musketeers, zippers at half-mast, jumped out of the toilets to save the day. Except Homicide Detective Stan Greenhouse was already there, gun aimed at our murderer. Bald, rage flushing his face, wearing a pin-striped suit and a tie that belonged in *Guys and Dolls*, Ed Mannucci spit curses at me. If Stan hadn't been such a gentleman, he would have joined him.

26

―――――― ❦ ――――――

While Stan ushered Ed to the precinct, Dmitri stripped me of his vest and carried me off to Roosevelt Hospital, moaning apologies in stunted English and flowing Russian all the way. I burped champagne bubbles. I laughed and clapped my hands to celebrate the success of my stunt. I ground my teeth against the pain. My kick had, in fact, refractured my fracture. I was given more Tylenol with codeine. My fibula was reset and I got a new cast. With the color of my choice. White for the purity of my intent. I reassured Dmitri that we were still partners.

Back at Mid-Town South, I made my statement and signed it. I had two corroborating witnesses. The Chanel-clad woman who had taken her time in the Port-o-San—she had locked herself back in at the sight of Ed Mannucci slipping a gun out of his pants pockets—and Flossie, who had seen Ed lift me off the ground. Assuming Ed was making a pass at me, she'd only been suspicious of his presence. Clothes manufacturers—too often tempted to copy what they had just seen—no longer made the invitation lists.

"If I'd seen a gun," Flossie stated, "I'd have taken it for a camera and knocked it right out of his fat hand."

And I would have been minus a neck.

I called Ed's wife, Sally. She'd helped me zero in on Ed and she'd let me eat her grilled vegetables. I felt I owed her. Ed called his attorney. Stan, without yet launching a word of reproof my way, booked Ed for attempted kidnapping and possession of an unlicensed weapon.

"Thanks for being there," I said after Ed was handed over to Raf's sweet-talking ways. We were sitting in the same windowless room with the baby blue walls I'd been in two days before. I made a mental note to bring a vase of flowers the next time. "Why were you?"

"I know you." He didn't look pleased.

I pointed out that Ed was our murderer.

"Evidence," Stan demanded.

"He came after me, isn't that enough? He thought he could kill me, and Victor and Sonny would get the blame. I was counting on that. If Flossie and Jerry knew about the hit and run, Ed Mannucci would know for sure. What they didn't know was that those two crooks were in jail. I set the trap over the phone this morning. I told Ed that I could prove he was Phyllis's lover and that he killed her."

"Evidence." Love him as I do, Stan can be monotonous.

"When I talked to Ed at Arno's the day after the murder, he called Phyllis 'Tootsie.' Later Jerry informed me that Phyllis liked to be called that in intimate moments."

"That's a little weak." Stan's eyes strayed over my shoulder. I was too full of my story to turn around.

"I asked Ed how well he knew Phyllis and he said that his wife went to high school with her, that he'd only met her when Saul set her up in Westhampton. The 'Tootsie' slip made him nervous."

Stan flicked open a file and shuffled some papers.

"Don't bother looking it up. Sally is four years younger than Phyllis. I got that from Roberta's employee files. Ed was the one who had been in the same class as Phyllis, along with Sally's friend Janice."

"It doesn't make him a murderer."

"Why did he claim not to know Phyllis's last name?"

"He didn't remember or, more likely, he didn't think it was any of your business." His eye twinkle turned on.

"Ed Mannucci didn't want me to look into Phyllis's accident." I twinkled back. Maybe Stan was going to skip the lecture. "I had to twist his arm to get Sally's phone number. Maybe he was counting on the fact that she wouldn't remember. She didn't, but she's a good bloodhound, she found the name for me."

"She asked her husband."

"I doubt that. I don't think Phyllis got mentioned in the Mannucci household. I suspect Sally knew that Phyllis and Ed had been lovers. Ed said Roberta fired Sally, but Roberta insists that Sally quit. I think Phyllis had something to do with that. Sally made a funny comment about filing her nails . . ." I eased myself back on the chair, my leg throbbing again.

"How was Mannucci involved with the accident?"

"I wondered why Phyllis had gone to St. Vincent's, down in the Village. At the time, she lived up on East Eighty-fifth Street, within easy reach of two hospitals. It didn't make sense. But what if someone had been with her that night, someone who wasn't supposed to be there? A married man, for instance? Then you'd pick a hospital where you didn't run the risk of bumping into anyone you knew."

Stan scratched his chin, the back of his ear, his eyes not meeting mine. Was I boring him? "Listen, love of my life. Dmitri found the ER nurse who was on duty at

St. Vincent's that night. She's seventy-eight years old, but she remembers!"

"Ginkgo pills, that's what keeps the light of day in my head," Eileen McDonough had said, shaking a white bottle. "Costs an arm and a leg, but, well, now that's worth every penny if it keeps my life in front of my eyes." She had smiled broadly, her cheeks pleating. Plump, with cropped-off white hair, clear eyes, and a button nose that gave her an impish look, Eileen sat erect on her bed. She wore gray sweats and white nurses' shoes. Dmitri and I sat on the empty bed next to hers.

"Now then," Eileen had said. "It's not just the pills that keep that night fresh in my head. It's the strangeness of it. There was a man that brought her in. He was hurt, too. Limping. One pants leg torn at the knee and the knee swollen and red. He wouldn't let me look at it, and when the admitting nurse asked his name, for the file, was he the husband, the next of kin, he lost his manners, he did. I stepped in and told him I'd have none of that in my ER and with the admitting girl not two days old at the job. He gave us a name then. Paul Kidd he called himself. A thumping lie because Paul Kidd was an OB/GYN at the hospital, they had just called his name over the PA system. But the man was too nervous to be aware of his nonsense. And I left it alone because he had a wedding ring on and the patient didn't.

"Oh, yes, there was man with her that night they brought her in, and no mention of it at the trial."

"Didn't the police look at the file?"

"No reason to, I suppose. She confessed to what she had done. She gave them all the information they needed. They did not doubt her."

"The file is yellow paper now," Dmitri said.

The old nurse nodded. "Now, then, I looked for it

before I left my work. I wanted to remember that night, you see. To look at the name. Dr. Paul Kidd." She stopped, her lips pressed together, as if savoring a forgotten taste. "He was long gone from the hospital and my life. But that night when that woman came in with her chin bleeding like a slaughtered pig, with her man limping and lying about his name, that night, or that morning, I should say, because it must have been near five o'clock into the next day by the time my work was done, that morning, I said yes to Dr. Paul Kidd. Him a married man and me, seeing the altar only for church on Sundays."

"Maybe the man who helped Phyllis that night," Stan said, "was a good Samaritan who didn't want to get involved with a police investigation." His eyes were still aimed at the door behind me, as if my face were an unwelcome sight.

"I'm willing to bet my new chest of drawers that man was Ed Mannucci," I said, leaning forward. "Phyllis and Ed were lovers then. That night Sally was busy giving birth to her son. Instead of going in the van Mrs. Morewitz had provided, Phyllis rented a car. Why? Because she was going to meet up with Ed. I say Ed parked his car near the party and got into hers. They were in the rented car together when the girl was killed. He kept quiet about it because he couldn't afford a divorce. Sally Mannucci's money had just set Ed up in business. "

A hiccup made me turn around. Sally Mannucci, red hair splayed over her mink coat, twitched her fingernails. How long had she been standing there?

"Go on," she said.

"I can't." I feared for my eyeballs.

"I'm a big girl."

I turned back to Greenhouse, cutting him my meanest look. He came back with Ivory soap.

"Go on!" Sally dropped down on the bench. "'Sally Mannucci's money had just set Ed up in business.'"

"This is all conjecture, Sally."

"Like hell it is." She lit a cigarette. Stan started to say something, then changed his mind.

"Phyllis had a lot of money in that safe-deposit box," I said. "Cash that she was keeping away from the IRS. She didn't earn it as a fitting model. I think she got the money by blackmail, and I propose that Ed was behind the wheel of that car in 1967 and that she'd been blackmailing him all these years. She went to jail for him, maybe for love, more likely for the money. And since Ed was her meal ticket, Phyllis offered to help undermine Roberta's business so he could take it over. Ask Jerry Sarnowski. It seems Phyllis was behind all the threats to Roberta."

Sally snapped open a silver change purse, careful not to break her nails. "I could have bought Riddle Solutions ten times over." She flicked ashes inside.

"Why didn't you?" Stan asked.

"I'd have to kill my mother first. It's her money. The trouble is, I love her." She turned to me, and spoke with clenched ferocity. "What about the Buddha that killed that bitch? It was locked up in Roberta's studio, and you can bet your fat tush my husband didn't have the keys, because I made sure he didn't."

"I think Phyllis took it with her when she went to the bathroom. I think Ed asked her to. It's an expensive piece with sentimental value for Roberta, an anniversary present from Saul. Maybe Ed suggested that they should smash the Buddha and send it back to Roberta as another sweet threat. Then Ed got a better idea. I'm sorry, Sally."

"You won't be the only one." Sally dropped her cigarette inside the metal change purse and choked it with a snap. "I'd like to see my husband, please."

27

———— ❦ ————

"You're wrong, Simona," Roberta said. She'd been waiting for me at the Bowery Bar, a new hot spot in the middle of downtown NòHo's industrial charm. It had once been a gas station and now looked like a fifties diner right out of an Edward Hopper painting. The after-show party Charlie had arranged was over by now. The fashion gang, my musketeers included, had gathered forces and rolled on to crash Todd Oldham's party at Industria. Lourdes had gone home to her son. Flossie had gone looking for Jerry. All that was left was the acrid smell of alcohol, smoke, and sweating hormones.

Mr. Nite, Mario, Roberta, and I were sitting in a black-and-white booth. Water glasses were half-filled with flat champagne. I had just retold my story. "What am I wrong about? The murder or the accident?"

"The accident, to start," Roberta said. Her face seemed to bear the weight of the world.

"Do you want to tell me what happened?"

Roberta sat back. "I was in the driver's seat the night

of February twenty-fourth, 1967. I killed that girl, and I have lived with guilt ever since."

Mr. Nite poured more champagne. Mario sipped coffee. I was too surprised to think.

"When Elsa Morewitz kicked Phyllis out of her house," Roberta said, "I locked myself in a bedroom upstairs. From the window I saw Phyllis sprawled in the backseat of her rented car. She was drunk, she was probably asleep, but I remember thinking—she's waiting for Saul, she knows he'll come to her even now that I've discovered their sordid affair. Her confidence enraged me. The bedroom had a terrace with stairs leading down to the garden. I ran down, threw myself into the driver's seat, and started the car before Phyllis had a chance to react.

"She laughed when she saw me. I nearly threw up from the smell of her, whiskey and rot. She got a kick out of married men. The more famous or richer the wife, the more she enjoyed it. Saul did not inspire any trite feelings of love, she assured me. It was the fast pleasure of stolen sex she was after, and the power she felt while being with me or the other wives, knowing she had taken something from us, something she could surprise us with at any time she chose.

"A car was behind, gaining on us. I could only see the headlights, but I was convinced it was Saul. That made me crazier. I accelerated. At a curve on the road ahead, I saw a break in the wall of rocks. A few feet beyond, the bay. It came to me then why I had jumped into the car. I aimed straight for that break. I wanted us both dead. Phyllis screamed. She leaned over the seat and grabbed the wheel from my hands. I felt the swerve, heard the crash into a tree. I hit my head against the window and lost consciousness. I never saw the girl."

"Phyllis took the rap for you so she could blackmail you for the rest of your life?"

"No. Phyllis left me in the car with the dead girl on the road. Not before taking a picture of me."

"The incriminating evidence in her safe-deposit box."

"A negative that I have not burned. She took the picture and then someone drove her away, the same man who took her to St. Vincent's, probably. Not Saul. He had stayed behind at Elsa's, pleading behind that locked bedroom door. Elsa was his witness."

"It was Ed."

"I would like it to be Ed."

"Why weren't you arrested for killing the girl?"

"Because I, too, had a knight-errant."

Mario coughed.

"Tell her," Roberta said, her voice creamy now.

"I took the Lighthouse Road to go home," Mario said. The paper globe of light above him dropped shadows down his face. "I like to drive near the water. It reminds me of home."

Roberta clasped his hand. "His nostalgia saved me. He lifted me into his car—I was apparently wandering the road in a semiconscious state—and took me home to Manhattan."

"What about the girl?"

"I checked her pulse," Mario said. "I listened to her heart. I brought Roberta's compact mirror to her mouth. No one could help her."

"Mario wanted to get me away as fast as he could. I apparently kept jabbering about Phyllis, and he assumed that she had been driving and purposely left the scene of the accident to place the blame on me."

"I did call the Manhasset police from a pay phone near Roberta's apartment." Mario fished a cigarette out of his breast pocket and stood up. "That's all I could do." He walked outside and blew the smoke from his cigarette against the glass wall of the restaurant, as if trying to fog out our view of him.

"I didn't tell Mario the truth. That I had killed that girl. I couldn't." Roberta slowly shook her head, the legs of her spider hat riffling the stale air. "For the first twenty-four hours I stayed in bed. In a panicked daze, if that's possible. I had a cut on the side of my head, a small one. Saul wanted me to go to a hospital, but I was too scared. The cut had bled in the car and I expected the police to arrest me any minute. I couldn't believe it when Phyllis admitted to killing the girl. She didn't mention me at all."

Mr. Nite offered more champagne.

Roberta palmed the glass. "I thought who else but Saul could have convinced her to take the blame? Mine was the hand that fed him. He couldn't afford to have me in jail. He'd pay Phyllis handsomely for her sacrifice. I even thought he had paid Mario to fetch me."

"Mario is in love with you," Mr. Nite said, his hand brushing hers. "He wears his love on the rim of his eyes, like tears."

"I found that out later," Roberta said. "After his wife and son left. Flossie told me. I called Sicily to speak to his wife, to tell her there had never, ever been anything between us. She wouldn't come to the phone. I wrote. The letters came back unopened. And all this time I didn't have the courage to tell Mario the truth."

"Tonight she told him," Mr. Nite said. "In the middle of her success party, she said, 'I am the one. I killed the girl.' And Mario, he told her, 'You are a good woman, Mrs. Riddle. *That* is the truth.'"

Roberta looked outside, beyond the glass door. Mario was giving a cigarette to a panhandler. "He's just like me. Blind to everything he doesn't want to see."

"Ach, Roberta Riddle, enough with the past. We are partners now, and I am a sentimental old man. I say tomorrow the newspapers will say Roberta has found her art again," Mr. Nite clasped her hand and shook it in the air, "but tonight she has won the match. She has found her heart."

Roberta gave her new partner a kiss on his soft cheek while I filched a San Pellegrino bottle from the booth behind me. "When did Phyllis start putting the pressure on you?"

This time it was Mr. Nite who excused himself.

Roberta watched him head for the rest rooms. "Ernest believes in discretion. Like Mario. Saul had no idea of the significance of that word."

I poured myself a glass of Italian bubbly water. "Tell me about Phyllis."

"The minute she got out of jail she demanded a party. That was the beginning. To add a twist to my heart, she told me Gloria Hernandez had given birth to a baby just a few months before I killed her. That's when I closed up the studio and went away. Phyllis was the one who was going to have a baby, but I didn't know it."

I drank. "Lourdes was supposed to be that baby." The San Pellegrino was as flat as the champagne.

"I didn't quite believe it, but I didn't have the strength to prove her wrong. I put blinders on and worked myself bloodless."

"Sunday, the night she died, twenty-eight years' worth of rage came out. I fired her without thinking of the consequences. Phyllis laughed in my face." She looked up with a flash of fear.

The thought of Sally Mannucci on the loose made me turn quickly.

"Mrs. Riddle," Stan said, "I know you trust Simona more than the New York City Police, but may I join you?"

"The moment of truth?" she asked.

"Call it getting the facts straight."

"Whatever. Please do join us." She waved her glass at Mario's empty spot. Mario was still out there, puffing, probably going through a whole carton rather than listen to more of the past. Mr. Nite hadn't come back either. He'd had a lot of champagne.

Stan brought up a chair. "Cheers." He lifted his Diet Coke. "We've got our murderer."

"You got Ed to confess!" I clutched his arm. "That's fabulous!" The cast stopped me from jumping on his lap.

Stan extracted himself. Coke had spilled over his shirt and tie. "Truth be told, I had very little to do with it. I simply let Sally Mannucci loose in the interview room. By the time she was through with her husband, he'd confessed."

"He killed Phyllis?" Roberta asked. "There's no doubt?"

"He gave us the whole story just as Simona had guessed."

"Guessed! My assumptions were derived from logical thinking and pure deductive reasoning."

Roberta exhaled a long, trembling breath. She'd turned ashen.

I touched her shoulder. "Are you all right?"

Stan offered her a glass of water.

Mario opened the door to come back in.

"I thought Mario was the murderer," Roberta said. "Because Phyllis was ruining my life, and he loves me. I was so certain and so afraid for him. That's why I asked for Simona's help." She quickly looked at Stan. "It's an ugly, sordid story, and I was in the middle of it. I didn't want to be alone. Simona is a friend, a woman, an Italian. She would understand me, sympathize with Mario. And the fact that she was your girlfriend made it even better. When the time came, I trusted her to make you understand and not treat us as common criminals.

After almost thirty years of living a lie, I wanted compassion."

"I never told him anything!"

"I didn't know that, Simona. Forgive me." She waved her arms. "Mario, come sit down. And Ernest, too. Detective Greenhouse has the best news."

"You haven't heard all of it," Stan said as Mario and Mr. Nite sat down. "Sim, you were wrong about the accident."

"How wrong?"

"Phyllis didn't kill Gloria Hernandez."

A rod dropped down Roberta's back. I found myself not wanting Stan to know the truth. Roberta had paid enough. So had Mario.

"Mannucci wasn't in the car with Phyllis," Stan said.

Roberta clasped Mario's hand. "I will help you straighten the facts. What really happened—"

"What really happened," Stan interrupted, "is that Mannucci was driving behind her. He'd just parked a few blocks down from Mrs. Morewitz's house. They had a little rendezvous planned at Sally's mother's place nearby. Sally was giving birth, and Sally's mother was in Florida.

"You drove right by him, Mrs. Riddle. His lights were still on, and he spotted you and Phyllis. He followed, wondering where you were taking her. You lost control on a curve, but Phyllis managed to grab the wheel and avoid ending up in Manhasset Bay. Mannucci swerved in the other direction, to avoid crashing into you. When he saw the girl, coming out of a path, it was too late. He hit her full force. Mannucci was lucky he wore the seat belt his fancy new car provided. Gloria Hernandez died instantly. He ended up with a badly bruised knee."

"I would like to laugh," Roberta said. "I should

laugh." Mario brushed fingers over his eyes. Mr. Nite stroked the Star of David on his chest. Stan looked at peace with the world. I was exhausted.

"You were set up, Mrs. Riddle," Stan said. "But then you got away." Stan looked at Mario, then at Mr. Nite. "How doesn't really matter at this late date. Mannucci convinced Phyllis to take the rap for him for love and a lifelong supply of money. He was in love with her then, so he thought that would be okay. She's been hanging from his neck ever since, demanding money, demanding his time. Her last request—he should divorce Sally. They'd take over Riddle Solutions, buy out Roberta and Charlie, and she'd run the place herself. That's when he decided it was time for murder."

Roberta sat in silence, eyes closed. "Are you sure, Detective Greenhouse?"

"It's over, Mrs. Riddle."

Mr. Nite stroked her wrist. "It has been a long day."

"A good day," Mario added.

Roberta lifted her face. "Why was Phyllis so cruel?" Her cheeks glimmered.

"Lawyers advance all kinds of reasons," Stan said. "Abuse, abandonment, insanity. Sometimes they're legitimate."

Mario shook his head. "Sometimes people are born bad."

"I wish I could feel sorry for her, but I don't."

Roberta slowly unfolded herself from the chair. Mr. Nite and Mario stood up. "Thank you, Stan. Thank you, Simona," she said, dabbing her cheeks with a handkerchief. "I think it's time to go home. Gentlemen," Roberta turned to her escorts, "may I give you a lift?"

The men accepted. She linked arms with them.

"Mrs. Riddle," Stan said, "did I pass the compassion test?"

Roberta laughed. "Beautifully. Thanks to Simona, no doubt." She kissed my cheeks. "Every one of us distorts the truth to fit the dictates of our heart. Sometimes, though, it is *not* our best defense."

Epilogue

———— ❦ ————

Stan did end up giving me a stern lecture about safety, folly, responsibility to loved ones, and I don't know what else. I was too busy working on his ear-lobes. As smooth and sweet as grapes. Seedless too.

Mr. Nite was right. Roberta's designs were a great success. So was his lingerie. They're talking about a new line. Riddle Under-Nothings. Charlie's already offered eighty sketches. Mr. Nite loves them. Roberta isn't making promises. The next few months at Riddle Solutions, Inc., will produce a hardy crop of exclamation points, I suspect.

Roberta's sixtieth birthday came and went. At her request, no party, no presents. My cast came off two days ago. Last night I gave a "Thank God it's over" party, my first in my new home on the Upper West Side. Roberta was at the top of the guest list. This was one celebration she accepted. The Riddle gang came, minus Jerry. Willy with a cute date, my musketeers—Dmitri, Mike, and Phil. Mrs. Cordova without her daughter, Anna, who is still waiting for the bureaucracy of justice. Raf brought his girlfriend, Tina. Charlie came with his mom. Lourdes brought her mother, husband, and a sleeping Hector. Eileen McDonough from her wheelchair declared that there was enough food to feed the crowd at St. Patrick's on Easter Sunday. Kathy Breen and her brother, not to be outdone, declared the apartment could have passed for a cemetery on All Soul's Day. Butterfly orchids from Roberta, three baskets of carnations from Mrs. Cordova; roses from Mr. Nite, Italian coffee beans from Mario, and dried sunflowers from my new partner. Flossie offered challah, the size-six green suit Roberta had flung to the wall, and the perfect name for my main dish. *Schmatta* pasta.

Halfway through the party, Dmitri cornered me in the hallway and accused me of not being very good at the "we" game. He didn't like having missed out on the ending.

"That'll teach you to go chasing models."

"I conduct business. Kilo of hair from Bettina, Irina, Lisa, and Charlene! Next time I stay with you."

We toasted to that next time, hoping it wouldn't involve murder.

Charlie and his mom got me in the kitchen. "We've talked it out. It's okay," Charlie said.

His mom beamed. "I love my boy."

I cornered Roberta in my bedroom.

"I never blamed Saul." Roberta was looking for her cloak. "My work has always come first." The party was winding down. "I loved him dearly, but I think it was my pride that he hurt the most."

"I have one curiosity left." I dug out the cloak, blue velvet lined in gray wool. "Something I could only ask in private." I eyed the black velvet cap she was wearing.

"You want all the truth."

"Why not?"

Roberta lifted her cap and crunched it in her hands.

Her hair, waves of blond-washed gray, lay flat where the cap had been. Roberta turned her head. A knuckle of white scar tissue cut a three-inch path high above her ear.

"The wound got infected," Roberta said. "I could let my hair grow long enough to cover it, but I liked to think of my hats as hair shirts. A humbling daily reminder." She slipped the cap back on and adjusted her curls in front of the dresser's mirror. "I didn't kill that girl, but I'm still guilty of a great deal of stupidity. I'm also vain and don't like to think someone might spot the scar." She looked at her reflection. "Proud, manipulative, power-hungry. Coco Chanel said it. 'He who doesn't enjoy his own company is usually right.'"

I dropped the cloak on her shoulders. "You have two men who are devoted to you. Flossie didn't leave you even after you fired her son. Charlie thought enough about you to say no to designing for Mannucci. Dmitri and I stuck by you. Not a bad group of friends."

"I'm not a nice woman."

"Who defines nice?"

"Your man. Stan Greenhouse. He's a *mensch*. Love him well."

I do. I am looking at him now, in his armchair, his kind, handsome face engrossed in a book. He is reading about Eleanor Roosevelt. I sit on the floor looking through turkey recipes. Thanksgiving is coming. Cooking the bird will be a first for me. I hope to wear Roberta's green suit.

The apartment smells of steaming broccoli.

Stan rests his stockinged foot against my ankle. "I forget how persuasive women can be. Sonny's acting coach, Rita. Sally Mannucci." His eyes smile and joy somersaults inside me. "You."

"Which reminds me," I say and lean against his knee, "your walls just scream 'off-white.'"

Appendix

FASHION FOOTNOTES

THE PAST TRACK

Several factors have contributed to making New York City one of the top three fashion capitals of the world.

As early as the beginning of the nineteenth century, New York was the major import center for dry goods and was a distribution center for clothing. Being home to the largest banking, shipping, and insurance companies, it provided the resources for the production of cotton in the South.

During the Civil War, New York became dominant as a manufacturer of cotton and woolen clothing, benefiting from its geographic location between the raw material of the South and the fabric manufacturers of New England.

Between 1880–1910 a mass migration of Eastern Europeans and Italians poured into the Lower East Side and provided the fledgling industry with both skilled talent and cheap labor.

*   *   *

The invention of the sewing machine by Elias Howe in 1846 was the first step in the development of the garment industry. In 1860, records of the American production of women's clothing appeared for the first time. Cloaks, with their heavy material, were the first to be manufactured, followed by women's suits.

By the end of the nineteenth century, as more and more women worked outside the home, a "new woman" style emerged, one made famous by the Gibson Girl: the shirtwaist (blouse), copied from men's shirts and worn with a blue serge suit. The shirtwaists were easily mass-produced. Instead of being produced in-house, which had been the norm for suits and coats, shirtwaists were cut in one place, sewn in another, and finished in yet another. This production method led to the evolution of sweatshops.

When the Gibson Girl went out of fashion, the cotton shirtwaist was lengthened into a long, one-piece dress worn with a coat instead of a cloak. It was the beginning of the women's dress industry.

Between 1900 and 1910, the women's apparel industry doubled, whereas the general population increased by only 25 percent. Competition was fierce. Men, women, and children worked an average of sixty-five to seventy hours a week and weekly wages ranged from three to ten dollars.

One company fined workers fifty cents if they looked out the window and twenty-five cents if they laughed.

After a twenty-year effort, the International Ladies' Garment Workers Union (ILGWU) was founded in 1900.

In 1909 and 1910, the needle trades held their first successful mass strikes.

On March 25, 1911, a fire erupted at the Greenwich Village Triangle Waist Company. One hundred and forty-six workers lost their lives. Most were women. Many could have been saved if the rear exit door had not been locked. One hundred thousand people followed the funeral procession. The public's outrage over the deaths led to factory building inspections and fire-prevention legislation, and greatly increased the power of the ILGWU.

Today the average work week is thirty-five hours. The average weekly wage is $263.

By 1915, the small tenements and airless lofts of the Lower East Side could no longer accommodate the growing demands of the industry. Successful clothing manufacturers started looking uptown, near the railroad station.

In 1916, the Save New York Committee was formed to prevent the apparel industry from encroaching on the Fifth Avenue retail district.

In 1918, the real estate firm of Helmsley-Spear, together with a group of manufacturers, leased land from Trinity Church and built 498 and 500 Seventh Avenue. Three years later, 512, 530, and 550 Seventh Avenue followed.

It was the beginning of the garment center as we know it.

FAST STATS AND FACTS

In 1900, there were 472 New York City shirtwaist manufacturers. By 1921, 2,655 factories were making waists (blouses) and dresses. Today, the garment industry is New York's largest single employer, providing 250,000 jobs. It is also the city's largest manufacturing industry, with 4,500 factories and over 5,000 showrooms. The industry generates annual revenues of $14 billion.

U.S. consumers spend $125 billion on apparel, of which $70 billion is in women's apparel.

The industry offers five market weeks and sixty-five annual trade shows that are attended by an estimated 22,000 apparel buyers. Visiting retailers account for 10 percent—$100 million—of New York City's tourist dollars.

Approximately 100,000 manufacturing jobs have been lost to Asia and the Caribbean. Additional jobs have been lost with the expansion of regional fashion marts in Atlanta, Dallas, Los Angeles, Miami, and Chicago.

The International Ladies Garment Workers Union estimates that one fourth of all domestically sold women's garments are imported.

Out-of-town retailers have long complained that buying trips to New York's garment center are too expensive, dirty, and dangerous. It may be the main reason regional fashion marts are gaining in popularity. A Fashion Center Business Improvement District (FCBID) was launched in 1994 in an effort to bring those buyers back. The FCBID offers security guards, sanitation crews, and hotel and restaurant discounts.

Somewhere between 250,000 and 300,000 people

pass through the garment center in the course of a normal day.

Street litter collected in the first four months of operation: 189.3 tons.

American designers were considered nonexistent before World War II. French fashion was so loved by Americans that some stores removed American labels and replaced them with ones bearing French names.

After the war began in Europe, *Vogue*, in a prescient move, featured American ready-to-wear in its February 1940 issue. In June 1940, the Germans occupied Paris, and French haute couture designs stopped crossing the Atlantic. Dorothy Shaver, president of Lord & Taylor, filled her store windows with American designers, advertised their clothes, and featured their names. In 1943, the Coty Awards, the Oscars of the fashion world, were established to honor American fashion.

By the end of the war, American designers had become household names.

Forty percent of American women are a size fourteen or larger. Forty-nine percent are five four and under. Yet size eight—the halfway mark between two and fourteen—is still the standard of measure used by the industry against which the other sizes are scaled. There are, however, no industry regulations as to the measurements of that size eight, and through the years size eight has gotten larger to accommodate the increase in weight of the American woman.

TALKING FASHION

Herodotus, historian—"A woman takes off her claim to respect along with her garments."

Diana Vreeland, magazine editor—"Elegance is refusal."

Benjamin Franklin, statesman—"Eat to please thyself, but dress to please others."

Halston, designer—"I don't know any woman who doesn't want to look good."

Gloria Sachs, designer—"Style is a . . . true indication of who you are."

Karl Lagerfeld, designer—"Fashion is . . . the most typical expression of a moment."

Suzy Menkes, journalist—"Fashion today is about divine chaos."

William Norwich, journalist—"Fashion is the new Broadway."

Calvin Klein, designer—"No one really needs fashion."

Donna Karan, designer—"The last thing I have time to do is worry about my clothes."

Coco Chanel, designer—"When I had to choose between the man I loved and dresses, I always chose the dresses."

Issey Miyake, designer—"Clothing is one of the last areas where total personal options are left."

Giorgio Armani, designer—"Glamour in a woman starts with her own well-being."

Adele Simpson, designer—"Women are very smart. They know what they need to fit into their lives."

Yves St. Laurent, designer—"It's all in the fit."

Unknown—"Show me a woman who's not ashamed of her body and I'll show you a six-year-old child."

THINK ABOUT . . .

Fashion responding to political, cultural, and economic phenomena:

In the Gold Rush of 1849, men needed sturdy pants. Levi Strauss, owner of a dry goods store, came up with pants made of sailcloth, reinforced seams, top stitching, and a pocket strong enough to hold the weight of gold nuggets. Jeans were born.

During World War I, Alice Roosevelt Longworth launched a campaign to convince women to give up their steel-boned corsets. She gathered 28,000 tons of steel for the war effort, helping to free Europe and the female waist.

During World War II, fashion was dictated by the shortage of fabric. Two years after the end of the war, Christian Dior's "New Look," with its full, long skirts, signaled a hard-earned new era of opulence.

In the fifties, a thriving economy led people out of crowded cities and into suburbia. The need for comfort and conformity produced the hostess gown, the car coat, the circle skirt, and the Peter Pan collar.

The sixties saw the Vietnam War and the assassination of President Kennedy. The disillusioned and the rebellious took fashion into their own hands and produced the hippie look.

The popular Chinese jacket of the seventies was a direct result of new political ties between the United States and China.

The color coding of babies in pink and blue didn't start until the turn of the century, accompanied by a strong women's rights movement and theories suggesting that behavioral gender differences were learned traits. Before that, small children of both sexes were dressed in similar clothes, and blue was considered a feminine color.

After World War II, when women gave their factory and office jobs back to men and retreated into their traditional roles, pink for girls and blue for boys became standard.

HOW-TO GUIDE

To create a woman's garment:

The designer first makes a working sketch, known as a croquis (pronounced croak-ee), which shows the construction lines. The assistant designer then drapes the chosen fabric on a size-eight fitting model or a dummy. The shape is then transferred to a flat pattern. Cutting assistants, also known as "sample hands," produce a muslin toile prototype. Corrections are made to the prototype and to the sample pattern and a finished original sample is produced. Next, a production person costs out the sample, taking into account the quality and yardage of the fabric, in-house and contractor costs, the findings and trimmings used. Overhead is earned out of the markup.

Duplicate samples are made to display in the showroom and to send out to trunk shows all over the country. A production pattern is prepared when sufficient orders have come in to justify cutting (usually four hundred garments sized six to fourteen). The production pattern is then graded into sizes and a paper marker is made, which is used by the cutter as a guide to cut the fabric. The cut pieces are bundled together according to size and shape, and then are sewn together to make the finished garment.

CENTS AND SENSIBILITIES

A manufacturer will normally "keystone" the cost of a garment, that is, sell it at double the cost, which is also mysteriously called a 50 percent markup. The quoted showroom price of a garment is the wholesale price. The retail price is usually double the wholesale price. A garment that costs the manufacturer one hundred dollars ends up costing the consumer four hundred dollars.

If a garment doesn't "walk" (usually after thirteen weeks in the store), the retailer marks down the dress. Each store department has a certain percentage of markdown dollars. If the store goes over that budget, the manufacturer has to participate.

The retailers claim that they want the manufacturers to be partners. The manufacturers claim that they are partners in losses, never in profits.

BABES IN BOYLAND

The fashion industry has traditionally been considered a male-dominated business, but women designers have had a strong say in what is chic.

Some American women designers from the past: Fira Benneson, Elizabeth Havies, Adele Simpson (her theme was "young, pretty, and with a purpose"), Hattie Carnegie (the first lady of American fashion), Bonnie Cashin (she designed for the Rockettes), Ceil Chapman (the debutantes' favorite), Clare Potter, Dorothy Cox, Jane Derby, Ann Fogarty, Kiviette, Tina Leser, Vera Maxwell, Claire McCardell (considered the first true sportswear designer), Mollie Parnis, Nattie Rosenstein, Carolyn Schnurer, Sophie Gimbel, Pauline Trigère (Paris born), Jessie Franklin Turner, Valentina, Joset Walker, and Emily Wilkens.

More recent names: Linda Allard, Liz Claiborne, Patricia Clyne, Jennifer George, Cathy Hardwick, Betsey Johnson, Norma Kamali, Donna Karan, Anne Klein, Carol Little, Mary McFadden, Nicole Miller, Rebecca Moses, Diane Pernet, Carolyn Roehm, Cynthia Rowley, Isabel Toledo, Ellen Tracy, Joan Vass, Adrienne Vittadini, Diane Von Furstenberg, and Laura Whitcomb.

RUNWAY REPORT

The first fashion show with live models took place in
New York City in the ballroom of the old Ritz-Carlton
on November 4, 1914. It was the brainchild of Edna
Woolman Chase, editor of *Vogue*, who was looking for
a way to fill magazine pages because World War I,
begun in August, had shut down the French fashion
business.

Today, fashion shows are essential to the industry.
American designers traditionally showed their collections during market week, on runways installed in their
showrooms or in offbeat night spots. Retailers and journalists (approximately 12,000 in 1994) found it difficult
to run from one place to another, often with only a few
minutes to get there. Paris centralized its shows in tents
behind the Louvre Museum. New York followed.

In October 1993, under the auspices of the
Council of Fashion Designers of America, American
manufacturers moved market week to Seventh on
Sixth in Bryant Park.

The most celebrated American designers hold their sea-
sonal fashion shows in two large white tents behind the
New York Central Research Library:

The Gertrude Pavilion—named after the park's
statue of Gertrude Stein—is the larger of the two tents.
Entirely black inside, including the chairs, it seats 850,
has a total capacity of 1,165, and rents for $25,000 a
show. It will house two to three shows a day.

The Josephine Pavilion—named after the Josephine
Shaw Lowell fountain, which the tent partially
embraces—seats 610, has a total capacity of 800, and
rents for $14,200 a show. It will house three to four
shows daily.

Smaller shows are given inside the library building

itself—in the Celeste Bartos Forum, the Trustee's Room, and Astor Hall.

Seventh on Sixth's annual budget—$2 million.

Average cost of a runway model—$750 an hour.

Average cost to a designer for showing a collection—$200,000.

WHEN AND WHERE

January	Spring/Summer Haute Couture for the current year. In Paris.
March–April	Fall/Winter Ready-to-Wear for the current year. First Milan, then London, Paris, and New York.
July	Fall/Winter Haute Couture for the current year. In Paris.
October–November	Spring/Summer Ready-to-Wear for the following year. Milan, London, Paris, and New York.

Because the New York designers' shows are presented last, manufacturers have complained that by the time retailers come to Bryant Park, they have already used up their spending allowances.

Retailers have complained that they have to wait until they come to New York to know how much to spend where.

It's a kvetching business.

THE WILDER SIDE

Some New York City garment-center crime:

Loaded garment trucks have been hijacked in broad daylight.

Fake messengers arrive to pick up garment bags minutes before the real messengers.

Until recently the apparel business was at the mercy of a few trucking firms with Mafia connections. In the early thirties, Louis Lepke was said to have controlled the garment business with fifty trucks. In the eighties, the trucks of Thomas F. Gambino, president of Consolidated Carriers Corporation, had taken over.

In February 1992, in State Supreme Court in Manhattan, Gambino and his brother, Joseph, pleaded guilty to a single felony count of illegally restraining trade. Instead of going to jail, they paid a $12 million fine and agreed to get out of the trucking business.

The Mafia is still thought to own dress companies used to launder money.

Some manufacturers continue to exploit immigrants by farming out work to contractors and subcontractors who do not pay minimum wage. Some designers, aware of the exploitation, ignore the problem.

Although certain distinctive fashion styles are protected by U.S trademark, the theft of simpler, more basic fashion ideas is not punishable by law.

SEEING DOUBLE

Back when global communications were slower, the friendly department store saleslady was instrumental in the copying of clothing.

As the new Paris fashions came into the store, designers and their assistants would hole up in a dressing room, quickly and quietly sketching the styles the saleslady brought in.

Copying from the French was considered acceptable, but American ready-to-wear designers formed the Fashion Originators Guild to protect themselves. The guild would sell garments only to retailers who promised not to buy copies of members' designs. In 1941, the Supreme Court declared the guild an illegal monopoly, clearing the way for the U.S. knockoff industry.

To knock off a garment today, you need two or more of the following:

A fabric salesman at the trade shows in Milan and Paris willing to reveal which designer just bought what.

Moles in the designers' studios.

Photographers ready to part with copies of their collection shots, which you fax to your contractor in Hong Kong. In twenty-four hours, he ships back a sample by overnight mail. The next day the knockoff gets shown to buyers in your showroom.

A friendly or hungry guard who'll let you crash the shows.

A knockoff consultant in Europe. For $500 to $1,000 a day the spy will walk into a designer

boutique with sharp eyes and a hidden camera
and scoop the latest.

A fax.

The fashion press.

A computer. The New York shows have gone on-
line.

Knocking off is an expensive science. Large American
clothing manufacturers send two or three people from
each division—children's, men's, women's—to the best
hotels in Milan, Paris, London, Florence, and
Amsterdam (strong in the junior market). Dropping out
of black limos, they scour the top boutiques for the latest chic and then fly home with body bags full of samples. Back in the studio, the company "designers" study
color, fabric, and detail and make adjustments for the
American market.

Eighty percent of Parisian designer boutiques sell
their clothes to manufacturers and merchandisers from
the United States, Canada, Australia, Japan, and South
America, fully aware that their clothes will be knocked
off.

Some knockoff manufacturers don't bother to make
their own samples. They use what they've bought in
Europe, simply shifting labels.

BAD NEWS

Many new small garment workshops have cropped up outside the garment district and Chinatown, according to a recent *New York Times* article. The shops are highly mobile, opening and shutting down before the Labor Department reaches them.

Recently a Chinese sign posted outside a garment factory in Brooklyn asked for workers. A Chinese-speaking reporter applied for the job and was hired.

After working for seven straight days, the reporter was promised that in three weeks she would be paid $54.24 for eighty-four hours of work. That adds up to 64 cents an hour. The legal minimum wage is $4.25.

An eleven-year-old girl, a veteran of the sweatshops since she was nine, sat next to her mother to sew printed labels onto the waistband of shorts. The label read: "Made in the U.S.A."

READY TO LAUGH

Business is bad at Abe and Leo's dress company. So bad that Leo can't take it anymore. From his office on the seventeenth floor, he looks down on the hustle and bustle of Seventh Avenue. Mentally he says good-bye to his mother, to his wife, to his children. To Abe. He loves them all. If only business were better!

Leo opens the window and takes the plunge.

On the way down, he passes his competitors' windows. They are working fast and furiously. Just before hitting the sidewalk, Leo yells up to his partner, "Abe! Cut velvet!"

Mort of Weintraub's Men's Suits has just come back from a vacation in Rome. Maria, his seamstress, is all excited to hear that he's seen the Pope.

"Really? The Pope? Were you close to him? Did he smile at you? Could you see his eyes?"

"I was real close," Mort says, tugging on a jacket button to make sure it'll hold. "So close I could touch the man."

"Oh, my God! What was he like?"

"A forty-four short."

Mr. Shapiro shuffles into Goldfarb and Sons and asks to talk to the boss. "I've got the spring line here. Ties, shirts, jackets."

"Mr. Goldfarb isn't seeing anyone. Mr. Goldfarb passed away."

"Really? Ach, that's terrible." Mr. Shapiro shuffles out.

Forty-five minutes later, he's back. "I've got the spring line here. Ties, shirts, jackets."

"Mr. Shapiro, I told you. Mr. Goldfarb can't see you. He's dead."

"That's terrible." Mr. Shapiro shuffles out.

Thirty minutes later, he's back with the same spiel.

"Mr. Shapiro, why do you keep coming back? I told you Mr. Goldfarb is dead!"

Mr. Shapiro smiles for the first time that month. "I like hearing it."

WHAT'S HOT

Schmatta Pasta

2 ounces dried porcini mushrooms
8 tablespoons olive oil
1 pound white mushrooms, cleaned and sliced
1/2 pound shiitake mushrooms, cleaned and sliced
1/2 pound portobello mushrooms, cleaned and sliced
Salt and pepper to taste
2 slices bacon, diced
4 cloves garlic, peeled
1 (28-ounce) can peeled Italian tomatoes
1/4 teaspoon crushed red pepper flakes
1/2 cup flat-leafed parsley, chopped
1 pound fresh lasagne*
1/2 cup grated Parmesan

Soak dried porcini mushrooms in 1 1/2 cups of warm water for 30 minutes. Remove the softened porcini from liquid and rinse under water. Chop. Drain mushroom liquid through a sieve lined with a paper towel and reserve.

Bring a large pot of salted water to a boil.

Heat 2 tablespoons of the olive oil in a large skillet. Sauté fresh mushrooms in batches over high heat until water has evaporated. With each batch, add oil as needed (reserving 2 tablespoons). Season with salt and pepper.

*Dried lasagne can also be used. Crack in half before boiling. Cook until *al dente* (approximately 10 to 12 minutes).

In another skillet sauté bacon until crisp. Remove bacon and discard bacon grease. Heat the reserved 2 tablespoons of oil in the same skillet and cook garlic cloves until golden. Add tomatoes, mushroom liquid, bacon, and red pepper flakes. Cook over high heat for ten minutes. Remove garlic and season to taste. Add all the mushrooms and mix well. Cook for another five minutes to heat through. Add parsley.

Tear lasagne into three-inch pieces to make the *schmatte*. Drop lasagne pieces (rags) into the boiling water. Mix well to keep them from sticking to each other. Cook until *al dente* (three minutes) and drain.

Pour half the sauce and half the Parmesan in a large serving dish. Add *schmatte* and mix well. Pour rest of mushroom sauce and rest of Parmesan on top. Mix again and serve.

Note: Recipe can be prepared in advance and kept in refrigerator for two days, or can be frozen. If not serving immediately, cook the pasta for only two minutes. Reheat pasta and sauce in 400-degree oven until piping hot (fifteen minutes or so).

Serves six.

Forget about fitting into that dress. Just enjoy!

Acknowledgments

I would like to thank the following for illuminating the garment industry for me: Susi Billingsley, Sal Cesarani, Nancy Ebker, Barbara Grande, Sharon Gray, Adrianne Grayson, Cathy Guyler, Arthur and Maxine Kohler, Ralph Rucci, Joan Steele, and Huey Waltzer.

I am grateful to Betsy Blaustein, Kenneth B. Lerer, Bob Livingston, Jane Magidson, and Aimée Philpott for their generosity.

To Stephen Lash a big belated *grazie*.

My support team has, as always, been invaluable: Larry Ashmead; my agent, Ellen Geiger; Jason Kaufman; Judith Keller; Drs. Barbara and Joseph Lane; my editor, Carolyn Marino; Maria Nella Masullo; and Sharon Villines.

To Stuart I owe my happiness.

I am indebted to the following for providing the facts:

The New York Times
Wall Street Journal

New York Observer

USA Today

Harper's Bazaar

The New Yorker

The Fashion Center

The ILGWU

Making the Modern Woman 1890–1920, an exhibit organized by the National Museum of American History and the Smithsonian Institution Traveling Exhibition Service.

Chase, Edna Woolman. *Always in Vogue*. Garden City, New York: Doubleday, 1954.

Cho, Emily, and Linda Grover. *Looking Terrific*. New York: Putnam, 1978.

Fairchild, John. *Chic Savages*. New York: Simon and Schuster, 1989.

Guerriero, Miriam, and Jeannette Jarnow. *Inside the Fashion Business*. New York: Macmillan Publishers, 1987.

Kennett, Frances. *Coco: The Life and Loves of Gabrielle Chanel*. London: Gollancz, 1989.

Rubin, G. Leonard. *The World of Fashion, an Introduction*. New York: Harper & Row, 1976.

Steele, Valerie. *Women of Fashion*. New York: Rizzoli, 1991.